IMPRACTICAL MAGIC

A WITCHES OF CLEOPATRA HILL NOVEL

CHRISTINE POPE

Dark Valentine Press

This is a work of fiction. Names, characters, places, and incidents are either the product of the author's imagination or are used fictitiously. Any resemblance to actual events, places, organizations, or persons, whether living or dead, is entirely coincidental.

IMPRACTICAL MAGIC

ISBN: 978-0692694633
Copyright © 2016 by Christine Pope
Published by Dark Valentine Press

Cover design by Lou Harper
Book layout by Indie Author Services

To learn more about this author, go to
www.christinepope.com.

IMPRACTICAL MAGIC

CHAPTER ONE

Ryan Ortiz stuck his head into Colin Campbell's office, dark eyes dancing. Judging by the grin his coworker wore, Colin got the impression that Ryan was up to no good, or at least had stumbled across something he thought was guaranteed to liven up their workday. "You've got a visitor."

"Yeah?" Colin didn't look up from his laptop's screen, pretending he was focused on the mind-numbingly boring article he was currently writing about the installation of new solar-powered parking meters in Tucson's downtown district. The week had been quiet so far, and without any sensational crimes to cover, he'd been relegated to writing the sorts of articles his editor claimed were necessary but which made Colin want to bang his head into a wall. Did anyone even read these things?

He knew it really didn't matter whether or not he acted interested in Ryan's latest revelation, because Ryan was going to dole out his story in bits and pieces the way he always did. However, Colin couldn't let himself get too irritated by that habit, because Ryan was the closest thing to a best friend he had. Three years earlier, they'd bonded over a love of craft beer and mutual commiseration about their crappy divorces, and despite his friend's tendency to exaggerate for effect, at least Ryan was generally there when you needed him.

"Yeah." Ryan leaned up against the doorjamb and crossed his arms, apparently nonplussed by Colin's lack of reaction. "Some older woman. She said she wanted to talk to a reporter, but it had to be you."

Colin allowed himself to lift an eyebrow. "Why me?"

"She says she'll only talk to the reporter who wrote the articles about the Escobar case."

That reply did make Colin look away from his laptop and swivel his desk chair so he was facing Ryan. "Seriously? The Escobar case?"

"That's what she said."

The Escobar case had been a nasty one. Colin had the fortunate—or unfortunate, depending on how you looked at it—ability to recall pretty much every detail of the cases he'd covered, and so he remembered all too well that Matías Escobar had been found guilty of the kidnapping, ritual torture, and murder of a young woman named Roslyn McAllister. From up in Jerome, Colin remembered. Her body had been discovered in a seedy apartment building here in Tucson, along with some paraphernalia which seemed to indicate that Escobar and Jorge and Tomas Aguirre, his cousins, had been into some pretty sick stuff, a weird mixture of Santeria and Satanism and God knows what else.

The Aguirres had also been convicted as accessories to the crimes, and all three of them were currently serving life sentences, although the cousins would be eligible for parole at some point in the distant future. There'd been pressure to give Escobar the death penalty, but because he didn't have any priors, the jury had decided to give him life instead.

At any rate, the story had been splashed over the Tucson papers for some weeks because of its sensational nature. There wasn't much doubt that Escobar would rot in prison for his crimes, but because Tucson wasn't known for its spectacular murder cases, this one had held the public's interest for longer than it might have in a place inured to those kinds of crimes, such as L.A. or New York or Detroit.

"Open and shut," Colin told Ryan. "That was probably one of the quickest murder trials I've ever seen. And Escobar isn't going anywhere anytime soon, so what does this woman want? She have new evidence or something?"

Ryan shrugged, but despite his outward indifference, curiosity gleamed in his dark eyes. "She wouldn't say. Or at least she wouldn't say it to *me*."

Despite himself, Colin's was intrigued. Besides, he could probably finish writing this damn parking meter article in his sleep. He might as well hear what the woman had to say. If nothing else, she might make the next fifteen minutes or so pass a little more quickly.

"Okay," he said. "What the hell."

"You promise to spill her deep, dark secrets in exchange for some Kilt Lifter?"

"On tap?"

Ryan looked offended. "Is there any other way to drink it?"

Grinning, Colin said, "Send her over."

His friend disappeared down the hallway while Colin tapped his fingers on his desktop and glanced around to make sure everything in his office was more or less fit for him to receive visitors. The place looked reasonably tidy, though, mostly because he hadn't been given anything to work on that required the stacks of messy notes he preferred. Assignments like the parking meter article sure weren't given that kind of in-depth treatment.

He was proud of his office, though, proud that he wasn't stuck out in the cube farm with the junior reporters. His last promotion had brought him this office, in addition to a semi-decent raise. Well, it would have been decent enough if he hadn't been forced to hand over a large chunk of it to his ex.

Soon, he thought. *Four more months. Four months, and then you're finally off the alimony train.* Considering he'd been making those payments for almost three years now, four months should be a breeze.

"Mr. Campbell?"

He looked up at the unfamiliar voice and saw a woman he'd never met before standing in the doorway to his office. As Ryan had said, she was older, most likely in her middle or late sixties, with hair that had once probably been blonde or light brown but was now the dishwatery gray-yellow that seemed to be the color of choice for women of a certain age in the greater Southwest region. Even so, she was trim and well-dressed, with bright pink toenails peeping out from the sandals she wore. It might have been the first week in November, but temperatures were still just kissing the low eighties in Tucson.

"Colin," he said automatically. "Please sit down, Ms.—"

"Ms. Kosky," she said. "But please call me Eileen."

"Eileen," he responded as she took a seat in the spare task chair he kept in one corner in case of visits such as this one. "Can I get you anything? Coffee? Water?"

"No, thank you," she said. Her fingers were clutched around the purse she carried. He noted that her nails were bright pink to match her toes. And, just as he was studying her, she seemed to be studying him. "You're really the Colin Campbell who wrote all those pieces on the Matías Escobar case?"

"Yes."

"You don't look old enough."

He wanted to laugh, but instead he replied gravely, "I'm thirty-two, Ms.—Eileen. I've been at this for a while."

His response seemed to satisfy her, because she nodded. Maybe she'd been unwilling to trust anyone under thirty, but since he'd attained the magic age of reliability, he was worthy of her respect. She said, "I really hadn't thought about it for some time, because that was all months ago, but then I saw this in the paper this morning…." She reached in her purse and pulled out a newspaper clipping, then laid it on his desktop.

A little surprised, he reached for the clipping. Yes, the physical version of the *Tucson Daily Sun* went out every morning, or he wouldn't have a job. Also, there was that whole "daily" thing in the title. Even so, he was always startled to be confronted by evidence that people were still reading the hard-copy version, rather than online.

The bit she'd cut out seemed to be from the lifestyle section, the part of the paper he frankly didn't pay much attention to. It wasn't his job to write up the wedding and birth announcements, the obituaries. The clipping showed a photo of an attractive young couple, the groom Hispanic and in his middle twenties, the bride apparently a few years younger, with wavy hair that was a mid-tone gray in the black and white photo but was probably light brown or maybe even reddish in real life.

Caitlin Lysette McAllister and Alexander Maximilian Ernesto Trujillo will be married at St. Augustine's Cathedral, Tucson, at 5:00 p.m., Saturday, the 12th of November. The wedding will be followed by a reception at The Arizona Inn.

The bride is the daughter of Mr. and Mrs. Richard L. McAllister of Jerome, Arizona. The groom is the son of Mr. and Mrs. David J. Trujillo of Tucson.

The bride, 22, currently attends the University of Arizona. The groom, 27, who also went to UA, majored in Communications and Marketing, and currently is a marketing manager at KWTN in Tucson.

Caitlin and Alex, after honeymooning in Scottsdale, will continue to reside in Tucson.

Colin set the clipping back down. "And...so? They seem like a nice couple." He didn't really want to think about how he and Shannon had seemed like a nice young couple once upon a time. That seemed a little too much like jinxing this Caitlin and Alex before they even got started.

Eileen Kosky raised one penciled eyebrow. "Well, it's because they were *there*."

"There…where?"

"At the shopping mall in Phoenix."

Around about that point, Colin began to think his visitor might be a few cans short of a six-pack. He also was thinking that Ryan was going to owe him more than just a couple of beers for putting him through this. "Maybe you'd like to go back to the beginning. You saw Caitlin McAllister and Alex Trujillo at a shopping mall in Phoenix?"

"Yes." Eileen took the clipping and put it back in her purse. What she planned to do with it, Colin had no idea. "I was up visiting my sister in Phoenix last March, and we decided to go shopping, maybe see a movie. We like to do that—one month I'll go to visit her, and the next she'll come down and see me here in Tucson."

That bit of information didn't seem to require a reply, so Colin only nodded.

"Anyway," she continued. "Patty had just parked the car, and we were walking toward the mall entrance—you know, over by Dillard's?"

He didn't, being blessedly unfamiliar with most of the greater Phoenix area's shopping centers. But, rather than profess his ignorance, he decided it was better for him to nod again.

"So we were headed toward the entrance when we heard what sounded like several people having some kind of argument in the next parking row. Well, naturally we looked to see what was going on, because maybe it was something that we should call mall security about. And that was when we saw *him*."

"Alex Trujillo?"

"Well, yes, he was there, but the first person I noticed was the one who got sent to prison. You know, Matías Escobar."

The name made Colin sit up straighter. "You saw Escobar before he was arrested?"

"Oh, believe me, there was no law enforcement around right *then*. He was holding on to a pretty Mexican girl, and it sounded as if he was arguing with the couple from the clipping, Alex and Caitlin." Eileen paused then, a puzzled expression crossing her features. Like so many fair-skinned women of her age who lived in Tucson or Phoenix, her face was heavily lined from too much exposure to the sun, but beneath those lines Colin thought he could see traces of the young woman she'd once been. He had a feeling that, once upon a time, she'd been kind of a knockout. "What's strange is that I'd really forgotten all about it. So had Patty, apparently. It wasn't until I saw that article in the paper yesterday morning that it all came back."

"The argument they were having with Matías Escobar?"

"Yes, but that wasn't the really strange part."

"What was?"

Eileen Kosky's well-manicured nails fiddled with the clasp on her purse, and her gaze wouldn't quite meet his. For someone who'd requested this interview—or, according to Ryan, had almost demanded it—she appeared awfully reluctant to continue with her story.

After a long pause, however, she said, "I know this is going to sound very strange—"

"Try me," Colin cut in. "You spend enough time as a reporter, you hear all kinds of weird stuff. It takes a lot to faze me."

His declaration didn't seem to move her, though. She still hesitated, fingers tapping on the brass fittings on her purse. Then she took a breath, as if coming to some sort of inner decision. "All right. They were arguing, but Patty and I couldn't hear exactly what they were saying. Then that young man—Alex— he lifted his hands, and there was this bright flash of brilliant blue light. And the next thing we knew, Matías Escobar was lying on the ground."

Well, Eileen Kosky had been right about one thing. That did sound strange. No, scratch that. It sounded downright weird. And impossible. So Colin did what he always did when confronted by something that seemed impossible. He started looking for the most plausible explanation. "Maybe he had a Taser—"

"It wasn't a Taser," she said, her tone emphatic. "I've seen those on TV. This looked nothing like that. It was just a burst of light, almost like a transformer exploding. You know, with that bluish tinge? Except not that big, and it didn't seem to hurt anyone except Matías Escobar. And then these two men came hurrying up—"

"Mall cops?"

She shook her head. "No. One was tall and quite good-looking, and the other was shorter and heavier. They had two young Hispanic men with them, and a girl with long dark hair. The men started talking to Alex and Caitlin—"

"Wait," Colin said. "So Escobar was still knocked out cold on the ground?"

Eileen gave a negligent wave of her hand, as if she considered the question irrelevant. "I suppose so. Anyway, those two men started talking to this Caitlin and Alex, but we couldn't hear what they were saying. And then—" Eileen Kosky broke off then, her penciled brows pulling together in confusion. "Actually, I can't remember exactly what happened next. It's like there's a gap in my memory or something. The first thing I remember after that was being in Dillard's and standing and looking at a shoe display with Patty."

"Does Patty remember seeing the blue flash?"

A lift of her shoulders. "She says she doesn't. I called her this morning to ask if she remembered anything about that day, and she said she remembered going to the mall but that was it." Another shrug. "She's my older sister, you see. Sometimes things slip her mind, but usually nothing as unusual as this."

Colin wondered how much older than her sister this Patty was. Eileen Kosky seemed sharp enough, despite the crazy story she'd just told. He supposed that having a "senior moment" when you were somewhere in your seventies probably wasn't that odd. And yet....

Something felt strange here. He'd gotten the feeling while he was working on his articles about Matías Escobar that certain information was being suppressed, that there were aspects to the story that someone didn't want to get out. Colin's numerous requests to question the suspect directly had all been denied. Also, the D.A. had been very careful to keep the case focused on the girl who was murdered, Roslyn McAllister, even though both she and her friend had been kidnapped by Escobar and his partners in crime. What was the other girl's name, anyway?

Danica. Danica Wilcox.

She hadn't been there for the trial, but he remembered how he'd caught a glimpse of her at Escobar's sentencing. An extremely pretty girl with long dark hair, but a strained, haunted look in her hazel eyes. He couldn't really blame her for that. Anyone would have probably felt that way after going through what she'd survived. She'd been flanked by a handsome dark-haired couple in their late forties. Parents, he'd assumed.

"Can you describe the girl who was with the two men?" Colin asked. He figured that was a good way to find out if there was any truth at all to Eileen Kosky's story. None of the papers—including his— had published any photos of Danica Wilcox, so if Eileen was able to describe her more or less accurately, then it would prove that she actually had seen the young woman in question on that warm afternoon in late March.

"Yes," Eileen said at once. "She had very dark hair, long and wavy, almost down to her waist. She was tall and slim. Very pretty, really. She probably could model, if she wanted to. We weren't close enough to see her eye color, though."

"Thanks, Eileen," Colin told her. Yes, one could argue that her description could have fit a lot of girls, but it also fit Danica Wilcox perfectly. "And the men you saw with her in the parking lot that day?"

"Well, two of them were Matías Escobar's accomplices. I remember that because I saw their pictures in the paper, too. But the others...." She shrugged, pretending a nonchalance Colin was pretty sure she didn't actually feel. Once again he glimpsed that flicker of worried confusion in her face, as if she thought she should know the answer to the question but didn't. "I know one was tall and good-looking, and the other one was much shorter and a little chubby. I can't remember any details, though."

"It's all right," Colin said, hoping he sounded more or less reassuring. "Did those two men seem to be with Escobar's accomplices?" He hoped to hell they weren't connected. Otherwise, the Tucson P.D. might have missed a very important clue, and there could still be several very dangerous men out on the street.

"I don't think so. Not that I remember, anyway," she replied, the exasperation clear in her voice this time. "I *should* remember. It's not like me to forget things like that."

He believed her. Sure, parts of her story sounded pretty far-fetched, but he'd interviewed enough certifiable crazies to know that Eileen Kosky was definitely not crazy. "Let's go back to Alex and Caitlin," he said gently. "Do you remember anything else they did?"

"No. I think they talked to the other girl, the one Matías had with him."

And who the heck she'd been, Colin couldn't figure out. A friend of Danica's, maybe?

Eileen paused for a moment, another of those frowns pulling at her brows. "I got the feeling she and Alex Trujillo were related somehow. Their coloring and bone structure...."

"His sister?" Colin asked. If Escobar had been trying to make off with Trujillo's baby sister, Colin could understand why the young man might have attacked him with...whatever that was. He still believed that it had to have been some kind of Taser, or maybe a stun gun, and Eileen Kosky had amplified the effects in her mind to make them sound a lot more spectacular than they'd actually been in real life.

"Maybe. Since I couldn't really hear what they were saying, I don't know for sure."

"And you don't remember what happened afterward, how you got into the store?"

"Well, I'm sure my own two feet carried me in there," she replied, sounding irritated enough that he knew he'd touched a nerve. "But otherwise, no.

It's like those shows where people get kidnapped by aliens and lose minutes or even hours of their lives."

"Do you think you were kidnapped by aliens?" he asked, unable to keep a hint of amusement out of his voice.

"Of course not," she snapped. "I don't believe in that sort of thing. But something very strange happened in that parking lot, and it seemed like the sort of thing someone should know about. I thought of you, because you were the one who wrote all those stories about Matías Escobar in the first place. But if you don't believe me—" She began to rise from her chair, and Colin immediately put out a placating hand.

"I'm not saying I don't believe you," he said. "It's just my job to ask questions."

Those words seemed to mollify her somewhat, and she sat back down. "So you'll look into it?"

"I think it bears looking into," he replied. As outlandish as her story sounded, elements of it intrigued him. Who was the Hispanic girl, and who were the two men who'd been talking to Alex Trujillo and Caitlin McAllister? Why hadn't Danica tried to get away from her captors?

He'd have to start poking around on his own time, though; he knew that Ned Tavener, his editor, would never give him permission to start investigating a case that involved weird blue flashes of light and missing time. No, he'd probably make a caustic remark about possibly looking into a position at the *National Enquirer,* and there would go the office and title Colin had worked so hard to earn. "But it might take some time. Do you have a number where I can reach you?"

"Better to email me," she said. "EileenK589 at Gmail." Apparently noting his raised eyebrows, she said crisply, "I do know how to operate a computer, Colin. I just don't like typing on my phone because the keypad is so darn small."

"Well, I have to agree with you on that one," he said, smiling. "So I'll email you, Eileen, if I come up with anything that might help explain what you saw in the parking lot that day."

"Thank you." This time she did get up from her chair. "Thank you for taking me seriously."

"Not a problem."

She let herself out, and Colin's smile faded. He turned back to his computer, then went to the paper's website and navigated to the lifestyle page. There was the online version of Caitlin McAllister and Alex Trujillo's wedding announcement, only this time with the photo in color.

Yes, Caitlin's hair was red after all. Very red. Well, with a last name like McAllister, he supposed he shouldn't be too surprised that she'd have such stereotypical Scottish coloring. Hell, for all he knew, maybe she was distantly related to him, generations and generations back. His family had come over in the early 1800s, but still....

He leaned back in his chair, staring at the photo. Saturday, the twelfth of November. The day after tomorrow. He knew St. Augustine's well enough; it wasn't that far from the *Daily Sun*'s offices. Not that he usually worked on Saturdays, but....

A grin pulled at his mouth, and he navigated away from the web page with the McAllister/Trujillo announcement on it. After all, it was probably better that no one here at the paper knew what he was planning.

Because it sure looked like he was about to crash a wedding.

CHAPTER TWO

TRAPPED IN THE CAREFULLY CONTROLLED MADNESS OF THE dressing room area at St. Augustine's, Jenny McAllister wondered—not for the first time—just what the hell she'd been thinking, volunteering to be Caitlin's maid of honor.

On the surface, her decision to take on that role had seemed like the obvious thing to do. She and Caitlin were cousins, after all, and who better to step into Roslyn's shoes than her own sister? Yes, Caitlin and Danica Wilcox were closer friends, but at the time Jenny had made the offer, Danica hadn't seemed capable of doing much beyond tying her own shoes. Now, of course, she was doing much better, but....

You will not go there, she told herself. *You will not begrudge Danica her happiness, not after everything she went through.*

Easier said than done. Jenny didn't have anything against Danica...except maybe a small, unpleasant undercurrent of resentment that Danica had managed to survive Matías Escobar's torments, whereas Jenny's own beautiful sister Roslyn had not...but still, it sometimes hurt to see how happy Danica was now, with her handsome fiancé and her now seemingly perfect life. True, she'd had to travel back in time more than a hundred years to find her Mr. Perfect, but still....

On days like this, it seemed as if the phrase "always a bridesmaid, never a bride" had been carefully crafted to stick in her craw. Jenny had been either a bridesmaid or a maid of honor in five other weddings before this one, and she vowed this would be the last time. It definitely didn't help that she was an anomaly in her own witch clan, a woman who was on the wrong side of twenty-nine and still unmarried. Witches and warlocks tended to marry young, some sixth sense telling them who their "one" was while they were still in their early twenties, but Jenny had never been that lucky.

"Have you seen Great-Aunt Ruby's earrings?" Caitlin asked, sounding panicked. She was dressed, hair done, and looking so beautiful in her ivory silk gown with its re-embroidered lace that Jenny knew she needed to push her gloomy thoughts aside and focus on the person this day was really about. "I've looked and looked—"

"They're in that little crystal tray on the dressing table," Jenny said calmly. That was what maids of honor were supposed to be—calm and in control, and also able to let the bride know that no crisis would arise that couldn't be handled. All right, a wedding planner could probably fulfill that same role, but no McAllister bride had ever hired a wedding planner, and Caitlin had decided she didn't want to be a trailblazer when it came to that sort of thing, even though she'd mentioned once or twice that she would have preferred to hand some of the work off to someone else, since she was trying to organize the wedding while also going to school full time.

And then there was that matter of Alex putting a wedding announcement in the local paper. One could argue that no one paid attention to those sorts of things except the families of the people actually getting married, and so it really wasn't that big a deal, but it just hadn't seemed like a very good idea to Jenny, or to the McAllister elders, either, not when the survival of the witch clans had always depended on keeping a low profile. They'd advised against it, but Caitlin had just shrugged and said that because Alex had a prominent position at a local television station, it made sense for them to make the announcement.

Well, done was done. Jenny watched as Caitlin slipped Great-Aunt Ruby's diamond and rose gold drops into her ears, then made a minute adjustment to the delicate band of filigreed copper that held back her carefully curled hair.

"You look gorgeous," Jenny said sincerely. The faintly blush-toned ivory of the strapless wedding gown suited Caitlin's coloring perfectly, where pure white probably would have washed her out. And Jenny had to admit that Caitlin had been kind to her bridesmaids, choosing simple sheath dresses in a dark coral hue that almost anyone could carry off. The color suited Danica's near-black hair and hazel eyes just as well as it did Jenny's own honey-blonde tresses and blue-gray eyes.

"I do?" Caitlin asked, sounding somewhat surprised.

"Like you stepped out of a magazine."

Danica came into the room then, carrying the box that held the bouquets. They were simple bunches of creamy white roses, with just a kiss of the softest coral pink around the edges of their petals. Behind her was Alicia Trujillo, Alex's little sister, who was the third bridesmaid.

"It looks like pretty much everyone is settled in," Alicia said. "So if you're ready, Caitlin—"

Caitlin pulled in a deep breath, then nodded. "I'm ready. I mean, I don't *feel* ready, but—"

"It'll be fine," Jenny said. "It always is."

She'd spoken those words of reassurance as a way of reminding Caitlin that there had been plenty of McAllister weddings before this, and there would be plenty after, and they always went off more or less without a hitch. That was part of the beauty of having witch blood; if you had the whole clan focusing their energies on making sure you had a perfect day, that was pretty much what would happen.

Also, it probably didn't hurt that Mr. "Lucky" Lucas Wilcox himself was here, too, part of the Wilcox contingent that had come down with Danica. Having him around basically ensured that everything would go exactly as planned.

Caitlin gulped in another swallow of air, then nodded. "I'm fine. It'll be fine. I mean, it's just Alex."

Alicia raised an eyebrow at that, and Caitlin hurried on, "Oh, you know what I mean. We've been living together for months now. It's not like he's going to change into someone else. He's just…my Alex."

Pulling Caitlin's bouquet out of the box, Danica said dryly, "Then go marry the boy. Let him make an honest woman of you."

That remark made Caitlin chuckle. "Don't tell me being with Robert's made you all prudish and Victorian."

"Hardly." A wicked light danced in Danica's eyes, and she added, "He may be from the Victorian era, but a prude he is most definitely not."

Jenny decided she'd heard enough, and was wondering how to steer the conversation in another direction when the universe appeared to take pity on her. She heard the first strains of the organist playing Pachelbel's "Canon," signaling that it was time for the girls to get into position. "Okay, everyone," she said, "grab your bouquets and get ready to go. It's showtime."

There was a brief flurry of activity after that, but the group managed to get out of the dressing room and over to the entrance of the chapel, where they lined up in the proper order. Just across the way, Jenny caught a glimpse of Alex's older brother, Diego, grinning at her. Damn, there was a good-looking man. Too bad he was married.

Of course he is, she thought then. *All the good ones are.*

But she didn't have time to brood over that sad fact, because Diego was linking his arm in hers and guiding her down the red carpet runner that led to the altar. The space was scented with the fragrance of roses and lilies, with something smoky and warm behind it. Probably traces of leftover incense; this was a very thoroughly Catholic church. And Caitlin and Alex would be married in a Catholic ceremony, something her parents hadn't been too thrilled about. But the de la Paz clan were both witches and fairly devout Catholics, whereas the McAllisters were a lot more freewheeling when it came to religion. Caitlin had said she didn't mind, that Alex respected her own beliefs and wouldn't try to force anything on her, and so she was perfectly happy to follow his family's traditions when it came to their wedding.

At least the services weren't being conducted in Latin. Did they even do that anymore? Jenny had to admit that her knowledge of the Catholic Church's practices was kind of foggy. Anyway, that sort of thing would have made her eyes glaze right over. As it was, she let her attention wander while the priest seemed to talk interminably, using what she couldn't help thinking of as the Webster's unabridged wedding ceremony text.

The church really was quite lovely, with its lofty dark-beamed ceilings and stained-glass windows. Back in Jerome, weddings were held everywhere from people's homes to hotel meeting rooms to fancy restaurants. Not churches all that much, so it was interesting to look at the architecture. The cathedral did make a rather spectacular setting, and Jenny could see why Alex had chosen this particular venue.

More interesting, though, was the people-watching. The de la Paz clan was very large, much bigger than the McAllister family, so their side of the church was packed to the gills. Even so, a good number of them must have had to stay home. Jenny wondered how that had been handled. Some kind of lottery? Or had Luz Trujillo, the new *prima* of the de la Paz clan and Alex's mother, helped Alex and Caitlin make those determinations based on how closely related a particular witch or warlock was to the groom?

Jenny hadn't been involved in that part of the process, so she really didn't have any idea. She did know that five hundred people had been invited, and it sure looked as if they were all here. There wasn't an empty space in any of the pews, not even the ones on the McAllister side, which also boasted a good number of Wilcoxes. Right there in front, sitting next to Caitlin's parents, were Angela and Connor Wilcox. True, Angela had been born a McAllister, but she still carried the Wilcox name now that she was married to Connor.

And she's half Wilcox anyway, Jenny thought, *since it turned out her father was a Wilcox, too.*

Some McAllisters still weren't entirely thrilled about that turn of events, nor the ongoing integration of the two clans, which had been enemies for generations. Actually, at first Jenny had been pleased by the thaw in relations between the Wilcoxes and the McAllisters. After all, a lot of the Wilcox men were awfully good-looking.

Unfortunately, she hadn't had any more luck making a connection with one of them than she'd had with those of her McAllister cousins considered distant enough to be safe to marry.

Or the civilians she'd dated, thinking maybe that was the answer. Her own mother was a civilian, a non-witch, and her parents' marriage was still going strong, some thirty-plus years later. But Jenny had somehow managed to strike out with the civilians, too.

Shifting her weight from one foot to the other, but trying not to be too obvious about it, Jenny let her gaze wander back over to the de la Paz side of the church. Yes, Diego Trujillo was married. That didn't mean there probably weren't plenty of eligible men in that clan. Or maybe not, if they all tended to get married as early as the McAllisters did.

Among that sea of almost uniformly raven-hued heads, someone's warm brown hair caught her eye. Jenny looked more closely, and hoped it wouldn't seem as if she was staring. Yes, the man sitting in the back pew definitely didn't look like a de la Paz. In fact, with his light brown hair and fair skin, he looked far more like a McAllister, although she knew she'd never seen him before. She would have remembered him. Handsome, but in a rugged yet boyish way. His jacket looked slightly rumpled, too, as if he'd retrieved it from the depths of his closet for this special occasion and hadn't bothered to steam out the wrinkles.

Maybe a friend of Alex's from college? She supposed that was possible, although the stranger looked older than Alex, probably past thirty, and so a few years older than she was. Well, that still didn't mean anything. She'd never gone to college; until Wilcox territory opened up during the past few years, there hadn't been a four-year university it was easy for a McAllister to attend, but she knew not everyone headed straight to college right after high school. That could explain why the stranger looked like he had a good five years or so on Alex.

Even so, something about him didn't feel right to her. The unknown man was watching the ceremony intently, but she noticed he sat as close to the end of the pew as possible, as if he wanted to keep away from his neighbors. Not that Jenny could really blame him, since a couple of squirmy kids who looked like they were around kindergarten age also occupied that pew, and were only separated from the stranger by an exasperated-looking mother.

But at least they weren't so noisy that they interrupted the ceremony. Alex and Caitlin were so wrapped up in each other and the words they were saying that they probably wouldn't have even noticed that kind of disruption, but, judging by the way Luz Trujillo's dark gaze kept flicking toward the back of the church, the *prima* of that clan most definitely would notice, and would most likely would have had a few words with the mother about keeping her kids in line.

Jenny actually felt a little sorry for the little boy and girl, since she was sure they probably would have rather stayed home than sit through this interminable ceremony. Right then, she just wanted it to be over herself so she could get to the good part—the reception and all that lovely champagne. She figured she'd earned a glass or two. Or three or four.

But even though her feet were starting to hurt, and she worried that her stomach was going to growl at any second, she couldn't help feeling moved when the priest proclaimed that Alex and Caitlin were now husband and wife. And the look in Alex's dark eyes when he bent to kiss his new bride—well, it awoke a deep, hurtful ache in Jenny's heart.

She wanted someone to look at her like that.

And then she couldn't help feeling ashamed, because at least she was here, and not buried in a corner of the McAllister plot in the Cottonwood cemetery. Roslyn would never have anyone look at her the way Alex had looked at Caitlin. She'd never see the sun shine again, or watch the moon rise over the Mogollon Plateau to the east of town. She'd never have children, or grandchildren, would never again

entrance an audience with the power of her beautiful voice.

All because of Matías Escobar.

The familiar burning ache of hate rose in her
then, and Jenny forced herself to push it back down.
She'd been over this same ground too many times
during the last six months. All the hate in the world
wouldn't bring Roslyn back.

She managed to plaster a fake smile on her lips,
since she knew that was what would be expected of
her. And sometime during the hubbub of getting
Caitlin and Alex out to their limo so they could have
their photos taken and still make it to the reception
area on time, that smile turned genuine. It was just
too hard to see their obvious happiness and not
respond.

Because Jenny had come down a day early to
help with the preparations, she had her own car, giving her a spurious sense of freedom. Her younger
brother Adam and his wife Mason had driven down
with Jenny and Adam's parents, since they knew
parking was going to be tight. They were staying in
the same hotel as Jenny, the place where the reception would be held, although on a different floor.
Her parents had already made plans for all of them
to go out to breakfast together the morning after the
wedding.

Usually Jenny wouldn't have minded, since she got along fine with her parents, and she liked her sister-in-law very much as well. Right then, though, the prospect of having to play happy family made her want to grind her teeth.

That's the crappy part about being a witch, she thought. *We all have these rigidly defined clans and these rigidly defined territories, and everyone's supposed to play by the rules. You can't just get in your car and keep driving and leave it all behind, no matter how much you might want to.*

Well, except Angela's mother. She'd kept driving and never looked back. Unfortunately, that hadn't worked out so well for her in the end, dead in a motorcycle crash at twenty-two, leaving her infant daughter for Angela's Aunt Rachel to raise.

Since the first set of photographs that would be taken at the reception site would include only the bride and groom, Jenny knew she had a little time before she had to drive over to the hotel, about fifteen minutes away. No rest for the wicked, though—she went through the church with a couple of the de la Paz cousins, helping to pick up any discarded programs and generally tidying things up before she was able to make her escape not quite half an hour later.

At least the hotel was close by. Jenny was able to grab one of the last parking spaces before hurrying over to the large event space where the reception was being held. Inside, the place felt packed—mostly because everyone seemed to be crammed into the bar area—but she managed to squeeze through the throng and make her way to the less crowded part of the room where everyone would sit down for dinner.

After a quick glance around, she determined that Alex and Caitlin were nowhere in sight, which meant they must still be off getting their pictures taken. Just as she turned, she almost bumped into the brown-haired stranger she'd spied earlier in the church.

He had a flute of champagne in either hand, and held one out to her. "Here," he said, his voice as pleasant and friendly as his features. "You look like you could use this."

"That bad, huh?" she responded, gratefully taking it from him.

"Well, you're carrying it well, but I've been to too many weddings not to recognize the 'I need a drink' look common to maids of honor the world over."

She couldn't help chuckling at that remark. It didn't stop her from taking a large swallow of the champagne. It hit her stomach with a flare of warmth and a welcome fizz. "Thank you." Since he seemed nice, and she didn't have any place she absolutely had to be in that moment, she added, "I'm Jenny McAllister."

"I know," he said, and she gave him a blank look.

"How? We haven't met before, have we?"

"No." He tapped the breast pocket of his dark gray blazer, where she could see one cream-colored edge of the wedding program peeking out. "I saw your name in here."

"Ah." She sipped some more champagne, and that gave her the courage to ask, "Friend of the groom?"

"In a manner of speaking. I was his T.A. at UA. I'm Colin Campbell."

Something about the phrase made her want to laugh, but that could have been the champagne talking. But at least it explained why Colin seemed older and still could have known Alex. "Marketing?" she asked.

"No, journalism. He took a few classes but then switched over to communications and marketing. Probably smart of him."

Colin's tone was wry, compelling her to inquire, "Smart how?"

"Well, let's just say it's kind of challenging to be a journalist in the internet age. No one seems to think you should get paid for your work. Actually, I ended up getting out of it, too."

"Oh." She supposed she should have realized that, but frankly, the Verde Valley wasn't exactly a hotbed of in-depth journalism. They had the *Verde Valley Independent* for the local stuff, but otherwise most people either watched TV or hit the web to get their information, depending on their generation and habits. "That's too bad."

"So what do you do?" he asked, clearly wanting to change the subject.

Typical question for this sort of gathering, especially coming from a civilian who had no way of knowing that he was surrounded by witches and warlocks of various clans and talents. But it grated on Jenny, because she didn't have a very good answer to that question. For a while she'd worked as a dispatcher for the police department down in Cottonwood, but that job hadn't lasted very long. Even in a place as small as Cottonwood, she'd gotten more of a taste of the dark side of human nature than she'd really wanted, so she'd quit. Unfortunately, leaving the job hadn't allowed her to escape reality's darker aspects. No, they'd intruded on a bright March day last spring, when the phone call came to tell her that her little sister was dead.

Hoping he hadn't noticed her hesitation, Jenny said, "Oh, a little bit of this and that. Lately I've been helping to run the art gallery downstairs."

"'Downstairs'?" he repeated, looking confused in an adorable sort of way.

"I'm from Jerome. Old buildings, apartments and flats on top of businesses. The business downstairs from me is an art gallery. And the owner is a ci—well, she lives in Scottsdale, so she wanted someone local to manage it for her."

Colin drank some of his champagne, then said, "I visited Jerome about ten years ago. Cool place. You like living there?"

She shrugged. *Did* she like living there? She really didn't have much of a basis for comparison. The former mining town had always been part of her life, along with its small, mixed population of witch-folk and civilians. Her clan was careful about who they allowed to live there, always choosing those who could be trusted to keep quiet about the powers their neighbors possessed but never talked openly about.

But getting the flat above the art gallery had been sort of a coup, since several of her cousins had cast covetous eyes upon it when it became available. Why the elders had decided Jenny should have it, she wasn't quite sure, except maybe they had taken pity on her because she was nearing thirty and was still unattached, and so deserved to get something of a break. Anyway, it was a great space, with a bedroom and an office, and a front deck that overlooked Main Street and provided amazing views of the entire Verde Valley, all the way to Sedona's red rocks. It was definitely something to sit on that deck and drink a glass of wine and watch the rocks turn redder and redder as the sun set.

"It's fun," she said. "Small. Everyone knows everyone else."

"So is that a good thing or a bad thing?" he asked with a grin.

The light that danced in his hazel eyes was definitely something she could get used to. "I guess it depends on who you ask."

"Well, what if I asked you?"

Was he flirting? It felt like he might be flirting. Jenny couldn't say for sure, because she pretty much sucked at that sort of thing. But she decided she might as well go along for the ride. If nothing else, it was refreshing to be talking with someone who didn't know anything about her or her background, or the sister she'd lost so tragically. "I'd say it's a good thing some days and a bad thing on others."

"Diplomatic. Or maybe evasive."

"Realistic?"

"I'll go for that." He raised his champagne flute, and she clinked her glass against his, unable to suppress a smile. There was something infectious about the way his mouth quirked, not really smiling, but edging toward it.

It seemed the best thing to do was to drink some more champagne. There were probably a million things she should be doing right then, but it felt good to stand there and not-quite-flirt with a good-looking stranger. It wasn't as if Alicia or Danica couldn't handle something if Caitlin suddenly required one of her bridesmaids to be there for her.

But then Jenny heard her Aunt Tricia—Caitlin's mother—calling for her, and she knew playtime was over.

"Duty calls," she said, and looked around for a place to set down her champagne flute.

"I'll take that," Colin offered, plucking it out of her fingers. "Maybe I should hang on to it. You up for a second round later?"

He was going to stick around, wasn't going to take off after he'd had a few free drinks. Something in her relaxed slightly.

"I'll be around," she said with a grin, and went off in search of her aunt.

CHAPTER THREE

GOD, SHE WAS GORGEOUS. FOR SOME REASON, COLIN hadn't been expecting that, even though the photos of her late sister showed that Roslyn McAllister had been an extremely pretty girl. But Jenny....

Wow. He'd done his best not to stare too hard as she disappeared into the crowd, but that simple dress she was wearing had hugged her backside in a far too distracting way. And the long blonde hair bouncing down her back—

He went and got another flute of champagne, although he knew he really should watch it. This was supposed to be a fact-finding mission, not some frat party blowout. Not that most frats served champagne at their parties.

So he headed off to a corner of the room and did his best to look inconspicuous. From what he'd been able to tell so far, there seemed to be three fairly distinct groups here. The first, and by far the most numerous, were obviously Alex's family, although it seemed a lot of them had the last name of de la Paz rather than Trujillo. The second batch were McAllisters, a few red-haired like the bride, including her mother, but most of them with sandy brown or dark blond hair. And then there were the darkly handsome Wilcoxes, including Danica's parents, whom Colin recognized from the trial.

They all looked far more relaxed now, talking and laughing, Danica's father holding a glass of red wine, while his wife and daughter had champagne. As did the tall man, maybe a few years younger than Colin himself, who was clearly with Danica and who had the chiseled looks of an actor or model. He wasn't, though, or at least he didn't ping Colin's radar that way. He'd known enough actors and guys who modeled when he was in college and out of it, and they all had a faint aura of knowing exactly how good-looking they were. The guy standing next to Danica didn't, for whatever reason. Which didn't prove much. But still, something about him felt a little off, even though Colin couldn't quite put his finger on what the difference was.

He supposed he should just be glad that he'd gotten this far without being called out as a gate crasher. True, the crowd was large, and mixed people from three different families, but even so, Colin thought he was conspicuous enough that someone should have wondered who the hell he was. Then again, several people had probably spotted him talking to Jenny, and so must have decided that he was either her date, or maybe just a friend.

The hard part was yet to come, though. A reception as big as this was obviously going to have set seating arrangements, with place cards and all that crap. About all he could do was hang back, maybe pretend that he was talking with the bartender, until almost everyone had sat down and he could scope out the gaps at the tables. No wedding ever had one-hundred-percent attendance; there was always someone who didn't show up, whether their absence was due to illness or bad traffic or sheer absentmindedness.

He hoped one of those gaps would occur at a McAllister table. His story about being Alex Trujillo's teaching assistant at UA would be a lot easier to sell to them, since they wouldn't know him nearly as well as Alex's own family. Also, Colin thought he would blend a lot better with the McAllister contingent.

Maybe I can convince them I'm a distant cousin or something, he thought. *At the very least, I wouldn't have to be explaining my connection to Alex to them.*

Probably not, though; he watched as everyone flowed from the bar area into the main dining room, and, judging by the way the McAllisters interacted, they seemed like a pretty tight-knit group. Trying to insinuate himself in with them didn't seem like a very good idea, as much as he would have liked to listen to what they were saying and attempt to glean some more information about Jenny.

Which isn't why you're here, he told himself again. He could try to rationalize that Jenny was Roslyn's sister, and so maybe she'd have some inside information, but he knew that wasn't the reason he wanted to know more about her. He wanted to know more about her because of…her.

Stupid, and possibly dangerous. He was here under false pretenses, and if she figured out he'd come snooping around because of journalistic curiosity, she'd probably tell him to go straight to hell, that her family's tragedy wasn't an excuse for him to play junior detective. At least, he was pretty sure that if their situations were reversed, he'd feel exactly the same way. And then there had been the way he'd lied to her already, hinting that he'd turned his back on journalism when the money started to dry up.

Maybe it would be smart for him to slip out now. This was a fool's errand, anyway; he didn't honestly think that Eileen Kosky had seen anything truly out of the ordinary in that mall parking lot, only Alex Trujillo using a stun gun or something similar to dispatch Matías Escobar.

And yet….

Colin glanced into the dining room, saw Jenny settling herself at the head table. Someone must have just said something amusing, because she was laughing, head tilted back to show that fine throat of hers, long blonde hair spilling down toward her waist. So many women these days used extensions and crap like that to make their hair look better, but he didn't think Jenny McAllister had resorted to those sorts of subterfuges. Her sister had had the same hair, long and honey-blonde and full. It must run in the family.

Standing there and staring, Colin knew he wasn't about to leave. He quickly looked around and noticed a table off in one corner that seemed to be composed of some Wilcoxes and some McAllisters, which meant they probably didn't know one another very well. And there were two empty seats at that table. Perfect.

He sauntered over and sat down, and then sent everyone what he hoped was his most charming smile. His sister Kate had always hated that smile— "when you put that thing on, Mom lets you get away with murder," she'd grumbled more than once—but Colin had found it useful on several occasions, up to and including talking his way out of the speeding ticket that one female cop had been about to give him.

Well, he'd just have to hope his smile would pass muster here.

"Hi," he said as he settled into his seat. "I'm Colin."

The group at the table sent him various looks of greeting or inspection, depending on who was doing the looking. Next to him was an extremely attractive woman in her thirties, her dark hair in an elegant coil at the back of her head, and just beyond her sat a man maybe a few years older, dark and handsome like most of the Wilcoxes Colin had seen so far.

"Nice to meet you," the man said. "I'm Lucas, and this is my wife Margot."

She turned a cool smile on him, the sort that made Colin acutely aware that he'd done a half-assed job of steaming his neglected sport jacket. He also had to hope he didn't have anything stuck in his teeth. "Hello, Colin," Margot said. "Are you a friend of Alex's?"

"Yes," Colin lied. Margot's dark eyes seemed to pierce right through him, and he had to pray that she couldn't smell the lie. "My girlfriend was supposed to come with me, but she got a migraine at the last minute, so I had to fly solo today."

"Well, we won't bite," Lucas said with a grin. Unlike most of the other people at the table, he had what looked like a glass of Scotch on the rocks at his place setting, instead of champagne.

"Unless you ask nicely," said a man sitting across the table, obviously a McAllister, with his sandy hair and blue eyes. He looked a few years younger than Colin, and sat next to a man who also appeared to be in his middle twenties. Their chairs were a little closer together than one might expect from two guys attending a wedding, leading Colin to believe that they weren't exactly just friends. "I'm Kirby, by the way. And this is Matthew."

Matthew gave a sort-of wave, but it seemed clear enough that he was just fine with letting Kirby do the talking. Colin couldn't blame him for that; coming to these sorts of affairs could be taxing enough without having to deal with the inevitable disapproval a gay couple might get from some of the relatives.

Then Margot asked how Colin knew Alex, and he trotted out the same line he'd used on Jenny. It seemed to work, because Margot just nodded, while Lucas inquired whether Colin was from Tucson as well.

That was safe enough ground, and he talked about the city and going to school here, and which restaurants to go to and which to avoid, and whether it was worth it for Lucas and Margot to delay their return to Flagstaff so they could go to the Saguaro National Monument the next day. Inconsequential stuff, and Colin found himself gradually relaxing, worrying less and less with each course that was brought out as to whether anyone at the table would catch him in a lie.

So far, so good, though, and by the time the dinner plates were removed, he thought he'd be able to get out of this evening more or less unscathed. All right, he also hadn't managed to dig up one useful piece of information, except that Caitlin apparently was starting to make quite a career for herself as a writer, something Colin hadn't heard anything about until this evening.

Not that he would have, since he didn't read much fiction, and definitely not fantasy, the sort of thing she wrote. Still, hearing that she was doing well at such a young age made an unwelcome little flare of jealousy burn somewhere inside him. Here he was, writing puff pieces about parking meters for the princely sum of $35K per year, while Caitlin had somehow managed to get two novels out there already, with a third on the way.

And he didn't even want to think about the crappy lifestyle and diet pamphlets he was churning out on the side, making an extra thousand or so each month writing for some ebook mill based in California, just so he could afford to keep up his alimony payments and still live in an actual apartment instead of the back seat of his car.

You'll be done with that soon, he reminded himself. *Just a few more months. And then you'll never have to write another book on aromatherapy or juicing ever again.*

His expression must have shifted, because Lucas shot him a speculative glance but didn't say anything.

Luck seemed to be sticking close by Colin that night, though. In the next moment, there was some commotion at the head table, and then the groom's brother stood up and made the usual speech about how the new couple had found the right person when they found each other, and how he was sure they'd be very happy together. This was followed by everyone tapping on their glasses, forcing Alex and Caitlin to share an obligatory kiss. Her cheeks were flaming almost as red as her hair, and Colin got the impression that she hated being the center of attention. Unfortunately, that sort of thing was kind of hard to avoid when you were the bride.

But then Jenny stood as well. She held a champagne flute in one hand and smiled, but there was something too tight about her expression, as if she wore it because she had to and not because it was something she would have voluntarily done. From the little Colin had been able to dig up about Caitlin and Roslyn McAllister, it seemed the two were cousins but also very good friends. If Roslyn hadn't been murdered, would she have been Caitlin's maid of honor instead?

Hard to say, and Colin doubted he'd ever have the chance to ask Jenny that question. She made a nice little speech as well, although he noticed how tightly she clutched her champagne flute, knuckles white and the muscles in her slender bare arm tense. If it had been fragile crystal instead of the sturdy glassware used by the catering company, he had a feeling that glass would have shattered in her grip.

"And I know," Jenny said, "that we're all very happy to have the de la Paz and McAllister clans joined like this, in the same way we McAllisters recently joined with the Wilcoxes. So let's drink to the bright future of everyone here, especially Caitlin and Alex!"

Everyone raised their glasses and drank, and Colin did, too, although he found himself puzzling over Jenny's words. Clans? They were in southern Arizona, not the Scottish Highlands. And something about the way she'd phrased that toast made it sound as if they'd just signed a peace treaty or something, instead of simply getting married.

He didn't have much time to puzzle it out, though, because then it was time for the couple to cut the cake, an event surrounded by a lot of clapping and cheering, although Colin couldn't see much of what was going on, thanks to the positioning of the table where he sat. Not that he cared; he wasn't much for sweets, especially when paired with champagne. It was good champagne, too, something that would have gone better with a nice salty cheese.

But when the cake came around, he took a small slice and had a few bites for courtesy's sake, listening to the group at his table discuss whether Connor and Angela—whoever they were—would come to Jerome for the holidays this year or would stay up in Flagstaff. Colin filed the names away for future reference, just in case, but he was only listening with half an ear. So far no one had mentioned Roslyn McAllister, let alone her murder, and the conversation had been full of references to people he didn't know. And certainly Alex Trujillo hadn't created any displays of blue light. So far, the whole thing seemed a bust. A pleasant bust, with plenty of champagne and a very nice meal of pork tenderloin with achiote/cherry sauce, but still.

Then Alex led Caitlin out to the dance floor for their first dance. An old standard, "The Way You Look Tonight," which surprised Colin. It seemed sort of old-fashioned, and he wondered which of the couple had chosen the song.

After they'd had their customary minute or so alone, though, more people moved out onto the dance floor, Lucas and Margot among them, his dark eyes twinkling down at his wife, as if at some private joke. And Colin shifted in his chair, wondering if this was his cue to get out before things got too awkward.

His eyes locked on Jenny, who stood off to one side, looking uncomfortable and apparently pretending as if it was completely normal for her to be there all alone, without a partner. The best man, Alex's brother, was dancing with an extremely pretty Hispanic woman, obviously his wife, which meant Jenny had been left at loose ends.

Without even stopping to think about what he was doing, Colin got up from his chair and wove his way through the crowd until he was standing in front of her. She startled, and then a surprised smile touched her lips as she seemed to recognize him.

"I think I left your champagne flute behind," he said. "But it would have gotten in the way."

"Of what?" But her big blue-gray eyes were sparkling. She knew exactly why he was there.

"Of asking you to dance."

One of her eyebrows went up. "Well," she said, "I think you could have probably asked me while holding it, but I agree that it would have been a problem once we actually started dancing."

"So…do you want to?" God, that sounded idiotic. He was really out of practice at this sort of thing.

But Jenny seemed to take pity on him, saying, "Sure. It'll save me from having one of my cousins give me a pity dance."

Colin wasn't sure whether he should take that remark as an insult or not, but he decided to brush it aside. Anyway, he really did want to pull her into his arms and lead her out on the dance floor. He wouldn't claim to be that great a dancer. On the other hand, he thought he could manage something slow like the current piece without embarrassing himself too much.

So he held out his arms, and Jenny moved into them, seeming to fit just about perfectly. She was on the tall side, especially with those three-inch heels she had on—he still hadn't figured out how women could stand around for hours on end in those things, let alone dance in them—but since he was just a shade over six-two, there was still a decent height difference between them, just enough to have her nose brush right beneath his chin.

Damn, she smelled good, too. Colin didn't know if it was her perfume or something she used to make her hair that shiny, but he liked it, a soft scent that wasn't too floral, sort of warm and welcoming, like the scent of sugar cookies on a cold winter day.

"So...." He cleared his throat. "Do you have a lot of cousins?"

"Tons of them." A tilt of her head, and those misty-toned blue-gray eyes were looking up at him. "We McAllisters are all over the place in Jerome. And the Verde Valley, too."

"So not all your family is here."

"Not even close. The de la Pazes—I mean, Alex's family—are pretty ginormous, too. I think my Aunt Tricia—that's Caitlin's mom—and my mother sat down and figured out some kind of lottery to make it fair as to who got in and who didn't. Luckily, I didn't have to be involved in that part of the planning."

"Just making sure everyone showed up on time and no one's bouquet got lost."

She grinned, fun little crinkles appearing at the corners of her eyes. "Sounds like you've been involved in a wedding or two yourself."

"A couple," he admitted. Well, that was true enough, if you counted his wedding to Shannon and then his sister's wedding, where he'd been an attendant but not, thank God, the best man. And then there were the weddings of friends from college, and his cousins, and a few he'd had to cover during his early days of working at the paper, before he got moved up to the more important stories…anyway, he'd sort of lost count after a while.

"So yes, all that kind of stuff. I stepped in when Danica—" She broke off then, as if she'd realized she was about to tread on ground she probably shouldn't be covering with someone she barely knew. Speaking quickly, Jenny went on, "Well, there was some stuff going on, and I was kind of a pro at this maid-of-honor thing by then, so I offered."

"That was nice of you," Colin said. Inwardly, though, he was wishing she hadn't cut herself off. Danica Wilcox had been kept out of the public view for most of Escobar's trial, but Colin knew she had to have suffered some kind of effects from her kidnapping ordeal.

A shrug. "She's my cousin. She deserved to have her day go smoothly."

The song ended then, and Colin, with some reluctance, let Jenny slip out of his arms. She flashed him another one of those brilliant smiles, then said, "I've got some more bridesmaid-y things to manage. Are you going to stick around?"

"Absolutely," he replied at once. So much for his notion of slipping out when no one was looking. But what man in his right mind would take off when a woman who looked like Jenny McAllister was asking him if he planned to stay around for a while?

"Great." One last smile, and then she was off toward the head table, where Alex and Caitlin had returned, although neither one of them had sat down. They seemed to be talking with the couple Colin recognized as the bride's parents, maybe trying to decide how many songs to get through before stopping things for the bouquet toss or the garter throw.

Since Colin wasn't really interested in either of those things, he wandered out of the dining room and into the hallway outside, then out through one of the sets of French doors that opened on the courtyard. All the trees were swagged with white fairy lights, and floating candles drifted on the surface of the swimming pool. Clearly, the Trujillo/McAllister wedding party had pretty much taken over the entire hotel, and Colin found himself wondering how much all this had cost. Fifty grand? Probably at least that; Shannon's parents had paid for most of their daughter's wedding, and Colin had tuned out a lot of it, mostly because he found it sort of horrifying the way people would spend money on what was, after all, just a single day in a person's life. That money would have been far better spent on a down payment on a house or something, even though he had to admit he wouldn't have been able to lay claim to that asset, either, considering the way the divorce had turned out.

Pushing his bitter thoughts aside, he made a mental note to do some checking into the de la Paz and McAllister finances. Everything was most likely on the up and up, but it never hurt to do a little digging.

The breeze was cool, the warmth of the day nearly gone by now. Overhead, the bright desert stars were pinpricks in the dark sky, although it wasn't entirely black, not with the lights of Tucson reflecting up into the heavens. The music drifting out from the reception seemed distant, otherworldly, and Colin frowned.

Just what was it that Eileen Kosky had seen? Once again he felt assailed by that sensation of futility, that he'd come here on a wild goose chase and had completely wasted his Saturday night.

All right, he hadn't completely wasted it. He'd met Jenny McAllister, and that was something.

Jenny McAllister, who lived approximately three and a half hours away from him.

He let out a sigh and jammed his hands in his pockets, vaguely wishing he hadn't given up cigarettes his senior year of college. At least if he still smoked, he'd have something to keep himself occupied. As it was, he began to wonder again whether now would be a good time to slip away. Maybe Jenny would be disappointed, but better disappointment now than later, when she realized he didn't have a whole hell of a lot to offer her. And that he'd begun things with her by telling lie after lie. Jesus.

"Hey," she said then, and he started, turning to see that she was approaching him in the semidarkness, her high-heeled sandals swinging from one finger.

Something about the sight of her bare feet, with her pretty painted toes, was almost insanely erotic. He swallowed, but his voice was steady enough as he said, "Hey yourself. All done maid-of-honoring for the evening?"

"I hope so." She headed over toward a table and chairs not too far from where he stood, then more or less collapsed into one of the seats. "I know my feet sure do."

"Those heels are pretty high."

With a *clunk*, she set them down on the tabletop. "Especially for someone who spends most of her days in boots or flip-flops, depending on the time of year. Jerome isn't exactly high-heel friendly."

A decade had passed since he'd visited the former mining town, but he recalled its steep sidewalks well enough. No, it wasn't the sort of place that was exactly conducive to teetering around on three-inch heels. Glad that she'd appeared and relieved him of the burden of slipping away into the night, Colin went over and sat down in the chair next to hers.

For a moment, neither of them said anything, but the silence wasn't awkward. Colin had always liked that quality in a woman, that she'd be okay with not talking and didn't feel as if every moment had to be filled up with conversation.

Then Jenny let out a sigh. "Damn. I should have grabbed one of those bottles of champagne on the way out. Things are winding down, so I doubt anyone would miss it."

"I'll go get one," Colin offered. "As long as I can name-drop you if one of the waiters challenges me."

"Permission granted," she said with a grin.

He got up and headed back inside. As she'd said, it did look as if the reception was starting to quiet down. A slow song played, and a number of couples still moved on the dance floor, but he could see how the room was starting to look a little empty around the edges. Ranks of champagne bottles and their attendant flutes sat on a side table near the bar, so Colin snagged a bottle and some glasses. Despite his worries, no one seemed to be paying him any attention, and he made it back outside without incident.

"Bless you," she said as he sat down next to her.

"You're welcome," he replied, then began prying out the cork with his thumbs. "I don't know what happened to the waiters, but I probably could have grabbed an armful of these things without anyone noticing."

"Well, we'll start with the one and go from there."

Something in him began to heat up at the promise in those words. He risked a sideways glance at her as his fingers still worked the cork, but he couldn't tell much from her expression. It was almost blank, as if she'd used up all her smiles during the day and the evening that followed, and now she just wanted to be calm and relaxed.

Well, he couldn't blame her. Even weddings that went off without a hitch—as far as he could tell, anyway—tended to have you feeling more or less steamrollered by the end of the day. And if she wanted some muscle relaxant and quiet conversation to take the edge off, he'd do what he could to oblige her.

The cork shot out and arced neatly into the pool, narrowly missing one of the floating candles. "Oops," he said.

"Don't worry about it," she said, waving her hand. "They've got to have someone come around and fish out all those candles, so I assume they can get the cork at the same time."

That sounded logical enough. Anyway, he wanted to focus on her, on the way the little votive in its glass holder on the table sent dancing lights shimmering in her golden hair and turned her blue-gray eyes almost green. He poured champagne into one of the flutes, then held it out to her.

"To Caitlin and Alex," he said.

She didn't smile, but nodded instead, as if that was all she had energy for. "To the happy couple."

They both drank. Another silence descended, although this time it felt more strained than the last one. Colin wondered if Jenny was thinking about her sister, who should have been here. Of course, he didn't dare ask her. He couldn't let on that he knew anything about her family's history with Matías Escobar, of the tragedy that had descended on them out of the proverbial blue.

Then Jenny said, "Goddess, I'm glad that's over."

That remark did surprise him. Not that he was overly religious or anything, but he didn't have a lot of experience with pagans. Probably better not to mention it, though. And because she'd let that piece of information slip, he figured he should be honest with her on at least one point. "Yeah, my own wedding was a pain in the ass."

She shifted in her seat, eyes flashing with surprise—and, he thought, disappointment. "You're married?"

"Divorced."

Relief seemed to ripple over her. "Oh. I'm sorry."

"Don't be."

A shake of her head, and a long lock of hair slipped over her shoulder. Where else but southern Arizona could a woman be comfortable wearing a sleeveless dress while sitting outside at nine o'clock at night in early November? "Well, still. I am sorry when I hear that anyone has had to go through that."

Tone slightly teasing, he said, "What, the McAllisters don't believe in divorce?"

But she didn't smile. "It happens. Not as often as it does with a lot of other families, though."

"What about you?" Maybe he shouldn't have asked, especially since Jenny did seem pretty unattached, but he wanted to know. Just because she was flying solo tonight didn't mean she might not be going through her own breakup.

"Never married." Her tone was short, as if she was only answering because she knew it would be rude to ignore his question. "Never came close, actually."

"Really?"

This time she did smile, if somewhat ruefully. After swallowing some more champagne, she said, "You sound surprised."

"I am. I mean, don't take this the wrong way, but you're kind of amazing."

"How could a woman take a compliment like that the wrong way?"

"You'd be surprised." Since her glass was almost empty, he refilled it, then topped off his own drink.

After sending him a grateful glance, she drank again. At the rate they were going, he might have to go in search of more champagne soon. Not that he would have minded, but he still had to drive home after this. "Well," she said, then paused, "I'm glad you think I'm amazing, because you're kind of amazing yourself."

Maybe that was the champagne talking, but Colin couldn't help feeling right then that he was damn glad he'd crashed this wedding after all, even if he hadn't been able to discover a single out of the ordinary thing about Alex Trujillo or his new bride. Well, except that she had a cousin who made every woman Colin had ever dated look like a sack of potatoes. "Now you're just messing with me."

"I am not," she said indignantly. "Sometimes I forget that there are real people in the world. Interesting people."

"There aren't real people in Jerome?"

She waved a hand. "Not—well, it's hard to explain. And I probably shouldn't be explaining it to a ci—" Her words broke off then, and she shook her head before tipping about half her glass of champagne down her throat. "Never mind me. It's been a long day."

"True." He allowed himself another sip of champagne, knowing it would probably be his last. The drive from the hotel to his apartment wasn't that far, but he didn't want to take any chances. "So maybe I should let you crash. Sounds like you've earned it."

Disappointment flickered in her eyes. She hesitated before saying quickly, as if pushing herself to get the words out before she lost her nerve, "Do you live close by?"

No, she couldn't be asking...could she? "Uh... pretty close. About ten minutes away."

Another pause. Then she said, "You want to get out of here?"

There was only one correct answer to that question. He grinned at her and said, "Absolutely."

CHAPTER FOUR

Too much champagne. Way, way too much champagne. Jenny knew that somewhere in the back of her mind, the part that was still functioning, but she didn't much care. Colin asked her about her car, and she told him that she was staying here at the hotel, so it didn't matter if she left it behind. He looked relieved by her reply, but also sort of nervous. Had it been a while for him, too? He'd mentioned being divorced, but of course she had no idea how long ago he'd split from his ex-wife.

She pushed that thought to the back of her head as she followed him out to his car. It didn't matter who he'd been with in the past. Well, maybe it did, but she'd make sure he used protection.

This was crazy. Totally crazy.

But then she was getting into a dusty black Honda Accord, and he was apologizing about the car. As if she cared. She liked him because of his smile and the sound of his voice and because it seemed as if he was listening to her, really listening, when she talked, instead of looking impatient and wondering when she'd shut up so they could get on with the important stuff. Anyway, if he was divorced, he'd probably been set back financially by the whole thing. Again, not his fault. And she wasn't a Wilcox, all wrapped up in material stuff like big houses and fancy cars. Maybe not all of them were like that, but she couldn't deny that Jerome would turn lousy with BMWs and Mercedes and Land Rovers whenever the Wilcox contingent came up for any kind of social gathering.

Jenny didn't know Tucson at all, had let her phone guide her into the hotel's parking lot through the directions on Yelp, so she had no idea where Colin was taking her. It was crazy to be going home with a guy she'd just met, someone she knew nothing about. He didn't look like a serial killer. But then, did they ever?

Her gift wasn't telling her anything, either. Gift. There was a joke. More like a curse. All witches and warlocks had a special talent, something stronger than the simple magical gifts of being able to light a candle with their minds, or draw simple circles of protection, or brew up a tea that would knock a cold out of your system in nothing flat. Her brother Adam was a weather-worker, and poor dead Roslyn had had the gift of singing perfectly on pitch, of hearing a song once and being able to interpret it without a single mistake ever afterward.

Whereas she, Jenny—well, people in the clan called her a mind reader, but that wasn't really what she could do. It wasn't like when you saw psychics on television or in the movies, and they could know what people were thinking practically word for word. Most of the time, she couldn't hear people's thoughts any better than someone who had no witch blood at all. But every once in a while, something in her mind would flare into life, and it was as if she could see into the minds of everyone around her, could understand every single thing they were thinking. As if she was standing in the television department at an electronics store, and all the TVs would come on at once, blaring their programs at maximum volume in the sort of cacophony that made her ears want to bleed.

She hadn't had an episode for more than a month now, and had been worried the whole time during the wedding that her gift would turn on her, and she'd be treated to a simulcast of all the wedding-goers' thoughts while she was trying to make sure Caitlin's day went off without a hitch. That hadn't happened, though, which was part of the reason why she'd been throwing back the champagne. Relief, and also the knowledge that when she was tipsy, if her talent did trigger for some reason, it would come through somewhat muted, the alcohol blunting the effects of the brain cyclone.

No wonder she'd had no desire to live anywhere except Jerome. It was so tiny that she could manage a lot better than if she'd been living someplace densely populated, like Phoenix.

Or Tucson.

If she could look into Colin's mind right now, what would she see? Satisfaction that he'd managed to score what looked like a sure thing? No, that didn't seem right. His voice sounded friendly and relaxed as he talked about Tucson, and how he knew some fun places to eat if she was going to be sticking around for a few days…but she could also see the way his fingers tapped on the steering wheel. He was nervous. If he'd had as much to drink as she had, maybe he'd be a little less tense, but then he wouldn't have been in any shape to drive.

They pulled into the parking lot of a large apartment complex. She couldn't see much of it, except that it was ringed by palm trees, but something about it felt shabby, not kept up as well as it should have been. Maybe his divorce had been an expensive one, and this was all he could afford.

She told herself that she should be the last person to judge a place based on its outward condition. True, her flat over the art gallery was very nice because the woman who owned the building was from Scottsdale and sort of anal-retentive, but a lot of Jerome, especially once you were off the main drag, had passed shabby years ago and was now well on its way toward ramshackle.

Colin parked in a covered space toward the back of the complex. "I'm on the second floor," he said, then shot a worried glance at her sandals, now back on her feet. She might have been well on her way to being drunk, but at least she hadn't forgotten to put her shoes back on before following Colin out to his car. "You going to manage those stairs okay?"

"I'm fine," she replied, although she wondered if she would in fact be able to manage. Three-inch spike heels weren't exactly in her repertoire on a regular day, let alone one where she'd probably drunk the equivalent of an entire bottle of champagne by herself. But fortune favored the bold, right?

She pushed the car door open. Colin, looking vaguely alarmed, hurried out of his own side of the car so he could be there for her when she launched herself outside. Good thing, too, because she wobbled the second her feet hit the pavement.

At once his arm went around her waist, steadying her. Much better. It actually felt really good to have him holding her like that. He seemed strong. Steady. Even so, she knew there was no way she was going to make it up the stairs in those damn shoes. Not unless he carried her, and she didn't think they were quite at the point in their relationship where she could ask such a thing of him.

Oh, but sleeping with him is an entirely different matter, the more or less sober part of her mind jeered at her.

Well, it was different. She wasn't the type to regularly indulge in one-night stands—actually, this would be a first for her—but expecting a guy you just met to carry you up an entire flight of stairs was a bit much.

So she said, "Hang on a sec," and bent to undo the buckles on her ankle straps. Luckily, Colin held on to one arm while she performed that maneuver, or else she probably would have lost her balance and done a complete face plant right there on the walkway. Then she straightened up, shoes dangling by their straps from one of her fingers. "There we go. All better."

Colin's expression appeared dubious to her, but maybe it was just the crappy sodium vapor lighting in the parking area. It tended to make everyone look pretty ghastly. He didn't say anything, though, but only kept his steadying grip on her arm as he guided her along the sidewalk, then up the stairs.

Jerome had more than its fair share of stairs, and she'd negotiated enough of them while in a less than sober state that she could manage well enough, now that she wasn't wearing those three-inch torture devices. Those damn things were going up on eBay the second she got home.

"I wasn't really expecting company," Colin said as he inserted his key in the lock to the apartment's front door. "But I don't think it's too much of a disaster."

"Don't worry about it," she replied breezily, although she found herself hoping that his bedroom wasn't a complete mess. Having sex while surrounded by a guy's dirty socks and discarded beer cans wasn't exactly her idea of a good time.

To her relief, the apartment he escorted her into was a little cluttered, with books and actual magazines and newspapers scattered on the coffee table and the table pushed up against one wall in the dining area, but it didn't look dirty. He headed toward the kitchen, saying, "Do you want some water. Or"—a brief pause, as if he'd realized he probably shouldn't be making the offer but didn't have a graceful way of backing out now— "maybe some wine? I think I have a bottle of chardonnay stashed in here somewhere."

"Chardonnay," she replied at once. Another mistake, no doubt, but if you were going to do the whole drunken one-night-stand thing, you might as well go for the gold.

A nod, and he started rummaging around in the refrigerator. Jenny heard bottles clinking together and guessed they were beer. Actually, a beer sounded pretty good, but she still possessed enough of her faculties to know that drinking beer on top of all that champagne was a spectacularly bad idea.

He emerged with a bottle of pale straw-colored wine, along with a pair of stemless glasses, the kind you got when you did a wine tasting, although she couldn't quite make out the logo on them. Some kind of a hand, maybe?

After clearing a space on the coffee table, he set down the bottle and the glasses, then pointed toward the well-worn leather couch. "Have a seat?"

She plopped herself down, then dropped her sandals off to one side of the sofa. Colin sat down as well before getting to work on removing the cork from the bottle. The label wasn't one she recognized, although it had a hand on it, just like the glasses. So he must gave gotten them at the same place.

Raising an eyebrow, she asked, "Su Vino?"

"They're in Scottsdale," he explained. "You probably don't see too much of their stuff up in your neck of the woods."

"No," she said. "In Jerome we try to buy as much of the local wines as we can. Although I won't say we don't cheat and get the cheap stuff at the grocery store as well."

"Sounds familiar," Colin said with a grin. "I don't go around loading up on Su Vino, but my parents belong to their wine club, so they tend to slip me a bottle or two when they come visit."

"Oh, do they live in the Phoenix area?"

"They do now," he replied as he poured about an inch of wine into each of the glasses in front of them. "I was born here in Tucson and went to college here, but then my father got a really good job opportunity up in Tempe, so they've been living up there for about the past five years."

"Ah," Jenny said. Would it be rude to ask what his father did? She wasn't sure. So much of civilian life seemed to revolve around where people worked and what they did for a living, whereas in the witch clans, the jobs people held—if they worked at all—were mostly for show, or protective camouflage to explain their financial status. There was the occasional exception, like Alex, who really did seem interested in having an actual career rather than something that would let him pass for normal in the "real" world. "So you weren't interested in going with them?"

A shrug. After taking a sip of his wine, Colin replied, "Well, by then I'd gotten married, and we were trying to make things work here, so...." The words trailed off, and he drank some more chardonnay. "Obviously, that didn't end so well, but I didn't have any desire to leave Tucson. This is my hometown."

"Oh," Jenny said, knowing even as the syllable left her mouth how flat it sounded. She should have thought of that, realized that five years ago Colin would probably have been in his late twenties and making a life of his own. Civilians weren't as hung up on making sure their families stuck together, and people were free to go their own way. The alcohol must have fried her brain even more than she thought.

Besides, it was stupid beyond belief to be disappointed by his comment that he wouldn't want to leave his hometown. They'd spent, what, a couple of hours together, max? Not exactly enough time to be planning a future together and picking out china patterns. Since she didn't know what else to say, she picked up her own glass and took a large swallow of wine. Even in her fuddled state, she could tell it was good, crisp and without the oakiness you got from a lot of chardonnays. "Well, Tucson seems nice," she added, realizing how limp the words were.

"Very different from Jerome, I'm guessing."

"Yes, but then, pretty much everything is different from Jerome. It's sort of a one-of-a-kind place."

"True."

They lapsed into silence then, and Jenny sipped her wine again, wondering if he was going to make a move after all, and what she would do if he didn't. He sat there next to her in his slightly rumpled sport coat, his hair looking a little mussed, and he was so sexy—and so completely unaware of his own good looks—that she knew she was probably going to jump on him anyway if he didn't put down that damn wine glass and….

He did set down his glass. In the next moment, he was plucking her glass from her fingers, putting it next to his on the coffee table. And then he was leaning in, his mouth very close to hers, hazel eyes gleaming with need, and yes, some hesitancy, but it wasn't enough to stop him from closing the gap between them, his lips brushing against hers.

Ah, Goddess, about time. She loved the shape of his mouth, how it seemed to match up perfectly with her own lips. He tasted of chardonnay and champagne, light and intoxicating, sweet and sharp at the same time. Warm, welcome heat flowed through her, making her lightheaded. But no, she'd already been a little bit dizzy. This was different, though, sweeping her away with the sensation, her body somehow knowing this was exactly what she needed.

She slid down against the cushions, and he was on top of her, his hands cupping her face as he kissed her over and over, his need clearly as urgent as hers.

Maybe once they were done she'd have the courage to ask him how long it had been since his last time. Months and months for her…no, wait…it had been almost a year. She'd broken up with Daniel right before she quit working dispatch for the Cottonwood P.D.

And she needed to stop thinking about that. Just focus on Colin, on the delicious taste of his mouth, the slight scratch of his stubbled cheek against her skin. He moved lower, trailing kisses down her neck, and she couldn't help moaning then, because he'd hit her right in the sweet spot, right where her entire body would react in chills and a flush of heat.

Then he was pushing himself up off the couch, pulling her with him. She knew where he was headed, knew she wouldn't utter a single word of protest. This was why she'd come back to his apartment with him, after all. At least he was being considerate, and wasn't going to try this on the couch. Not that it wasn't fun to have sex in new and exciting places around the house, but she'd always preferred that the first time be in a real bed.

They stumbled down the hall and into a dark room. He didn't turn on the lights. Was he shy about that sort of thing, or was he being considerate because he didn't know whether she was body-conscious? Either way, she thought she liked him more because of it. Anyway, enough light trickled in from the hallway that she could more or less see what was going on.

The bed was rumpled, messily made, but at least the sheets looked clean. A few more books and magazines lay in the middle of it, and Colin hastily gathered them up and dumped them on the nightstand. Something about him taking care to do that rather than pushing them to the floor made him seem that much more endearing. Most guys wouldn't have cared if they messed up a couple of magazines if it meant they'd get laid more quickly, but obviously Colin did.

He turned back toward her, his mouth finding hers once again. His hand touched the zipper at the back of her dress, and he did hesitate then. "Jenny," he whispered. "Is it—is it okay?"

"More than okay," she replied. "I want you to."

That word was clearly all he needed to fling aside any doubt he might have been experiencing. He tugged the zipper down, and at once his fingers closed on the straps of her dress and pulled them down as well. She stood there before him in her bra and panties, and thanked the Goddess that this had been a special occasion, and so she had on a matching peach-colored satin bra and panty set that she'd bought to go with her bridesmaid's dress.

Maybe he noticed; he let out a breath, and his hands came around to cup her breasts, fingers strong and warm against the smooth fabric. She gasped—not in surprise, but because she hadn't expected even that slight touch to feel so amazing.

"You're—" He paused then, and shook his head. "You are way out of my league, Jenny McAllister."

His manner might have been diffident, but she'd seen the desire and admiration in his eyes, and so she wasn't about to let him talk himself out of this. "No, I'm not. You're insanely hot, Colin Campbell. So don't try to tell me otherwise."

Those words appeared to crumble any further arguments he might have made, because he pulled her to him, devouring her mouth with those kisses that felt as if they were leaving scorch marks on her skin. In the next moment, they were falling onto the bed, and she was tugging at his jacket, tossing it aside with far less care than he'd shown his books. His shirt followed immediately afterward, and she found herself running her hands over his chest, reveling in the feeling of his warm, smooth skin, the firmness of the muscles beneath. No, he obviously wasn't some muscle-bound jock, but it sure felt like he was in good shape.

He fumbled with the hooks on her bra, then got it undone and threw it over onto the chair a few feet away from the bed. Before she could even think, his mouth had closed on her breast, his tongue moving over her flesh. Another moan escaped her mouth, while at the same time his hand slid up her leg, slipped under her panties so his fingers could sink deep into her.

Oh, Goddess. It had been so very long, and her body was about ready to spasm in what had to be a world record when it came to how long it took a woman to orgasm. She didn't care, though; she wanted him to know what he did to her, how much she loved his touch, so passionate and yet gentle at the same time.

Her body clenched around his fingers, and she rode the wave as she clung to him, tears starting to her eyes as that amazing release seemed to echo in every cell, every nerve. He kissed her then, softly on the cheek.

That felt good, but she knew she didn't want soft. She wanted him…all of him.

Her fingers closed on the waistband of his briefs, and she pulled them down so she could take him with her other hand, wrapping around him, feeling how hard and heavy he was, how ready for her. Well, she knew she was ready for him.

Neither of them spoke, but as if by some shared signal they shifted their positions so she could straddle him. A stray thought went through her mind— *oh, shit, we forgot the condom.* Right then, though, she didn't care. There was the charm of Brigit to protect her, a charm used by generations of McAllister witches to ward off unwanted pregnancy.

So she slid down onto Colin, felt him fill her, and she had to keep herself from screaming out loud at the amazing sensation of their bodies locked together, the way everything seemed to fit perfectly even though of course they'd never done this before. But he was in an apartment, and she really didn't want his neighbors knowing every intimate detail of this moment she was sharing with him.

His hands slid up her stomach, caressing her breasts again. Truly amazing how strong and sensitive his fingers were, how they seemed to know exactly how to touch her. Another orgasm was building in her, and she hoped she'd be able to hold it off long enough for him to climax as well.

That didn't seem to be much of a problem, though. His eyes had shut, and his thrusts were getting stronger, pushing deeper into her. She'd never been with him before, but she thought she could tell that he was getting close. Good, because she knew she was, too.

He came hard, pounding into her, a wordless groan wrenched from his lips. Jenny's own orgasm followed only a moment afterward, and once again she had to squeeze her eyes to prevent tears of ecstasy from rolling down her cheeks. She'd pretended that she was fine, that she didn't need this amazing closeness with another human being, but she knew she'd been lying to herself.

An endless moment while they rocked together, each spent, but not quite ready to end their joining. And then he took her by the waist and helped her slip down to lie at his side, their bodies pressed together, warm and damp from their exertions. For the first time, she realized the room was close to being hot. Probably he'd shut off the air conditioning while he was out for the day. She didn't mind; something about the heat felt right, felt good.

His arms went around her, and he pulled her even closer. That felt good, too. It seemed like most of the guys she'd been with had wanted to get out of bed as soon as the act was over, to head to the bathroom or to the kitchen to get a beer, to go to the living room and turn on the television. Anything to avoid this moment of heartbreaking closeness when a person was at their most vulnerable.

Colin didn't seem to mind feeling vulnerable, though. He held her, and she could feel the way his chest rose and fell against hers, the way his heart was pounding. Maybe she was reading the signs wrong, but she thought that this had meant more to him than just a one-night stand.

It sure meant more to her. She wasn't sure what she should do about that.

Should she say something? Her head felt swimmy with champagne and the lush heat of their love-making. If she said something, she might just screw everything up, and she didn't want that. She wanted things to remain as they were right now, beautiful and close and intense. Neither of them seemed too concerned about the unprotected sex they'd just shared. Jenny knew she didn't have much to worry about, because in addition to having Brigit's charm to protect her, she'd been on the pill for years because she liked how it worked to reduce the effects of her periods. Anything else, well, the McAllisters didn't have a healer, but the Wilcoxes did, which meant she didn't have anything much to worry about on that front, either.

Besides, she was so very tired. The day had suddenly caught up with her, and though she knew she should get out of Colin's bed and put her clothes back on, have him drive her to the hotel so she could get up the next morning and act as if nothing out of the ordinary had happened, she knew she was physically incapable of doing such a thing.

She laid her head against Colin's shoulder, and slept.

CHAPTER FIVE

HE DIDN'T WANT TO MOVE. HE WAS AFRAID IF HE MOVED, he'd wake her up, and then this whole amazing dream would vanish into thin air like the fairytale it must be. Girls like Jenny McAllister did not come home with guys like him.

But there she was, a stray beam of sunlight pushing past the closed mini-blinds and touching her hair, turning it to purest gold. Her beauty astonished him, especially now, with her hair tumbled and the mascara she'd worn for the wedding smudged under her eyes. That didn't matter. Smeared makeup couldn't hide the fine lines of her cheekbones, the straight, perfect nose, the curve of her mouth. Its corners were turned up slightly, as if she smiled at something in her dreams.

Was she dreaming of him? It seemed pretty presumptuous to think that he occupied her thoughts, even in sleep, but he was glad she looked happy. She'd done her best the day before to make it seem as if everything was just fine, but he'd seen the strain that lurked in those big blue-gray eyes. She hadn't been fine. She'd just put on a public face and made sure her cousin's big day had been as happy and trouble-free as it possibly could be.

As Colin looked down at Jenny, a pang of guilt flashed through him. Last night had been blurred by too much lust and alcohol, but now, in the not-so-cold light of a Tucson morning, he realized what he'd done. He'd gone to that wedding on false pretenses, lied to everyone around him, and then gone to bed with the sister of the girl whose spectacular murder had occupied a good deal of his professional life not so very long ago.

Jesus.

She stirred then, opening eyes that reminded him of the sky over the ocean. He'd only seen it once, when he was in junior high school and his parents had taken him and his sister Kate to California, but even so, the colors of the sea had haunted him ever since.

For the barest moment, their gazes locked while Jenny was still sleepy and relaxed. Her mouth began to curve into a smile.

And then the realization of where she was and what she'd just done seemed to awake in those big blue eyes, and her whole body went stiff. No, she didn't pull away from him, but she might as well have.

Then she did smile, but he could tell it was forced. "What time is it?"

He glanced over at the clock radio on the nightstand. "Almost eight-thirty."

"Shit. I mean—" She broke off there, this time moving away from him so she could push herself up to a sitting position. "I'm supposed to meet my parents for breakfast at the hotel."

"What time?" he asked, trying to sound casual. His first instinct was to think she was brushing him off as politely as she could, but he told himself that her story might very well be true. After all, she was down here for a wedding. Getting together to do family stuff made total sense.

"Ten o'clock." She slid over to the edge of the bed and reached downward, presumably attempting to find her discarded panties.

"Well, that's plenty of time." Colin did his best not to stare at the her bare back, at the way the covers had slipped down to reveal the rounded curve of her ass. He had a feeling Jenny wouldn't much appreciate the ogling. "We're less than ten minutes from the hotel here. I'll drive you as soon as you're dressed."

That offer made her throw a startled glance at him over her shoulder. "Oh, no, I couldn't ask that of you. I'll call a cab."

A cab? Seriously? "You don't need to call a cab. I don't mind driving you. Really."

Apparently she'd located her underwear, because she didn't answer at first, was instead doing her best to slip into it without showing off every inch of her body. He didn't know how successful she was, because he was trying so very hard not to stare. Anyway, if he really was going to drive her, he needed to locate his own clothes and get himself together.

He slid off the bed and went to the chair where most of his things appeared to have landed. After he'd gotten into his own underwear and started buttoning up his shirt, he figured it was probably safe to look over at Jenny. By then she was mostly covered, had just finished zipping up the back of her dress.

Her expression was dubious. "I don't know."

Despite his guilt over not being entirely truthful with her, Colin couldn't help experiencing a flare of anger. Was she really that determined to do the walk of shame, complete with early morning cab ride back to the hotel? Maybe he was reading too much into the way she'd responded to him the night before. Maybe she really didn't have any emotional investment, now that she'd gotten her itch scratched.

Voice hardening, he said, "I mean, if you just don't want to spend any more time with me, I get it."

At once her eyes widened, and she shook her head. "No, that's not what I meant. I—" She floundered for a few seconds, then said in a very small voice, "I just didn't want to push myself on you."

Oh, well, time to banish that notion. In two strides he crossed the room, then pulled her into his arms. Her mouth opened, as if she'd intended to say something, but he kissed her, stopping her words, just in case they might have prevented him from tasting her again, feeling her body up against his.

They broke apart, and she pulled in a deep breath. "Okay. That is—okay. You can drive me back to the hotel."

He wished he could go with her to breakfast, but that probably wouldn't be a very good idea. It was just that he knew she'd have to head back to Jerome at some point, and he didn't want to give up any opportunity he might have to spend time with her. "Great. On one condition, though."

Her look became guarded. "What?"

"You have dinner with me tonight. You will still be here, won't you? When do you go back to Jerome?"

"Not until tomorrow," she replied. "My parents are heading up there this afternoon, but I wanted to stay on a little longer just to wrap up any loose ends.

I figured I'd go shopping or something after they left."

"I can take you shopping," he said. *I can take you anywhere you want to go,* he added mentally, but he didn't dare say that out loud. It was just a little too impetuous, a little too romantic, for this early stage of the game. Better to start with dinner and see where things went from there.

This time she just looked amused. "You'd be bored out of your mind."

"Not if I was with you."

She was quiet then, watching him. Something shifted in her expression, but he didn't know her well enough yet to determine what it was. "All right. How about I text you after I'm done with breakfast and my parents are on their way out of here?"

"Sounds perfect. Let me give you my number."

They progressed into the mundanities of exchanging their contact information, and then it was time to hurry her down to the car and get her back to the hotel. She probably wouldn't have time to wash her hair, but she should be able to slip in a quick shower.

Best not to dwell on that, though. He knew he'd get himself in trouble if he started imagining what she might look like in the shower, water cascading over her perfect body.

Besides, if he was really, really lucky, he might just get a chance to experience that for himself...if all went well tonight.

An awkward kiss—thank God for the mouthwash Colin had thoughtfully left out on the bathroom counter—and then he was driving off in his ten-year-old Honda, leaving Jenny to hurry into the hotel before anyone could see her wandering around in the same dress she'd been wearing the night before. Thank the Goddess that her parents had been assigned a room in a different wing of the place.

A quick check of the clock radio told her that she had about forty-five minutes to go before she was scheduled to meet her parents in the restaurant downstairs. She peeled off the sheath dress and flung it on the bed, then grabbed a clip from where she'd left her cosmetics bag on the counter in the bath-room and pulled her hair up and out of the way.

The hot water felt good. It washed off some of the night before, although Jenny didn't know if she really wanted to completely get rid of the scent of Colin's skin, which seemed to have invaded her senses. But it also wasn't a good idea to show up at a familial breakfast while smelling of the hot sex you'd had the night before, so she scrubbed herself down as thoroughly as she could in the limited time avail-able, then hurried out so she could get dried off and do at least a rudimentary makeup application. If she hadn't made plans to see Colin again, she probably would have made do with just some mascara and lip gloss, but she wanted to look as good as she could. So...shadow and blush, a bit of liner, gloss in a soft raisin-wine shade. Then to get dressed in jeans and an embroidered peasant blouse, and her favorite nude flats.

It was just a hair past ten when she came downstairs and headed toward the restaurant. At the same time, the elevator doors opened, and Jenny's brother Adam and his wife Mason emerged into the lobby.

Jenny slowed down so they could meet up with her. They both looked fairly casual, too, although Mason was also wearing a nice top with her jeans and low-heeled boots.

Her dark eyes twinkled as she greeted Jenny. "So, what happened to you last night?"

"What do you mean, what happened to me?" *Goddess, that didn't sound defensive or anything....*

"Well, you were talking to that mystery man, the one who didn't seem to be related to anyone, and then you just disappeared."

Apparently Mason had been paying more attention than Jenny had thought. If it had been just the two of them, she might have told the truth, but no way was she going to confess to a one-night stand with her brother Adam looking on. "Nothing

happened. We talked for a while, things were winding down and I was tired, so I went up to my room."

Mason's eyebrow lifted, but right then Jenny and
Adam's parents appeared, and she abandoned the
topic. Luckily, it didn't seem as if either Marcus or
Lysette McAllister had noticed their daughter's dis-
appearing act from the night before, as they greeted
her normally enough, then said their good mornings
to Mason and Adam.

The dining room was crowded, but they had reservations, so in no time the party was escorted to a
table off in one corner, where they had a fine view of
the grounds and the swimming pool. Jenny looked
at the blue water, shimmering in the sun, and wondered if anyone had fished the champagne cork out
yet.

But that memory made her think of other things,
activities she probably shouldn't let enter her mind
while she was sitting at a table with her parents and
her brother and sister-in-law, and so Jenny picked up
her menu and pretended to be absorbed in its con-
tents. What really sounded great right then was coffee, lots and lots of it.

As if picking up on her unspoken request, their
waiter appeared and took their drink orders, then
headed off toward the kitchen.

"So," Jenny said, figuring she should get the conversation moving in a safe direction, "are Caitlin and Alex off yet?"

"I think Tricia said they'd planned to leave around nine-thirty," Lysette replied. "There's someplace up in Scottsdale that's supposed to have an amazing Sunday brunch, and they wanted to head there first before they go to the condo."

The "condo" was more like a full-on house, from what Jenny had heard. It belonged to the de la Paz clan and was shared among the family for special occasions. So Caitlin and Alex were going to spend the greater part of a week in the lap of luxury before they headed back to start their life together. Well, truthfully, they'd already begun their life together, since they'd been living together since June, but Jenny supposed it was nice that they'd get some time in different surroundings as a way of separating the life where they'd been living together from the one they'd be sharing now that they were married.

"That sounds nice," she said, but absently. Her mind was still on Colin Campbell, on the astonishing fact that he wanted to spend more time with her, wanted to have dinner with her while she was still in town.

Still in town. There was the real problem, wasn't it? Tomorrow she'd turn into a pumpkin and have to head home to Jerome. Go back to being a dysfunctional witch in a clan full of people who mostly had their act together. Unfortunately, it seemed as if there was usually one screw-up in a clan each generation, and she figured that title had fallen to her this time around. A talent that didn't work right, a string of failed relationships…yes, she was a real prize. Not for the first time, she wondered how many people in the clan had secretly wished she'd been the one to fall victim to Matías Escobar's dark magic, rather than her much-beloved sister. Deep down, she knew that wasn't true, but she still couldn't keep the ugly thought from resurfacing every once in a while.

"…sure you don't want to head back with us?" her father was saying, and Jenny blinked.

"What?"

Marcus McAllister sent her a curious look but said mildly enough, "I was just asking if you didn't want to change your mind and go home today. It seems as if everything is pretty well wrapped up, and I'm sure you could work it out with the hotel."

And miss seeing Colin again? she thought. *Not a chance in hell.*

However, she just said, "No, I want to stay. I wanted to do some shopping. Might as well while I'm here."

"That's fine, Jenny," her mother put in. "Lord knows the shopping isn't so great up in our neck of the woods."

Adam looked mildly disgusted, but Jenny knew that was because he spent his whole life in jeans and flannel shirts and hiking boots, and so didn't give a good goddamn about the limited shopping opportunities in the Verde Valley. Mason appeared slightly more sympathetic, although she'd grown up in Flagstaff, in Wilcox territory, where at least they had a decent mall.

To Jenny's relief, they changed the subject, instead going on to discuss how Danica and Robert had found a house they wanted to buy.

Mason said, "It's off Fort Valley Road somewhere, so it's got some land around it, and isn't right in the heart of things. I think sometimes our modern life gets to be a bit much for Mr. Rowe."

"Really?" Jenny's mother said. "It looked to me like he was adapting beautifully."

"Well, he is doing really well, all things considered, but there's something to be said for having some peace and quiet."

Adam grinned and said, "But Mason, I thought you liked living in the heart of things."

The two of them shared a flat in Flagstaff's old town district. It was great if you wanted to wander downstairs and be only a few doors away from a bar or restaurant, but Jenny could see how having that sort of activity around at all times could be exhausting. Especially if, like Robert Rowe, you hailed from a century that didn't have cars or the internet or cell phones.

"I love it," Mason said pointedly. "But I also wasn't born in 1858. Anyway, they found a house, and it sounds like they're planning their wedding for sometime in May."

Another damn wedding. The only good thing about this one was that Jenny knew she wouldn't get dragged into it, except as a spectator. It would be Mason's job to play field marshal for her sister Danica's nuptials.

But that was a crappy thing to think, and Jenny pushed away the shame that rose in her, even as she managed a smile at the waiter, who'd appeared right then to bring them all their coffee—except Jenny's mother, who was a tea drinker—and take their orders. Jenny hadn't even really done much more than glance at the menu, but she'd seen enough to quickly order a Greek omelet and a side of fruit and sourdough toast. All things considered, she was doing pretty well, but although she didn't have an actual hangover, her stomach was telling her that it needed something to soak up the remnants of her excesses from the night before.

The rest of the group chattered away, with Adam and Mason talking about how Adam had just lined up an awesome restoration job at one of the old Victorian houses just outside Flagstaff's downtown, but Jenny wasn't paying that much attention. She drank her coffee, and wondered what Colin was doing right then. Was he the type to go out for his breakfast, or was he a stay-at-home coffee-and-Chobani kind of guy?

Probably the latter, or something close to it. All you had to do was look at his car and his apartment to know he wasn't exactly rolling in cash. She really didn't care, because as a McAllister, she had her own money. Colin's finances weren't the issue. No, it was the man himself who was the real problem.

Because she liked him. Liked him a lot, even after only being around him for one evening, spending one night in his bed. She hadn't really met anyone like him before. All her former relationships with civilians had been with active, outdoorsy kind of guys—a fireman, a cop, the hunky Forest Service ranger who had the Mingus Mountain gig one memorable summer. Colin didn't seem like any of them at all, but Jenny thought that might be a change in the right direction.

Except for the little problem of him living down here in Tucson. Sure, Caitlin had bailed on Jerome to live down here, but Jenny didn't think she'd be able to do the same. She wasn't cut out for big city life, shopping expeditions or no. And she didn't like the heat. It got hot up in Jerome in the summer, but nothing like the weather they experienced down here in the southern part of the state.

And here you are, projecting all sorts of problems and roadblocks when you haven't even had a second date yet, she thought. *Getting a little ahead of yourself, aren't you?*

Maybe just a little.

She refocused enough to answer a couple of questions about her flat and the art gallery. Her mother, probing, just trying to be helpful, although Jenny knew Lysette was worried about her. What was that like, to be a civilian surrounded by witches, to know your own offspring possessed powers you didn't have and couldn't entirely understand?

Jenny's own trials with attempting to control her apparently uncontrollable talent had only made matters worse. They'd tried everything—the elders had showed her techniques for focusing her concentration, her cousin Jason had encouraged her to smoke pot, her mother had suggested seeing a psychiatrist, only to have that particular idea shot down almost at once. Going to a shrink wasn't a very good idea when a massive part of your existence involved keeping your true identity a secret. She'd wondered at Danica's parents sending her to a psychiatrist after her ordeal with Matías Escobar and the Aguirre cousins, but they'd been at their wits' end. Anyway, Danica herself had put the kibosh on that idea, ditching the therapy after only a few sessions.

For Jenny, the only thing that seemed to work at all was yoga and meditating. Most of the time she started out her morning that way, with a routine of simple poses, followed by sitting on her deck in the lotus position, eyes closed, mind blank while she breathed in Jerome's fresh mountain air and centered herself in her body. If she kept up that daily ritual, her talent barely intruded at all.

But because of the hubbub of Caitlin's wedding, Jenny had skipped her routine the past few mornings. She didn't want to admit how relieved she was that she still seemed to be okay. When she'd woken up in Colin's bed this morning, she'd been horribly frightened that her talent would descend, and she'd be able to look into his mind and see everything he thought about her.

The worst hadn't happened, though. He'd been a gentleman, insisting on driving her back to the hotel. And she was going to see him again later today.

Part of her thought that was a spectacularly bad idea. What was the point in getting even more attached when he was so geographically undesirable? True, she could find out after spending a few more hours in his company that she really didn't like him as much as she'd thought she did, but Jenny had a feeling she wouldn't be that lucky.

The food came, and she plowed greedily into her omelet, practically feeling the protein flood into her body. Everyone around her seemed similarly occupied, so all was quiet at the table for a while. When the conversation picked up again, it was more family chatter—a rumor that Angela might be pregnant again, which Jenny thought was more wishful thinking on her parents' part than anything else. The twins might be close to preschool age, but Angela hadn't said anything about wanting to give them a little brother or sister. Most of the time, she still looked a little frayed around the edges from having to run after a couple of three-year-olds. Jenny knew that if their positions had been reversed, she'd be holding off on having any more kids until Ian and Emily were in kindergarten.

Or possibly junior high.

The check came, and Jenny's father grabbed for it at once. She didn't bother to protest, and neither did Adam or Mason. All their funds came out of the same pot, anyway, more or less, although of course Mason had her own money, Wilcox money. Which was probably a lot more than the stipend all the McAllisters received, although Jenny had never had the courage to ask her sister-in-law about it. She just knew that the Wilcoxes always had enough cash to do pretty much whatever they wanted, whether that was buying houses or cars or, in several cases, their own planes.

The group headed out to the elevators after the bill was settled up. As they were waiting, Marcus asked, "You still sure you want to stay down here? We could all caravan back."

"Oh, let her be," Lysette said, before Jenny could reply. "After everything she did to help with this wedding, she deserves some 'me' time."

Jenny shot her mother a grateful look. "Well, I don't know about that, but I do want to explore Tucson a little bit before I head home. I'll see you all tomorrow afternoon sometime."

Marcus McAllister gave a resigned shrug. "Just thought I'd ask."

Then the elevator arrived, and Jenny gave her parents a quick hug each, and made her goodbyes to Adam and Mason. Once the doors had closed, she let out a relieved sigh and headed over to the wing where her own room was located.

Now it was time to have some fun.

CHAPTER SIX

UNTIL JENNY'S TEXT APPEARED ON HIS PHONE, COLIN HAD been certain she was going to blow him off. He knew she would decide that she really didn't want to see him again, and head back to Jerome before he even realized she was gone.

There it was, though—*I'm a free bird. When do you want to come and get me?*

He wanted to reply, *Right this instant,* but realized that would sound just a little too needy. Instead, he tapped out, *I need to finish up something, but I'll be there in about a half hour.*

Her answer came back almost immediately. *Okay, see you then.*

Colin responded with, *Okay,* and set down his phone. What exactly he would do to fill up that half hour, he really didn't know, but he figured he should probably tidy up a bit, just in case they came back here after dinner.

In case? In the desperate hope, more like it.

The apartment really wasn't that bad—and she'd seen it the night before, after all—but he still went ahead and made sure his books and magazines were stacked neatly instead of strewn all over the place. A fresh batch of towels in the bathroom, just in case. And then he ran over the surfaces in the kitchen and bath with some Clorox wipes.

When he was done, he thought the place looked pretty presentable. Well, at least as long as Jenny wasn't too picky. She sure hadn't seemed that way the night before, but then again, she'd had a lot of champagne to drink.

Anyway, the activity filled up the time, as he'd hoped, and so he was able to head out with about ten minutes to spare, meaning he should pull into the parking lot at her hotel right when he'd said he would be there. She hadn't told him her room number, so he parked in the visitor area and pulled out his phone.

I'm down by the guest drop-off, he texted.

The reply came back so quickly that he flattered himself she must have been waiting, phone in hand. *I'll be right down.*

And she was, appearing a few minutes later through the doors that led to the reception area. Her bright hair fell down her back, and she had on a pair of slim-fitting jeans and some pretty ballet-style flats. He'd found her gorgeous the night before, in her chic sheath dress and her hair done just so, but right then, watching the sun shimmer along her loose hair and her mouth purse slightly as she paused to pull some sunglasses out of her bag, Colin thought she was probably the most beautiful woman he'd ever seen.

She caught sight of his car and waved, then hurried over. Belatedly, he realized he probably should have gotten out and come around to open the door for her, but she didn't seem disappointed by his apparent lack of chivalry. She climbed into the passenger seat and shot him a hesitant smile. "Hi."

"Hi," he replied. Things already felt awkward, but he did his best to smooth over the silence that followed their greeting by saying, "So...I assume the mall first, since you've already eaten?"

"That would be great." She paused, and pushed her sunglasses down her nose, presumably so she could get a better look at him. "Unless you need to get something to eat? I could have another cup of coffee or something."

"No, I'm fine." While he doubted his breakfast had been as good as hers, he'd had coffee and toast and yogurt, and he knew that would hold him for a while. Maybe they could get a snack somewhere, not really big enough for lunch, but something to tide them over until dinner. He backed out of the parking space and pointed the car toward Oracle Boulevard. Once they were safely out into the flow of traffic he asked, "So is everyone headed home?"

"Probably. My parents were already packed, so I think they were going to hit the road pretty quickly. I'm not sure about Adam and Mason, but I don't think they planned to stick around much longer, either."

Some of the names sounded vaguely familiar, but portions of the evening before had been blurred by the champagne. Not all, though…there were several spectacular moments that he remembered in vivid detail.

"Adam's your brother?"

"Right. And Mason's his wife. Her sister is Danica. She was one of the other bridesmaids."

Colin nodded, hoping he looked just a smidge confused. After all, he really didn't want Jenny to know that Danica's face was all too familiar to him. Yes, her family had worked hard to keep her out of the papers, but he'd seen her photos in the police reports, and then the real thing at Escobar's sentencing. Back then, she'd looked scared and somehow vague at the same time, as if she wasn't truly processing everything going on around her. A vast change from how she'd appeared at the wedding, bright and focused and beautiful. Maybe the change in her appearance had a good deal to do with the handsome man who was clearly her boyfriend...or possibly something more serious than that. Fiancé, maybe.

"Yeah, I know, there were a lot of us," Jenny said, a ripple of laughter in her words. "You were a brave man, coming to a shindig like that all on your own. I'm surprised Alex inflicted that on you."

"Well, he did warn me that he had a big family, and so did Caitlin." There, that sounded plausible enough without actually admitting to anything.

"Like I said, a brave man. But we both survived." She smiled then, and Colin could feel himself starting to relax. Whatever had been the source of her diffidence earlier that morning, it seemed to have gone for now. Maybe it had nothing at all to do with him, and was more about her nervousness in facing her family after a fairly spectacular one-night stand.

At least, he thought it had been spectacular. It was hard to tell what Jenny thought, because although she seemed friendly and open right now, most of her previous awkwardness gone, that could have been merely a façade. Or maybe she was one of those women who didn't consider sleeping with a guy that big a deal. For whatever reason, Colin had always attached a lot of importance to the act, and had been surprised early in his college career when a girl he'd gone to bed with after a party had been totally friendly the next morning...but also had absolutely no interest in seeing him again, except as a casual acquaintance at parties thrown by mutual friends. His eighteen-year-old self had been shocked. Weren't you supposed to be madly in love after having sex?

Apparently not. And while Jenny appeared glad to be with him, maybe she was just being polite because she was here in Tucson and wanted someone to show her around.

No, that didn't feel right. Colin didn't pretend to be an authority on women—far from it, or he wouldn't have failed so spectacularly with Shannon—but he hoped he knew enough that he could tell whether someone wanted to be in his company or not.

Because it was a fine Sunday afternoon, with the sun shining and temperatures in the upper seventies, everyone apparently had thought it was a perfect time to be indoors at the mall. He circled several times in the spots he thought were most likely to have an open parking space, with no luck. At last he gave up and headed toward the back forty. Yes, they'd have a hike, but it was better than driving around and around, attempting to locate the perfect spot.

"Sorry about that," he apologized as he locked the car. "I didn't think it would be this busy."

"It's fine," Jenny said. "I've got flats on. Anyway, I'm used to walking everywhere. At least there aren't any hills here."

Maybe it was Jerome's hills that kept her in such great shape. Making that kind of remark seemed far too personal, though, so he just said, "Well, that's true. There's a mall entrance off to our left, so we can go through there and you can look at the directory and decide where you want to head next."

"Sounds good." She flashed him a mischievous little grin, her eyes dancing behind her sunglasses. "I promise I won't drag you to *every* store."

"It's cool if you do. My afternoon's open."

That reply made her chuckle, but at the same time she shook her head, as if she couldn't quite believe that any self-respecting guy would willingly traipse all over a crowded mall with a woman he'd just met.

Once they were inside, though, he could tell that she planned to make this a targeted trip. She paused at the directory, nodding a few times, as if consigning her most important destinations to memory. And then they were off.

Dillard's first, where he hoped she wouldn't drag him to the lingerie department—mostly because it would be embarrassing in the extreme, and not because he wouldn't have minded seeing her model underwear for him. But no, she shopped for jeans and some new blouses, and a pair of sandals from the shoe department. Then it was over to Sephora for makeup, and a few more smaller clothing stores after that.

"I didn't mean to make you my beast of burden," she protested, after he took several of the heavier bags from her.

"It's fine," he replied. "I like to feel useful."

She raised an eyebrow at him but didn't say anything else, instead heading off toward another shoe store. Actually, if he stopped to add it all up, the amount she was spending was kind of staggering. Again he thought of the wedding he'd attended the night before, and how much it must have cost. Were the McAllisters rich? He wouldn't have thought that, considering how Jerome was kind of a funky place, not exactly Scottsdale or even Sedona. But Jenny had to have dropped close to a grand already, and wasn't showing any signs of slowing down. Maybe she'd been saving up a long time for this kind of shopping trip. He didn't know, and he sure as hell wasn't going to ask.

Once again, though, he made a mental note to start digging into the McAllister finances. And probably the Wilcoxes and the de la Pazes, too. Just in case.

After the sixth store, though—or was it the seventh?—Jenny shot him an apologetic smile and said,

"We should probably take a break. Could you eat something?"

By that point he probably could have eaten several somethings. They'd passed a Cheesecake Factory on the way in to the mall entrance, so he suggested that.

"Is it good?"

He stared at her blankly. "You've never been to one?"

"I doubt there are any closer than somewhere in Phoenix. It's a national chain, right?"

"Right. I won't say it's haute cuisine, but it's good for a snack."

"A snack sounds great. Lead on."

Even though the mall had been crowded, the restaurant wasn't too bad, probably because it was now a hair past two, and not really lunchtime any-more. He and Jenny were seated quickly enough, and when the waiter came by, she ordered iced tea.

Colin asked for the same, then gave Jenny a ques-tioning look. She shrugged and said, "Well, I figured we were going out for a real meal later, and after all that champagne last night, it seemed safer to stick with tea for now."

"I think you're right." He could have gone for a beer after all that marching around the mall, but tea would do for now, especially since it sounded clear enough to him that Jenny intended to stay the course and wouldn't dump him as soon as her shopping spree was over with.

They decided on hot spinach and cheese dip, and gave the waiter their order when he arrived with their iced teas. Once he was gone, Jenny said, "I'm not wearing you out, am I?"

There was a loaded question. But Colin thought he'd better answer literally. "Not at all. I got a lot of training getting dragged here with my mother and sister when I was younger."

Jenny took a sip of her iced tea. "Any other brothers or sisters?"

"No, just the two of us. What about you?" And he held his breath, wondering if she would tell him the truth, or whether she would say it was only her and Adam.

She did seem to go very still then, hands wrapped around her iced tea glass. "Well, there's Adam. And then there was my sister Roslyn."

"'Was'?"

Her eyes seemed to be focused on the spot where her discarded drinking straw wrapper lay on the tabletop. "She was…killed…about six months ago."

"Oh, Jesus, Jenny, I'm so sorry." And then he felt like a world-class asshole for putting her on the spot like that, especially when he'd already known the answer to his question. Jerk move to bring up the subject at all when she seemed to be having such a good time.

A wild impulse came over him that he should just tell her the truth now, before they could get in any deeper. He hated the lies he'd already told. Sure, she'd be angry, but....

But somehow, he couldn't make himself do it. He knew she'd gather up her bags and storm out and call a cab, and then he'd never see her again.

Anyway, she'd spoken again, and the moment was gone. "I'm actually surprised you didn't hear anything about it," she said, her tone bitter. "It was all over the news. At least, my parents said it was. I couldn't bear to hear or read about any of it. The Escobar thing?"

He put what he hoped was an appropriately shocked expression on his face, at the same time feeling like the world's biggest bastard for continuing this charade. When he'd come up with the idea of crashing the wedding, he'd never thought in a million years that he'd end up telling all these lies. "Oh, Jesus—that was your sister?"

"Yes, it was my sister." Suddenly, Jenny seemed very tired. She pushed at the wrapper from her straw with a finger, studiously not looking up at him. "That bastard killed my sister, and I just couldn't bear to see her name get dragged through it over and over again, as if it was somehow her fault that she'd come here on spring break and ran into the wrongest guy she possibly could." Still not looking at Colin, she picked up her iced tea and pulled a long sip through the straw. "She and Caitlin weren't just cousins, they were really good friends. They'd always promised they'd be each other's maid of honor—or matron of honor, I guess, depending on who got married first—and so after Roslyn was gone, I sort of had to step in, because Danica, who was also their friend, had to deal with her own kind of hell with Matías Escobar and wasn't in much shape for maid-of-honor duty."

"I'm sorry," Colin said. And he was…sorry for what Jenny and her family had gone through, sorry for these lies that just seemed to keep building up on one another. Shit, he'd never intended to get himself in this kind of a situation.

Another of those bitter little smiles touched her lips. "I'd say it's okay, but it really isn't. But it also isn't anything any of us can change, even if we all are—" She stopped there, as if realizing she'd been about to say something she really shouldn't. "Even if we all wish we could, that is." After sipping some more tea, she added, "But let's just say that I'm really glad this wedding is over. I'm happy for Caitlin, I really am, but…."

"But you can't help thinking about how your own sister won't ever get her wedding."

Surprise flashed in those big blue eyes, and Jenny nodded. "Something like that. Which I try to tell myself is stupid, because Roslyn wasn't even dating anyone seriously, and didn't seem to care all that much about settling down. But why should she? She was just a kid. She was barely old enough to drink."

Watching the mixture of sadness and anger move across Jenny's fine features, Colin wished they'd sat next to each other in this booth, rather than across from one another. He wanted to pull her close, put his arms around her, give her what comfort he could. Instead, he reached across the table and wrapped his fingers around hers. She started, but then he could feel her give him an answering squeeze, as if grateful that he'd offered her even that small gesture of compassion.

"I really shouldn't be talking about this—" she began, but Colin shook his head.

"I want you to. It's something that happened to you, to your family. I don't want you to think you have to hide anything from me." *The way you're hiding things from her? Asshole.* He really needed to find a way to steer this conversation to a different topic.

At that remark, her gaze dropped to the table-top again, and once more his spider sense started tingling again. There was something going on with the McAllisters—and the Wilcoxes and de la Pazes as well, for all he knew—but he couldn't begin to put his finger on what it might be. They all seemed like normal people to him. If he'd learned anything in his years of working on the paper, though, it was that "normal" could hide all kinds of weird shit.

"Thanks for that," Jenny said. "I've tried to do what I can to move on, to heal. But…she was my baby sister."

A strange pang struck him then. For whatever reason, he hadn't really tried to put himself in Jenny's position. But how would he feel if it was his own little sister Kate who had been the victim of a sadistic killer like Matías Escobar? He wasn't sure he would have been able to cope as well as Jenny apparently had.

Colin was saved from having to make a reply by the arrival of the waiter with their chips and dip. Whatever appetite he might have worked up by following Jenny around as she shopped seemed to have disappeared, but he thanked the waiter anyway. After the two of them were alone again, they were both silent, looking at each other. Jenny only seemed sad, and Colin didn't want to know what she might be seeing in his face. Right then he felt like a piece of shit.

Then she picked up a chip and dunked it into the dip. "We might as well eat this," she said.

"I suppose so." He also got a chip and dipped it into the artichoke/cheese mixture. Somewhat to his surprise, he found that it tasted good, waking an appetite that had only gone dormant and hadn't disappeared entirely.

"So, what is it you actually do, Colin?" Jenny asked in an obvious attempt to change the subject. "That is, I know you said you were Alex's T.A. in one of his journalism courses, but you made it sound as if you weren't doing that anymore."

Colin nearly choked on the chip he was eating. Without trying to look too obvious, he drank some iced tea, then said, "I'm not still at the university, if that's what you're asking. I also switched to communications and was still trying to get my master's, but then I was with Shannon and felt like I had to get a real job instead of staying in school forever, so...." Pausing, he cast about desperately for something that sounded plausible, something one of his former classmates was now actually doing. "So now I work in corporate communications."

"Corporate communications?" she asked. "That's actually a thing?"

"Yeah, you probably don't have much call for it in Jerome"—she flashed him a jaundiced look at that remark—"but basically, I write all the material for the corporate newsletters, quarterly reports, press releases. All that kind of stuff. It might not be the most exciting thing in the world, but it pays the bills."

Since he'd been watching her carefully, Colin noted the faint lift of an eyebrow Jenny gave at that comment. Well, true, on the surface it didn't look as if it was doing that well at paying his bills. The sad truth was, if he really had gone into corporate communications, he'd probably be making a good deal more than he was at his current job, even if you included the extra grand or so a month he earned from writing those godawful "self-improvement" pamphlets.

"Alimony is a bitch," he said, and Jenny gave a guilty start.

"You were married long enough for that?"

"Five years." That much was the truth. "Could have been worse, I guess. The judge only ordered spousal support for a three-year period, so I'll be done with all that in just a couple more months."

"That must be a relief."

"Well, I'd be lying if I said I wasn't looking forward to the day when I write that last check."

Jenny went quiet then, and broke a chip in two before dunking half of it in the dip. "At least it didn't seem to sour you completely on weddings."

"Oh, I'm glad I went." At least that wasn't a lie.

Their eyes met, and Colin's heart gave an odd little thump. Had it thumped like that when he first met Shannon? He couldn't even remember anymore; his first memories of her had been irrevocably colored by what had happened later on in their relationship, and so he knew he couldn't form an unbiased opinion when it came to analyzing his feelings about her.

Jenny, though…he was pretty sure he'd never had this kind of reaction to a woman before, especially not after spending so little time with her. Everything about her seemed to give him a thrill—the way she smiled, the low, sweet timbre of her voice, how her hair fell around her face. Even the sadness in her eyes. It made him want to take her in his arms and never let go.

She sent him a smile right then that made a distinct tingle go down his back and end up someplace he really shouldn't be thinking about. Especially not when they were out in public, surrounded by people.

"I'm glad you went, too. Although I'm surprised you didn't bring a date."

"Um, well…I did invite a friend from work. Purely platonic," he added quickly, before her brows had a chance to pull together. "But the invitation was for me and a 'plus one.' She wasn't feeling well, though, so I decided to go ahead and come on my own."

More lies…but what he was telling Jenny now should match up well enough with what he'd said to Lucas and Margot and the others at the table where he'd been sitting. He didn't know if any of them would actually check to make sure the stories lined up, but just in case Jenny made a casual mention, it should be okay. He hoped.

"Anyway," he went on, "is there much more shopping on your list?"

She gave him a sly smile. "What, have I worn you out already?"

"No," he replied. "But I figured I'd mentally prepare myself for another marathon."

"No marathon. I'm pretty much done, actually. There might be one or two places I want to hit on the way out, but that's it."

He didn't quite heave a sigh of relief, but Jenny must have noticed something in his expression.

"What, didn't your wife drag you all over the mall?"

"Not really." He wouldn't bother to mention that she preferred to shop on her own or online so he wouldn't have a good idea of how much she was actually spending. Well, not until the credit card bills showed up, anyway.

Jenny appeared to digest this, but the slightest of frowns touched the corner of her mouth, as if she understood that he wasn't telling her everything. Unlike a lot of women, though, she didn't seem inclined to press the issue. "So what is there to do around here besides shop?"

There was a lot to do in Tucson, but Colin had a feeling that Jenny wasn't really in the mood to go sightseeing or visit a museum or whatever else he could think of to fill up the time until dinner. Then he had an idea. She might shoot him down, but better to know now whether they shared any of the same interests.

"Do you have in IMAX in the Verde Valley?"

She gave him a pained look. "Please. The nearest theater has a total of six screens, and they're all dinky."

So far, so good. "You like superhero movies?"

Her head tilted to one side. "The kind where a lot of stuff gets blown up?"

Was that condemnation in her tone? God, he hoped she wasn't into romantic comedies or Oscar-bait dramas. Might as well go for broke. "Lots of explosions, yeah."

A sunny smile spread over her face. "That sounds *perfect*."

CHAPTER SEVEN

HOW HAD COLIN KNOWN THAT THIS WAS EXACTLY WHAT she needed? Maybe she should have been out in the fresh air, going to see the historic sites and museums around town, but none of that sounded particularly appealing. She just wanted to do something where she could check her brain out for a few hours.

So now here they were, watching the fate of the universe hanging in the balance on the biggest movie screen Jenny had ever seen in her life. Actually, she wasn't sure if she really cared for it that much—the setup was somewhat vertigo-inspiring—but she had to admit that it definitely immersed her in the action.

Neither of them had been interested in any snacks, but they'd gotten a large Coke and two straws. That felt slightly illicit, too, since she hardly ever drank soda. And it was fun the way every once in a while they'd reach for the drink at the same time and their fingers would bump into each other. Colin would always defer to her, which she thought was unnecessary but sweet.

And it just felt good to sit here in the dark with him next to her, looking like a completely normal couple. All right, they weren't really a couple, but it felt good to pretend. She liked feeling as if she was just a regular young woman out on a Sunday after-noon date with her boyfriend. No one around her knew she was a witch, or that she'd lost a sister under tragic circumstances. Okay, Colin knew, but he'd been perceptive enough to let the matter go when he could tell she didn't want to talk about it anymore.

She liked that about him. Actually, she liked a lot of things about him. Maybe some part of her had been waiting for him to do or say something to prove that he was a jerk after all, but he'd been nothing but funny and sweet and understanding. Which meant she'd need to find a pretty big reason for not continu-ing with this to see where it might be headed.

It was too bad that his marriage hadn't worked out, and that it had hit him so hard financially, but it sounded as if he was almost free of that particular burden. He must have gotten married fairly young to have been with his ex for five years and to have three years of spousal support on top of that. Yes, witches and warlocks tended to marry young, but they also tended to stay together.

Well, most of the time. Her cousin Evan had gone through a pretty spectacular breakup a year and a half ago, but at least he'd had the clan to bail him out and pay off his ex-wife so she wouldn't talk about exactly what made the McAllister family just a little different from the norm. Jenny had suffered her own guilt over that situation, mostly because she'd had one of her awful flashes of mind reading and had seen that Taylor was cheating on Evan with a Phoenix lawyer she'd met online. That was after the marriage had already begun to fall apart, though, and so she'd kept the vision to herself. Knowing the truth wouldn't have changed the situation and would have only hurt Evan that much more. Still, Jenny had filed the vision away with all the thousand and one other things she'd seen and wished she hadn't. She couldn't change what she saw, but she could force herself to ignore it as best she could.

Her mind was wandering. Not because the movie wasn't good, but because she had way too much occupying her thoughts. Once again she bent to take a sip of Coke, and once again she nearly collided with Colin. This time, though, he didn't back away. His lips brushed against her cheek, and his hand covered hers where it sat on the armrest that separated them.

Heat rushed all through her body, but she made herself take that sip of Coke anyway. As she did so, Colin settled himself against the back of his chair once again. Even in the darkness, she could see the way his teeth flashed as he grinned.

Tease, she thought, but she made herself sit back as well and pretend to be engrossed in the three-story images on the screen in front of her. It was hard, though, because she still felt flushed and distracted. Right then, she thought she had a pretty good idea of what was going to happen between them after dinner. Something about this Colin Campbell seemed to be well nigh irresistible.

Which troubled her, because he really wasn't her type. Yes, he was good-looking and tall and slim, but she'd always gone for more muscular men, guys who spent time at the gym or at least engaged in a good deal of outdoor activity. She kind of doubted Colin went to the gym at all. He might run—he had the long, lean muscles for it—but she had a feeling that was the only kind of exercise he bothered with.

They sat all the way through the credits, because Jenny knew that you had to wait for the "Easter egg" at the end to get a sneak peek at what might be happening in the sequel. Eventually, though, they clambered out of their seats and headed toward the parking lot. During the time they'd been in the theater, the sun had sunk almost all the way to the horizon, painting the sky and the oddly jagged mountains to the north and east of town in shades of copper and gold. The wind had picked up, too, cooling the air rapidly.

Jenny shivered.

Colin noticed at once. "Are you cold?"

"I'm fine," she replied. "It's a lot colder in Jerome than it is here. I guess I just wasn't expecting it in Tucson."

He didn't look all that convinced. "Well, it's not too far out of the way to swing by your hotel so you can pick up a jacket before we go to dinner. Does that sound like a plan?"

"Sure." She hesitated, then asked, "Are we going someplace dressy? Should I change?"

"No. You're perfect." It could have been the colors of the sunset painting the red in his cheeks, but Jenny thought he flushed slightly then. "I mean, what you're wearing is perfect. You don't need to worry about that."

She nodded, and they got in the car and headed out of the parking lot. Stopping by the hotel made a lot of sense, because then she could offload her packages at the same time she was picking up a jacket. Luckily, they'd all fit in the trunk of his car, thereby not offering any incentive to would-be thieves, but she might as well get rid of them while she had the chance.

As she'd been shopping, it hadn't really seemed like that much. When she and Colin began pulling bags out of the trunk, however, Jenny realized how much she really had picked up during her spree.

"Sorry about this," she said as they began to stagger toward the elevator. "I guess I went a little crazy. I don't get out much."

"It's fine," he said. "It's not like we had to hire a Sherpa or anything."

She chuckled at that, and led him down the hallway to her room once the elevator deposited them on the correct floor. It did feel sort of strange to have him come in there with her, after the experiences they'd shared at his apartment the night before. He wore a carefully neutral expression, though, and dumped the shopping bags he carried on the bed, then went to the window and looked out at the gardens below.

"Nice view," he commented.

"Thanks," she replied, which was kind of silly, since she really hadn't had anything to do with whether the view was nice of not. She went ahead and put the bags she carried next to the ones Colin had dropped on the bed, then headed over to the closet to get the suede coat she'd brought with her to Tucson.

After she'd shrugged into it, she turned to see that Colin was now looking at her, rather than at the view out the window.

"What?" she asked.

He shook his head. "Nothing. It's—this is going to sound stupid."

"I doubt that."

A pause. Then he came toward her, and her heartbeat began to speed up. Was he going to try something now? But the bed was all covered in shopping bags....

He didn't touch her. He stopped about a foot away and watched her for a long moment, during which she tried not to blink or flush or do anything to show how awkward she felt right then.

"I was just thinking how glad I was that I'd met you. It's lame, I know."

"I don't think it's lame," she said. Lame? That was one of the sweetest things anyone had ever said to her, and she'd only known him for barely twenty-four hours. "Well, if it makes you feel better, I'm really glad that I met you, too. Gives me some hope."

"Hope?" he asked.

"That there are still some decent guys in the world."

Something in his expression altered then. It wasn't exactly that a shadow passed over his face, but she could tell that what she'd said had affected him.

Then he shrugged and said, tone a little too careless, "Well, I'm glad I've restored your faith in humanity. But how about your appetite?"

"My appetite?" she said blankly. Maybe she'd overstepped her bounds, gotten too personal too fast. He'd seemed open enough, but….

"Yes, your appetite." He smiled then, but something about it looked almost forced. "Because where I'm taking you, you'll need to be prepared to eat a *lot*."

God, he was a shit. A *total* shit. Here Jenny McAllister was thinking he was this great guy—and he had to wonder what assholes she'd hooked up with in the past, if she was looking at him as some shining example of manly integrity—when in reality he was just a lying bag of crap.

He really needed to tell her the truth. And then he wondered how many of these margaritas on the rocks he'd have to consume before he worked up the courage.

On a Sunday night, the El Charro Café wasn't quite as busy as it would have been on a Friday or Saturday, but the place still hummed. Colin had brought Jenny here because it was a landmark, and because she'd commented that there wasn't as much good Mexican food in her part of the world as one might think. They'd both ordered margaritas on the rocks, shared some casual conversation about the movie and about their respective favorite restaurants, and the whole time he'd been watching Jenny's beautiful face and listening to her warm, sweet voice, and knowing that this would all come to a crashing end as soon as he told her the real reason why he'd been at Alex Trujillo's wedding.

With every passing moment, though, that prospect seemed more and more impossible. Colin told himself that it would be better to wait until they were alone. Really, why make a scene here and have her miss out on one of the restaurant's world-famous chimichangas? Better to take her back to her hotel, then sit in the car with her and tell her the real reason he'd come to Alex's wedding was because he'd been told by a very nice older lady that she'd witnessed Alex shooting some kind of blue fire out of his fingertips, and the reporter in Colin wouldn't allow him to pass up such a story without investigating it further.

Yeah, that would go over real well.

"Well," Jenny said then, "if the actual food is as good as the chips and salsa and this margarita, then I'm sold."

"Oh, it is." Colin took an over-large gulp of his own margarita. Liquid courage. Only he didn't feel particularly courageous right then. He felt like an asshole. A lying asshole. "So," he went on, "what are your plans for when you're back in Jerome?"

Something in her face fell, but she said calmly enough, "Same old, same old. My cousin Susan was watching the gallery while I was down here, but it's back to work once I get home."

"Have you always been interested in art?"

The question elicited a chuckle, and Jenny shook her head. "Not really. The gallery kind of came with the flat above it. But mostly what I've found is that people just want to experience art on their own and decide if a piece is something they want to take home with them. They really don't want someone jibber-jabbering about its meaning, or whatever."

He could see what she meant. Not that he'd ever been in a financial position to collect art, but if he were, he knew he'd prefer to choose pieces on his own, rather than have some gallery owner tell him what he should or shouldn't be buying. "That sounds like it could be fun."

"Some days it is, some days it isn't. I don't really like having to explain why an artist charges what he or she does. It's like some people think that creative types should just be able to live on air or something."

"And it's not exactly like you can tell your customers to go to hell."

Her mouth pulled to one side as she gave him a wry half-smile. "Well, I might have done that on one or two occasions when I couldn't take it anymore. I guess I should just be glad that the people I pissed off apparently weren't the type to go home and vent their frustrations on Yelp."

Colin wished he'd been there to see her telling off a couple of rich tourists. He could just see her, hands on her curvy hips, head tilted to one side with that golden mane of hers spilling down her back. "Yes, you should definitely count yourself lucky there. I have a couple of friends who own a restaurant—a very good restaurant—but even so, it seems like an uphill battle sometimes. You get someone who's had a crappy day or who had to wait a few minutes longer than promised for a table, and they act like someone just kidnapped their firstborn."

Jenny's eyebrows lifted. "Your friends own a restaurant? So why didn't we go there?"

Oh, crap. It was true that Linda and Greg's place was very good, but no chance in hell would Colin take Jenny there, not when she had no idea who he really was or what he did for a living. Luckily, he did have a good excuse ready to go. "You made it sound like you wanted Mexican food, and their place is Italian."

That response seemed to make sense to her, because she nodded as she took another sip of her margarita. "True. Well, maybe next time." Then she looked stricken, as if she'd just realized that she'd made it sound as if there would be a next time. "I mean—"

"It's okay," he broke in. "I want there to be a next time. I know it's tough with us living so far apart, but I know we can figure something out." Even as he spoke, he realized how he was digging himself deeper with every word. Problem was, he wanted to dig deeper. He wanted to be with Jenny McAllister, although he had absolutely no idea how to make that work after the way he'd lied to her.

She didn't reply right away, but swirled her straw through her half-drunk margarita. Right then, Colin wished he had the ability to read minds, because he would have killed to know what was going through hers. At last she gave the smallest lift of her shoulders. "I suppose we can," she said at last. "I mean, Caitlin and Alex did the long-distance thing for six months, and she was even farther away, in Flagstaff."

"In Flagstaff?" Colin asked, confused. "I thought she was from Jerome, like you."

"Oh, she is," Jenny replied, now looking a little amused. "But she was going to school at NAU. She transferred to the University of Arizona, though, so she could finish her degree down here in Tucson."

"Right." He supposed he should have thought of that. Truth be told, he was having some trouble keeping all of Jenny's relatives and their various connections completely straight. If he'd been on assignment, he would have been taking notes on the pad of paper he usually carried with him wherever he went, but he kind of doubted that would go over very well while he was on a date.

A date. That's really what this was, although neither he nor Jenny had uttered the word out loud. The whole thing was almost a foreign concept to him, since he hadn't been on a date since he and Shannon split up. He'd met women here and there, but none of them had caught his fancy enough for him to deal with all the complications of trying to woo one woman while managing the aftermath of a divorce from another. There had been a couple of very casual hook-ups, but that was it.

"So," Jenny said, giving him the sort of smile that seemed to indicate that this date would end very well, "does that mean you'll come up to Jerome next weekend?"

"If you want me to." As he spoke, though, he wondered how he was going to manage that, since he usually spent part of his weekends writing those damn diet and fitness ebooks. He was already behind, thanks to crashing the Trujillo/McAllister wedding and all the associated aftermath. Well, he'd just have to put in a few hours every night after he got home from work. It wasn't like he had what you could call an active social life.

"It'll be fun. There's a good band playing at the Spirit Room on Saturday night."

"The Spirit Room?"

"A local bar. It's haunted."

It was his turn to raise an eyebrow. "Don't you mean that it's *supposed* to be haunted?"

She chuckled, then plucked another chip from the wooden bowl at the center of the table. "Actually, it's pretty well documented that the Connor Hotel—the Spirit Room is on the hotel's ground floor—is *very* haunted. I'd suggest that you stay there and find out for yourself, but…."

"But?" he prompted, hoping she meant what he thought she'd meant.

"I'd much rather have you stay with me."

Colin smiled. "I think that sounds like much more fun than ghost hunting."

The food arrived then, and they ordered another round of margaritas before they tucked into the enormous plates that had been set before them. He might have been guilty as sin, but he was also hungry. And something about the look in Jenny's eyes told him that he'd better be well fortified for the evening ahead.

While they ate, the conversation moved on to mundane enough things—Jenny talked a little about her brother Adam, and how he was starting to make a name for himself as a carpenter who specialized in restoring vintage Victorian and Craftsman-style houses. In return, Colin told her about his own sister Kate, who was five years his junior and working on her master's in urban planning. He didn't mention his brother-in-law, though, since he really didn't like Jeff. About the only good thing Colin could say for him was that he didn't seem to mind Kate staying in school for a long as necessary. "I think she wants to rebuild Phoenix or something," he said with a grin, "but she's got her work cut out for her."

"So she's going to school in Phoenix?"

"Yes, at ASU. Which explains why she's still in school—she's kind of on the eight-year plan. Frankly, I think she would stay there forever if she could, but I guess you have to get out into the real world eventually."

Something about those words made a flicker of sadness pass over Jenny's face, and Colin wondered what it was that he'd said to disturb her. Maybe, being from Jerome, she didn't have a lot of experience in the "real" world. Or maybe she was just thinking about her own sister Roslyn, now gone forever, who would never get a chance to go to college or do anything at all. That had to be rough.

"Yes, I guess you do," Jenny said at last, her voice soft. "Although some of us have a harder time with that than others. But you—you seem more like the kind of person to face the real world head on."

"Well, I don't know about that," Colin protested. "There are some days when I really don't want to deal with the world at all. Unfortunately, we don't always have that choice."

"True." She pushed some rice around on her plate, not looking at him. "That is, I guess it's mostly true. I know some people in Jerome who haven't dealt with the real world in years."

"I guess it's a good place for that."

"You have no idea."

They both went quiet then, seeming to concentrate on the food before them. Colin guessed, however, that her thoughts were probably just as occupied as his were. What she was thinking about, though, he had no idea.

They passed on dessert. As they were driving away from the restaurant, Jenny said, "Do you want to go to the hotel, or back to your place?"

She'd already struck him as someone who didn't beat around the bush, but her openness as to where their evening apparently was headed did surprise him somewhat. "Uh…whichever you like."

"The hotel," she said promptly. "That way you can have room service before you head off to work in the morning."

Right then he was glad of the relative dimness inside the car. That way, he could hope that she hadn't seen the flush he knew heated his cheeks.

He'd always hated that about himself, and in the summer it wasn't so obvious, because he tried to get enough sun so he wouldn't look like a pasty office boy. It was November now, though, and he'd been working so many hours between his regular job and the freelance ebook writing on the side that he hadn't had a chance to sit out by the pool at his apartment complex even on warm sunny days.

"Okay," he said, hoping he sounded cool and collected, instead of having a pulse that had begun to race at the mere thought of a repeat of the previous night's activities. "You mind if I swing by my apartment first so I can get a few things? That way I can go straight to work from the hotel."

"That sounds like a great idea."

So he cut over a couple of streets so they'd have a straight shot to his apartment complex. It was a good fifteen minutes from the restaurant to there, however, a drive that was spent in companionable silence. Jenny stared out the car window, watching the streets flash by. Colin wondered how strange and foreign it must feel to her, to someone who'd grown up in a place as tiny as Jerome. Had she not traveled at all? No, she'd made a few comments that seemed to indicate she went into Phoenix from time to time, but clearly she was still not used to urban sprawl, to block after block of car dealerships and grocery stores and check cashing places and all the other "conveniences" of big city life.

After he'd pulled into his parking space and turned off the car, he turned toward Jenny. "Do you want to come up, or wait here?"

"I'll come with you."

Good thing he'd tidied the place up again, just in case. "I'll just be a couple of minutes," he told her after he let her in the apartment.

"No problem." She sat down on the couch and picked up a copy of *Arizona Highways* from the coffee table.

Cool, wasn't she? Good thing she seemed so relaxed, because Colin knew he sure as hell wasn't. Still, he tried to look like he did this sort of thing every day as he headed into the bedroom and retrieved his carry-on bag from the shelf in the bedroom closet. At least his workplace was casual enough that he could wear jeans and a polo shirt, neither of which were likely to suffer too much from being packed in a suitcase, even if they had to sit in there all night.

His toiletries didn't take up much room, or require much time to gather, so he was back out in the living room in less than five minutes. Jenny looked up from the magazine.

"That was fast."

"I like to travel light."

She grinned, then put the copy of *Arizona Highways* back where she'd found it and stood up. "You could probably teach me a thing or two. I'm terrible at packing. Probably because I never really go anywhere."

Was that the faintest edge of bitterness he heard in her voice? He didn't know for sure. During the time they'd spent together, he'd come to recognize some of her moods and expressions, but there was still so much about her that was a complete mystery.

"Well, you came to Tucson," he said. "That's a start."

"True. It has turned out to be a worthwhile trip."

Should he kiss her? They'd actually been fairly hands off all day, as if they both had realized that to share too much physical intimacy would only send them right back into bed together. And while he burned to kiss her, Colin told himself that it would be better to wait until they got back to her hotel room.

So he gave her a smile of his own and said, "I'm glad you think so," as he moved toward the door.

Jenny appeared to get the hint, and picked up her purse and let herself out into the hall so he could lock the door behind them. Then it was back to the car, and another quiet drive for the final leg that would lead them to the parking lot of her hotel.

He got his bag out of the trunk and couldn't help experiencing a flash of relief that they were walking onto a hotel's grounds. No one would find anything strange about him bringing a carry-on bag with him in this kind of place, whereas if they'd been going to her apartment....

Which was something he'd more or less promised her, meaning that the whole of Jerome would know exactly why he was staying at her place. Well, Jenny didn't seem to have a problem with that, so he told himself that he shouldn't, either.

By some stroke of luck, the elevator was empty when they got on, and the hallway that led to her room was also unoccupied. But then, it was Sunday night, probably not a peak occupancy time for the hotel. The management was probably happy that Jenny had stayed on for another day.

As was he.

She waved her plastic key in front of the lock, then said, "Damn," almost as soon as they were inside. Hurrying into the main part of the room, she went on, "Just give me a minute to get this cleared up."

For a second, he wondered what the heck she was talking about, then remembered all the shopping bags she'd left piled on top of the bed. "No problem," he assured her.

"I should have hung all this up when we first stopped in," she said. Then she pointed to the desk. "There's a room service menu. Maybe order a bottle of champagne?"

Colin wasn't sure what champagne would do on top of the margaritas they'd already drunk, but one look at Jenny told him she wasn't quite as blasé about what was coming next as she might have wanted him to think. And hell, he'd gone to work half hung over before, especially when he was in the middle of his divorce, so he figured he could handle the champagne, even if they did end up drinking the entire bottle.

While she was busy with pulling items out of bags and hanging them up in the closet—or, in the case of the shoes and accessories, merely piling the shopping bags on the floor of the closet—he called down to the restaurant and ordered the champagne. Not the super-expensive Dom Pérignon, which would have cost her nearly five hundred bucks, but the much more modest but still good Schramsberg, a champagne-style sparkling wine from California.

"On its way," he told her.

She stuck her head out of the closet and said, "Thanks," before returning to her work.

Since the bed wasn't completely clear yet, Colin sat down at the desk and pretended to be perusing the rest of the room service menu. Should he have ordered something to go with the champagne? Probably not; the two of them were already full enough after that meal at El Charro Café, so full that they'd both passed on dessert.

But he could look at the breakfast portion of the menu. Jenny had already more or less offered to buy him breakfast, a first in his life.

He'd just decided that he would probably get the Denver omelet when she shut the closet doors and let out an audible sigh of relief and said, "Well, that's done. How I'm going to get all that to fit once I get it home, I have no idea, but I supposed I can worry about that then."

"Small closets?"

She made a face. "You have no idea. But the view is so amazing that I have to forgive the lack of storage space."

"That good?"

"Oh, yeah. You can sit on the front deck—or porch, or whatever you want to call it—and look out across the whole Verde Valley, all the way to Sedona's red rocks. But you'll be able to see for yourself next weekend."

"Sounds great," he replied. And it did. Of course, it would probably sound even better if they didn't have this huge lie hanging in between them. What he was going to do about that, he had absolutely no idea.

A soft knock at the door, and Jenny hurried to answer it. Room service with their bottle of champagne. She took the silvery ice bucket and pair of flutes from the waiter, then murmured a thank-you. Belatedly, Colin realized that he probably should have gotten up and helped her with the transaction. And what about offering to pay? But she'd obviously put the champagne on her room's bill, and he had a feeling she wouldn't want to argue about it, especially since he'd sprung for dinner.

He did get up after she'd closed the door, hurrying over so he could take the ice bucket with its well-chilled bottle from her. She shot him a grateful look, then went and set the glasses down on the desk.

This time, he couldn't exactly shoot the cork into the pool. Colin settled for aiming at the heavy wooden door, figuring it was less likely to show any damage if he did manage to score a direct hit.

His aim was more or less true; the cork bounced off the doorframe and landed on the carpet a few feet away. Since the champagne had been chilled so well and clearly had been handled with care, it didn't foam up everywhere, but merely fizzed gently as he poured it into the glasses.

Jenny scooped hers up first, but waited while Colin set down the bottle and picked up his own flute. "So what should we drink to?" she asked.

A brief hesitation, as he weighed what he really wanted to say against what he probably should say. He knew he was already falling for her, even after only a day spent together. But…what the hell. His shoulders lifted just a fraction, and he said, "To beginnings?"

To his relief, she didn't flinch or look at him sideways. Instead, she nodded slightly. "To beginnings," she echoed, her voice firm.

They clinked their glasses together and drank. The champagne was good, better than the stuff that was served at the wedding, although it had been decent enough. Problem was, he could feel it hitting the tequila and doing interesting things to his system. Thank God that he didn't have to drive anywhere, didn't have to do much more maneuvering than getting Jenny over to the bed.

If the drink was affecting her in the same way, she didn't show it. She sipped quietly, almost as if she was thinking of something completely separate from their upcoming assignation. Was she having second thoughts and trying to decide how to back out without hurting his feelings?

Then she set down her glass and glanced over at him. Something raw was reflected in her eyes, something naked with need, with want. Right then, Colin wanted to know who had hurt her in the past, because he wanted to track the bastard down and punch him in the face.

"Colin," she whispered, and that was all he needed.

He put his half-empty glass down on the table and stood up. Without speaking, he extended a hand. She took it, her fingers strong and warm and soft against his. Desire flooded through him, and he knew he wanted to make love to her more than he'd ever wanted anything in his entire life. Yes, they'd had sex the night before, but he wasn't sure he would have classified that coupling as lovemaking. Rather, they'd both been burning with a need that had to be quenched, and it had been hard and quick and sweaty and satisfying. Now, though...now he needed to make love to her.

Jenny's mouth was sweet with champagne. He kissed her over and over, and after that they were falling to the bed, their hands moving over one another, undoing belts and buttons, jeans getting dragged off and flung to the floor. His fingers found the clasp of her bra and unfastened it, and then the exquisite fullness of her breasts was spilling into the palms of his hands. She let out a little sigh; he'd already learned how sensitive she was the night before.

So he took a nipple into his mouth, suckling her, while he reached with one hand to slip into her panties to feel how ready she was for him. And he did want to be in her, but first he wanted to taste her, taste all of her.

She startled slightly as his lips began to trail down her stomach, moving lower and lower, even as he eased down her panties. Something in her body seemed to tense; maybe she hadn't been expecting this, maybe none of the men she'd been with before had taken the time to really make love to her completely.

But a long, drawn-out gasp left her lips as he touched his tongue to her, caressing her, savoring her taste, the amazing beauty of this most secret part of her body. Her breathing sped up as he continued to make love to her with his mouth, and he knew she was close. God, he loved the way her body responded to him.

The climax shuddered through her, and he continued to lick and tease at her, knowing that she probably wasn't quite done. A minute or so later, he was proven right, as a smaller orgasm sent shivers through her frame. He pulled away then, lifting his mouth from her, and her hand reached down and wrapped around him, stroking him, her fingers strong and sure.

And skilled. If she kept that up for too much longer, he was going to come right then and there. Not that that was a bad thing, but he wanted to be inside her again. Nothing could compare to the sensation of being buried in her, of feeling her surround him completely.

Yesterday he'd been surprised that she hadn't asked him to put on a condom. He knew he was crazy for having unprotected sex with her, but for some reason, he wasn't worried. Which was even crazier.

Now, though, he did pause long enough to ask her, "Do you want me to get a condom?"

A low chuckle escaped her throat. "I'd say that was a bit like locking the barn door after the horse was stolen. Don't worry about it."

"You're sure?"

"I'm sure. I'm on the pill."

Well, thank God. He bent and kissed her neck, moved his hands over her breasts, and she moaned and pushed her body against his, practically begging him to enter her.

He didn't have to be asked twice.

He plunged into her, their bodies immediately picking up the rhythm, rocking away. Dimly, he heard the headboard hitting the wall, and hoped the room next to hers was empty. But that didn't matter enough for him to stop. He couldn't have stopped himself if he wanted to. In that moment, the world was only the two of them, spinning around and around, her soft, warm flesh pressed up against him, surrounding him.

His mouth came down on hers, and they were kissing, tongues touching as their bodies were joined as well. He knew he was going to climax soon, and prayed she would be more or less in time with him, because he couldn't hold this back, couldn't make it last longer. The release the evening before had been incredible, but somehow he knew this time around would cast his previous experience into shadow.

The orgasm thundered through his body, and he clenched as he released into her. Jenny's legs wrapped around him, driving him in even deeper, and then he could feel her clamping down on him, her climax only intensifying his own. They clung to one another while the world shuddered around them, as if neither of them wanted to acknowledge that they were two rather than the one they seemed to be in that moment.

To say that he'd never experienced anything like it would be an understatement. He'd thought sex with Shannon had been good—at least in the beginning—but it seemed like a pale shadow of the act compared to what he'd just shared with Jenny McAllister.

At last, though, they did pull away from one another. Colin brushed a hand down her cheek, marveling at the velvet softness of her skin. Her eyes were half shut, her forehead glowing with the faintest sheen of perspiration. He bent and kissed her, and she kissed him back, mouth open, as if she had to show him how much she still wanted to share herself with him.

I love you.

The thought came and went like the tiniest of flickers in his mind, but even so, he knew he was in trouble. He couldn't be in love with her. He barely knew her. This was just sex and champagne talking.

God, he wished that was true.

But somehow, he knew it wasn't.

CHAPTER EIGHT

THEY'D GOTTEN OUT OF BED AFTERWARD AND DRUNK more champagne. Not a whole lot, but enough so that about two-thirds of the bottle was gone. Maybe Colin hadn't wanted to seem wasteful. Jenny didn't know for sure, but she was willing to go along for the ride. The champagne did help to prolong the swimmy, almost ethereal feeling that had taken over her body. She'd had sex plenty of times, but this...this was different. He'd made love to her. He'd taken the time to make sure she was satisfied.

Goddess, was she satisfied.

Well, physically anyway. Sometime around three-thirty in the morning, Jenny had rolled over in her hotel room bed and had lain there for a long while, quietly watching Colin as he slept. His hair was a mess, his lashes thick and dark—a good deal darker than his hair—and he snored ever so faintly. Not enough to wake her up; she knew his snoring wasn't the reason she was wakeful now. She stared at him and felt something inside her turn over. This feeling—it was trouble. She knew that, but she also didn't know what the hell she was supposed to do about it.

If she'd had two brain cells to rub together, she would never have brought up the subject of having Colin come visit her in Jerome. They could have had just this weekend together. An amazing weekend, true, with the best sex she'd ever had, but one that also held no promise of any kind of future together. They could have walked away with some great memories, and that would have been the end of it. But when he got up in the morning and headed out for work, he wouldn't be leaving her life altogether. He'd only be leaving it until next Saturday.

Maybe there was some way she could take back the invitation to come stay with her in Jerome. No, that would be incredibly rude. And besides...she didn't want to take it back. She wanted to see him again.

She was pretty sure she wanted to see him every day of her life, which was probably impossible.

But did it have to be? Civilian and witch pairings were rare but certainly not unheard of, starting right with Jenny's own parents They were happy enough, or at least as happy as a couple could be who'd had one of their children murdered less than a year ago.

And you are getting way ahead of yourself, she thought then. *So you've had some mind-blowing sex with Colin, and he's actually treated you like a human being. That doesn't mean you should start picking out baby names yet.*

Probably not.

There was something comforting about having him sleep next to her, though. She liked it. She wanted to wake up next to him every morning.

Damn. She let out a sigh and rolled over, willing herself to sleep. Maybe by the time she awoke, she'd have acquired some common sense.

Colin had an alarm set on his phone so he wouldn't oversleep and be late to work. Its beeping brought him back to consciousness, and he stared up at the ceiling for a few seconds before he remembered where he was.

Jenny's hotel room, and there she was, hair a spill of glorious gold across the pillow. As he picked up his phone to turn off the alarm, she stirred, then pushed herself up to a sitting position. Her expression was bleary, but she'd retained enough presence of mind to hold the sheets up against her breasts so she wasn't entirely exposed.

Too bad.

"Time?" she asked.

"Six-thirty," he replied. "Sorry it's so early, but my office is halfway across town, and I have to be there at eight."

"It's fine." With her left hand—not the one holding up the sheet—she rubbed at her eyes. "Why don't you let me know what you want for breakfast, and I'll call room service while you're in the shower."

"Denver omelet."

She raised an eyebrow.

"I took a look at the menu last night."

"Ah." A pause, and then she added, "Coffee?"

"Of course." He stopped to assess exactly how he was feeling. It definitely felt like a two-cup morning. Or maybe three. Getting up and downing most of that bottle of champagne hadn't been one of his better ideas. "You might want to order a whole pot."

A small smile quirked her full lips. "Will do."

He untangled himself from the sheets, picking up his abandoned underwear during the process. Was it worth it to put them back on, just to walk into the bathroom? Mornings after were always so tough, especially when you were new to someone and hadn't really defined your relationship. And was this even a relationship?

His soul and heart and body wanted it to be. His mind...well, his mind was still trying to figure out exactly what was going on.

Colin decided against the underwear, and walked as casually as he could toward the bathroom, although he was all too aware of Jenny's eyes on him as he took those few short steps. Then he shut the door and released a small exhalation of relief. He'd always been more about the mind than the body, although he did run to keep himself in shape. But he wasn't sure he was up to an in-depth inspection by a goddess like Jenny McAllister.

The shower felt good, hot and invigorating, helping to blow out some of the cobwebs in his brain. He still wasn't any closer to figuring out how to break the news to Jenny that he'd come to her cousin Caitlin's wedding under false pretenses, but Colin did feel as if he was thinking a little more clearly. There was no point in denying his feelings for her, so he had to decide what his best course of action should be.

Sitting down and talking to her right before he had to take off for work was not a good idea at all. Might as well end their time together this weekend on a high note. No, he'd get through his work week, go up to Jerome on Saturday, and then clear the air while she was safely on her home turf. He'd explain that there hadn't been anything malicious in his actions, only a desire to know the truth behind the story Eileen Kosky had told him.

How well Jenny would react to that revelation, Colin had no idea. But at least there wouldn't be any more secrets between them.

He got out of the shower and towel-dried his hair, then wrapped himself in one of the plush terrycloth robes hanging from the hook on the bathroom door. His overnight bag was still sitting out on the floor next to the dresser, but he thought he could get dressed while Jenny was in the shower. If she even planned to shower while he was there. After all, she only had to take a leisurely drive back to Jerome today. From what she'd said, it sounded like she wouldn't actually be going to work again until the next morning.

When he emerged from the bathroom, the rich—and welcome—smell of coffee and eggs reached his nose. "That was fast," he commented as he headed for the table by the window where Jenny had set out their breakfasts.

"I don't think the hotel is too busy today," she replied, pouring coffee into the mug at the place setting across from hers. "There's cream and sugar," she added.

"I take it black, but thanks."

Her nose wrinkled slightly, but she didn't say anything as she poured a good deal of cream into her own coffee, followed by a small spoonful of sugar.

"So…you have a lot of corporate communicating to do today?"

Colin knew the question was completely innocuous, but inwardly he cringed at having to tell her yet another lie. "Some press releases, the verbiage for a new brochure. The usual."

"Sounds exciting," she said, then sipped at her coffee.

"It's very not exciting, unfortunately, but that's how it goes."

She nodded. Luckily, she didn't appear all that interested in asking him anything else about his upcoming work day—maybe he'd made it sound dull enough that she'd decided it was better to avoid the topic—and instead dug into her own breakfast, which consisted of scrambled eggs, hash browns, and a side of fresh fruit.

His omelet was excellent, and he ate with appetite, although he kept an eye on the clock on the nightstand. A quarter after seven. Not too bad, but he still needed to shave and get dressed, and if he left much past seven-thirty, he was going to be late.

"It's okay," Jenny said quietly. "I know you have somewhere you have to be."

Colin tried not to wince. "Was I that obvious?"

Her smile was luminous, even with her smudged mascara and sleep-tousled hair. Or maybe it was because of that. "Sort of. But really, it's okay. I knew you had to get up and go to work today."

"Still…."

"Just eat your breakfast. And try not to look so tragic. It's just work. Millions of people survive it every day."

"True." Something about her words made him realize that he really would have to leave her, would have to get in his car and drive away, go off to all the mundanities of his existence. There was something strong and splendid about her that made his everyday life seem very small. Which was ridiculous, wasn't it? She was just a woman. All right, an amazing woman, unlike anyone else he'd ever known, but still….

Anyway, he was being melodramatic. He'd see her again soon enough.

Six days from now. Ouch.

But because she was watching, and he didn't know what else to say, he finished off the rest of his omelet and drained his cup of coffee. "Gotta shave," he mumbled before heading off to the bathroom.

She just nodded, then turned back to the remnants of her scrambled eggs.

Shaving usually helped him to get his head together, made him mentally prepare himself for the day ahead, but Colin's thoughts kept wandering. He didn't want to go to work and write a puff piece about parking meters or whatever else his editor thought would resonate with readers' concerns. No, he wanted to throw his overnight bag in the back of Jenny's car and head home with her to Jerome.

At any other time, he would have chalked his restlessness up to working way too long without a real break; his vacation time was stacking up because he hadn't taken anything other than a long weekend away from work for going on three years now. He'd sucked his vacation days away while dealing with the divorce and had hoarded them ever since. What was the point in using them just for mental health days? It wasn't as if he planned to go jetting off to Cancun anytime soon.

But he hadn't even given a thought to playing hooky from work despite all that. No, right now he desperately wanted to prolong his time with Jenny, make this weekend stretch into a week, then a month, and then....

And then you really need to cool it, he told himself, scrunching his face so he could reach that hard-to-get-at spot down along his jawline. *A couple of great nights in the sack do not a lifetime together make.*

Come to think of it, that was part of the mistake he'd made with Shannon. They spent a wild weekend together out at the El Dorado hot springs, and he'd become so entranced with her that he'd decided she was the perfect person for him. Never mind that they really hadn't had much in common, except a taste for certain movies and certain kinds of music. Shannon had wanted someone with a real future, someone who could give her a comfortable lifestyle. It wasn't that she didn't expect to work; she got her teaching credential and taught first grade, which she loved. But she also knew she'd never get rich doing that, and a husband who was scraping by making a little over thirty grand at a local newspaper didn't exactly meet her expectations.

Well, that was one thing he could tell was different about Jenny McAllister. She had some money of her own, that much was obvious. All those purchases had been paid for with cash or a Visa debit card, not a credit card. He'd paid attention, because a woman who was so blithe about racking up credit card debt was not someone he wanted to get involved with. At any rate, she'd let him take her out to dinner, but she'd covered the champagne and breakfast here at the hotel, which meant she certainly wasn't out to take advantage of him.

Keep it up, he thought as he tapped the bristles from his electric razor into the bathroom trash can. *At the rate you're going, you'll be asking her to marry you the second you walk back out there.*

It did seem as if he kept coming up with reasons why Jenny seemed to be the ideal woman for him, even when he thought he was doing the opposite.

He went out and offered her a smile as he retrieved his overnight bag. She was sipping her coffee, the plate in front of her empty except for a few scraps of hash browns. Clearly, she wasn't too worried about her calorie intake. Then again, why should she be? She was slender without being thin, with a nicely curved ass and a full bust, but not too full. Just enough for all the proportions to be right.

And that was the wrong thing to be thinking, because he could feel himself stir at the memory of her warm flesh beneath him, at the way her breasts had spilled into his palms. Thank God for bulky hotel bathrobes.

Probably moving too quickly, he went back into the bathroom to get dressed. If he'd had more guts, he would have stayed out in the main part of the room, but he just couldn't quite manage the thought of having Jenny sit there and drink her coffee as she watched him climb into his boxer briefs and jeans. Yes, she might consider such behavior prudish, and Colin knew he'd have to live with that.

After stuffing himself into his jeans and pulling a polo shirt over his head, he ran a comb through his hair one last time, then sucked in a breath. He didn't wear a watch, preferring to use his phone to let him know what time it was, but he had a feeling he was running late.

Sure enough, when he emerged from the bathroom, a glance at the clock on the nightstand told him that it was now seven thirty-five. He might still make it on time—if the gods smiled at him and gave him a whole hell of a lot of green lights between here and work.

Jenny's expression was resigned. During breakfast, she'd appeared fairly serene, but he could tell from the look on her face that she didn't want to say goodbye any more than he did. Nevertheless, she got up from the table and came toward him, a trace of a smile on her eminently kissable mouth.

"I know—you're late," she said. "So get going."

"I'll call." Of that he was certain. Talking to her during the week would make the days go by more quickly. It would also torture him with the sound of her voice and the knowledge that she was hundreds of miles away, but he'd have to figure out a way to deal with that.

"You'd better," she replied, this time giving him a real grin. Then she kissed him on the cheek, moving to his mouth immediately afterward so she could give him a real kiss, one that tasted of coffee and cream.

God, that was enough to make him want to toss his overnight bag to the floor and drag her back to the bed...right after he made a call to work to let them know that he'd picked up bubonic plague over the weekend. Or maybe Legionnaire's disease. Something that would keep him out of commission long enough to spend as much time as he wanted with Jenny.

But he did none of those things, only kissed her back and said, "I've got to go. I'll call you tonight."

She didn't say anything, only offered him another smile. And then he was heading out the door and over to the elevator, which was blessedly unoccupied. His car looked shabbier than ever as he approached it in the parking lot, which was bathed in bright desert morning sun, but right then he didn't much care.

He got in and headed south, toward the *Tucson Daily Sun*'s offices. In a lot of ways, his editor was pretty laid back, but he did not like people coming in late to work. Being late to work meant you were also capable of being late to make a deadline, and missed deadlines were something that Ned Tavener just did not allow.

Luck seemed to be with Colin at first, though, as he blazed through several lights on Campbell Avenue, heading away from the hotel. The street bordered the university, and the sight of the familiar architecture made a strange pang go through him. Back when he'd been going to graduate school there and besotted with Shannon, he'd sure never thought he'd end up broke and divorced, having to write crappy diet ebooks in order to have any kind of spare cash.

Yeah, and you never thought you'd meet someone like Jenny McAllister, either, he told himself as he turned right on Broadway and headed toward downtown. *Let alone basically spend the weekend with her. I'd say you're doing pretty well, all things considered.*

Well, except for the way their entire relationship so far had been built on false pretenses.

Scowling, he pulled into the *Daily Sun*'s parking lot at five minutes after eight. Not horrible, but not great, either. And there was Ned's silver Audi, gleaming in the sun. Colin would have hated the sight of that car, except he knew Ned really didn't make all that much. His wife was a lawyer who specialized in trusts and probate, and that was where the car had come from.

Ned was nowhere in sight when Colin entered the building. He allowed himself a small sigh of relief and hurried into his office, then powered up the computer right away so it would look like he'd been there all along. Just as he was entering his password, Ryan Ortiz appeared in the doorway.

"So…?"

"So what?" Colin replied, eyes intent on the computer screen.

"So what happened with the wedding crashing?"

"Oh...nothing." Colin had told Ryan that there might be a connection to the Escobar case at the Trujillo/McAllister wedding, but he hadn't said anything more than that. Ryan had been curious, although only mildly so; his attitude had more or less suggested that he thought the whole thing was a snipe hunt, and if Colin wanted to waste his weekend chasing down leads provided by a crazy old woman, he was welcome to it. "Total dead end."

"That's too bad."

"My fault for following up on something that wasn't worth my time." More lies, but he sure as hell wasn't ready to tell Ryan about Jenny McAllister.

"Mmm." Ryan's dark eyes narrowed, and Colin tried to make himself appear more or less neutral, maybe with a tinge of impatience. Lord knows what he looked like in the harsh office lighting—he hadn't noticed any obvious hickeys or other marks on his neck or face, but he knew he looked tired after two nights in a row of too much to drink and not enough sleep. But then Ryan shrugged and went on, "Well, it sounds like I owe you that beer. We could go over to Hennessey's tonight after work."

The last thing Colin wanted right then another night on the town. All he wanted to do was survive this day of work, then go home and crash. Maybe get some writing done on that next pamphlet, because it was due on Friday, but nothing else.

"Rain check?" he asked. "I'm kind of beat."

"Yeah, you look it," Ryan agreed before shooting him a sarcastic grin and heading off to his own office.

On other occasions, Colin might have continued the banter, trading casual insults. It was the way he and the other reporter tended to interact. Right then, though, he was just glad that Ryan hadn't hung around. Sharing quips required way too much energy.

Colin opened Word and pulled up the parking meter article. His editor wanted the piece to run in Tuesday's edition, since the Tuesday paper always had an expanded local section. It was mostly done, thank God—just needed a little more polishing, and a follow-up email to double-check that Colin had all the dates for the rollout correct. He was glad that people didn't tend to bat an eye at emails, because they weren't merely a heck of a lot easier to deal with than phone calls. They also provided written documentation in case there was ever a question of accuracy.

The article sat there on his screen, the white "page" appearing to flicker ever so slightly. It wasn't the screen, though; Colin knew he was just tired. So working on something as simple as this should be a piece of cake.

Jenny's face drifted through his mind's eye, her wide smile, the glow in her big blue-gray eyes. No, she was exactly the last thing he should be thinking about right then. He needed to work. Anyway, he'd already promised her that he would talk to her that night.

But...there was that expensive wedding. The way Jenny had casually dropped probably a grand or more during her shopping expedition.

The blue-white light Eileen Kosky swore up and down that she'd seen in the parking lot outside Dillard's some six months ago, coming from Alex Trujillo's outstretched hands.

Colin stared at the computer screen for a long time, the words of the article blurring in front of him. Then he swore gently under his breath and minimized the Word document before bringing up Firefox. He had a feeling that a simple Google search wouldn't be all that much help, but he figured he had to start somewhere.

So he typed in *McAllister family, Jerome, Arizona.*

CHAPTER NINE

Jenny was glad of the long drive to get back to Jerome. She knew it would take that long to try to put Colin out of her mind, to make herself ignore the little ache she felt deep inside at the thought of not seeing him until next weekend.

He's a civilian, she reminded herself, but that seemed like a puny excuse. Her mother was a civilian. Big deal. If the person was right for you, the divide between witch and ordinary man didn't seem to matter all that much.

Traffic in Phoenix had been cloggy and slow, even though Jenny hadn't gotten on the road until a little after ten. She hadn't minded too much, since the congestion only pushed back her arrival time that much more. What she did mind was all the impatient big-city drivers, the ones who rode your bumper or cut in front of you at the last minute. She wasn't used to that kind of behavior. Not to say that everyone in Jerome or the Verde Valley as a whole was a model driver, but the pace was a lot slower there.

It was with some relief that she passed through the northern suburbs in the Anthem area and headed into more open territory. The freeway had its share of traffic, but it had opened up enough that she could let herself focus on other things.

Like the way Colin had cupped her face in his hands and kissed her. So tender, so wonderful. She'd never had anyone hold her like that, like she was a precious piece of porcelain he was afraid he might break.

He hadn't wanted to leave. She'd seen it in his eyes, in the lopsided smile he wore as he said goodbye, as if that was the best he could manage when faced by their separation. Goddess knew, she hadn't wanted him to go, either. But it was necessary. Good, even. Hopefully, this time apart would allow her to analyze her reactions to him, to think about him more clearly now that several hundred miles would separate them.

Maybe by the time he came up to visit her, she'd know what to do.

It was just after two when Jenny pulled into the alley that led to the carport behind her flat. She was lucky to have covered parking, even if it wasn't a full garage. Lots of people in Jerome didn't even have that, had to fight with the tourists for street parking.

Now, there would be a handy talent, she thought. *To always have the perfect parking place wherever you went.*

Her own pesky gift appeared to have remained dormant, even without her morning rituals of yoga and meditation. Well, she'd get right back on that the next day, just to be safe.

In the meantime, she had a whole lot of bags to drag up two flights of stairs. There was a staircase built into the back of the building, one that led directly from the carport to the back door of the flat above the gallery. Jenny had been glad of those stairs on more than one occasion, since they meant she could slip into her flat without being seen by anyone on the street. Unlike a lot of Jerome's business owners, who seemed to keep whatever damn hours they pleased, the civilian owner of the gallery expected Jenny to open the place at ten and close it at five—six o'clock on Fridays and Saturdays. Most of the time, that wasn't a problem. But once or twice she'd gotten hung up handling McAllister business and wanted to make sure that no looky-loos who might be peeking into the gallery's windows could see her sneaking into her flat.

Today, that wasn't an issue, because Susan was holding down the fort. Well, at least as much as was necessary on a Monday. In general, it wasn't exactly

a busy shopping or sightseeing day in the little mountain town, unless that Monday happened to be part
of a three-day weekend.

Jenny hauled the first batch of shopping bags
upstairs, then went down and collected the remainder, along with her luggage. By that point she was
feeling a little winded—too much alcohol and not
enough sleep the night before—so she left the hanging up and the organizing for later, and went into
the kitchen and poured herself some water from
the pitcher in the fridge. Then she took her glass and
went to sit on one of the Adirondack chairs on the
deck.

Everything was so quiet here. Now and again a
car would go past on Main Street, right below her,
but because it was a Monday, the traffic was light.
The line of the Verde River, off in the distance, was
clearly visible because of the bright autumn yellow
of the cottonwoods that grew on its banks. And
beyond that were Sedona's red rocks, looking redder
than ever in the slanting afternoon light.

A certain tension she hadn't even realized she'd
been carrying eased itself out of Jenny's neck and
shoulders as she sat there and looked at the view.
This was what she needed—the place where she'd
been born, its familiar vistas soothing her soul.

She let the idea of Colin Campbell enter her
mind—the flash of humor in his hazel eyes, that little

dent in one cheek that wasn't quite a dimple, but its first cousin. And then she tried to think about how she would feel if she never saw him again.

All of a sudden, the view beyond the deck wasn't quite as soul-nourishing as it had been a few minutes ago. Jenny had been afraid of that, but she'd needed to try. Deep down, she'd hoped her weekend with Colin had been only a fling, something she could easily let go once she was back home. That didn't seem to be the case, however.

Great, she thought, as she drank the rest of her water and stared at the distant ruddy shapes of Sedona's hills and mesas. *What am I supposed to do now?*

Almost from the start, Colin could tell that Google— or the internet in general—wasn't going to help him much on his quest. There should at least have been documents on file with the Yavapai County recorder's office showing any transactions involving real estate. That stuff was in the public record, after all. But he couldn't seem to find anything. It wasn't that properties didn't trade hands in Jerome; they did, although not with the sort of turnover he would have expected. No, it was that no one with the last name of McAllister seemed to be involved in any of those deals, which didn't make a whole hell of a lot of sense to him.

It was almost as if all those properties had come into the family early on, and then had been quietly handed down when someone passed away, or possibly traded when a family needed to upgrade to a bigger house. Colin had been able to discover that the McAllisters had come to Jerome in the late 1870s, but there was little else that he could find.

Which didn't mean that it didn't exist. It just meant that he'd have to do some in-person digging. Not in Jerome itself—his suddenly appearing there before his scheduled date with Jenny on Saturday would raise way too many questions—but in Prescott, which had been the capitol of the Arizona Territory when the McAllisters came on the scene. There must be some records there, some piece of evidence that would help to explain his nagging feeling that he was missing something big when it came to Jenny's family.

The Wilcoxes were a little easier, just because they didn't seem to have made any effort to keep the recorder in their county from setting down all their various real estate transactions. Colin didn't have the time to look into it too much, partly because the McAllisters were his real focus, and partly because it would have taken a team of investigators to track it all down. The Wilcoxes were a big and prosperous family, and they liked to buy houses. And shopping centers. And car dealerships. And probably any number of other properties that Colin just hadn't discovered yet.

But the McAllisters...that would be worth digging into. He'd realized, though, that the only way he'd be able to follow up on his investigation would be to take a day off from work. That damned parking meter article had been turned in, and Ned hadn't given him another in-depth yet, just a couple of short pieces that anyone on the staff could handle. And Colin had made sure to get at least a third of the way through the pamphlet that was due on Friday before he'd continued with his research into the McAllisters after he got home. Mostly poking around on Facebook, which felt creepy but was easy enough to do. Well, it should have been easy. But he hadn't been able to find much. If the McAllisters were on social media, they seemed to have made sure not to advertise their location when they set up their profiles.

So, okay, he'd need to take a sick day so he could drive up to Prescott and poke around in the records at the historical society there. He wouldn't let himself feel too guilty about pretending to be sick, since he'd dragged himself into work on more than one occasion when suffering from a cold or whatever. His sick days were piling up almost as fast as his vacation days.

He did suffer a few pangs when he called Jenny that night, knowing he'd already resolved to go to Prescott and continue to look into her family's history. The second he heard her voice on the phone, he found himself almost overcome by the impulse to confess everything. But he'd gotten a hold of himself, mostly because he knew telling her the truth over the phone was not the right way to handle this. Besides, was it really so wrong to dig up a few historical facts about the McAllisters? A lot of it was, after all, public record.

She'd sounded tired but not in a bad way. "Long drive," she told him. "And I'd forgotten how many stairs I'd have to drag all those bags up."

The rueful note in her voice made him chuckle. "But you survived?"

"Barely. Of course, they're all just sitting in my bedroom right now. I'm going to have to do a closet cull to get everything to fit. Goodwill is going to love me."

Colin found himself wondering what her bedroom looked like. Was it filled with antiques to match the town she lived in? Or was it more modern, simple? He hadn't really gotten a grasp on her personal style yet, although if what she'd worn on their shopping trip was any indication, she wasn't very tailored, more boho and informal.

"Out with the old," he said. Not that he had much personal experience with that sort of thing. He tended to wear his own shirts and jeans until they grew holes and were no longer fit for work. Spending any kind of money on clothes just wasn't his thing.

"In this case, there's a little too much new, but I'll get it figured out." She paused then and asked, "How was work?"

"Oh, the usual. I wasn't too late."

"Well, that's something."

They chatted a little more, but Colin noticed how they carefully skirted around saying anything too personal. And then Jenny said she had to go, but she'd call him on Wednesday.

Apparently she wasn't the clingy type. Or maybe she was trying to appear non-clingy, and that was why she'd scheduled their next talk for the day after tomorrow.

Either way, he couldn't help being a bit relieved. That meant he wouldn't have to worry about still being out in Prescott when she called again. He'd have the whole day to himself.

Just what he would find, he wasn't sure.

Lysette, Jenny's mother, came into the gallery on Tuesday afternoon, a time carefully calculated to give her daughter enough space after returning to Jerome, but also a time when the gallery would most likely be dead quiet and they could have a little moth-er-daughter chat.

Or at least, that was how Jenny saw it. She didn't mind, actually, because she wanted to talk to her mother about Colin. Maybe that was jumping the gun, but she thought she'd better get a few things straightened out in her head before she saw him again. When he was around, she tended to get so wrapped up in being with him that she pushed the less pleasant aspects of their relationship aside.

Lysette gave a quick glance around as she entered the gallery, then nodded slightly, as if satisfied that the place was empty of anyone except her daugh-ter. She leaned up against the display case that held jewelry made by several local artists—including the clan's own *prima*, Angela—and gave Jenny an inquir-ing look. "How was shopping?"

"Fine," Jenny replied. From the glint in her mother's eyes, it was pretty obvious that Lysette had more on her mind than simply how many pairs of new shoes Jenny had picked up in Tucson. So she came out from behind the counter toward the back of the gallery and said, "His name's Colin."

"I know. Margot told me."

Long ago, Jenny had resigned herself to the way news traveled in the McAllister clan faster than any text or email. Even so, she tensed, then crossed her arms and propped herself up against the display case opposite the one where her mother stood. "Oh, really? What else did Margot have to say?"

Lysette apparently decided to ignore the edge in her daughter's voice. "Not a lot, Jenny. But several people mentioned to me that you were talking with a young man who obviously wasn't a member of any of the clans that attended the wedding, and since Margot and Lucas were seated at his same table, it was only natural that she had a little more information than anyone else. She said Colin seemed like a nice enough person, although a little out of his element."

There was an understatement. A few civilians besides Colin had been at the wedding—mostly spouses of clan members—but as far as Jenny knew, he was the only one who had been there as just a friend, with no other real attachment to the people involved. "And?"

"And what?" Lysette sent her daughter a very mild look, the sort Jenny knew was intended to keep her from getting too riled up. "That's all. But when you disappeared after the reception and didn't come back until the next morning—"

"How did you know that?" Jenny demanded. As far as she'd been able to tell, there hadn't been anyone around to witness her hurrying up to her room while wearing the same bridesmaid's dress she'd had on the night before.

"Your father was opening the draperies in our room—a room that looked down on the parking lot. He saw—"

"Okay, I get it." Great. Just great. So there she'd thought she'd been able to sneak back in with no one noticing, and her father had been standing there the whole time, watching as Colin dropped her off at the hotel. About the only thing she could be grateful for was that the kiss she and Colin had shared right then was quick and awkward, not much more than a peck. At least they hadn't been standing in the parking lot playing tonsil hockey.

"So…." Lysette said. She tapped her fingernails against the display case. When she went on, her tone was very gentle. "Do you want to talk about it?"

It was on Jenny's lips to say no, she really didn't want to talk about it. Problem was, she *did* want to talk. She really didn't have any close friends among the McAllisters, mostly because the girls she'd gone to school with and hung out with as a teenager and an early twenty-something were now all married and had kids. They didn't share much common ground, despite being members of the same clan.

But she and her mother had always been close, whereas Roslyn had been her father's special pet. He still hadn't begun to recover from that blow, even if he did manage to wear a brave face most of the time.

Jenny pulled in a breath and faced her mother, taking in the big blue eyes and honey-colored hair that both she and Roslyn had inherited. Lysette McAllister was fifty-two, but she looked nearly a decade younger than that. Right then, Jenny found herself hoping—not for the first time—that she'd age as well as her mother had.

"Mom, when did Dad tell you?"

Lysette didn't ask her daughter what in the world she meant. Instead, she let out a little sigh, a pucker of concern pulling at her dark gold brows. "Is it that serious already?"

"I—I don't know." Jenny played with the silver bangles she wore on her right wrist, not looking up at her mother. "It might be. He's—I don't know. I like him a lot." There was an understatement. She really didn't want to acknowledge the feelings that stirred inside her, because it was stupid to be thinking that way about someone she'd only met a few days earlier. "He's smart and funny and treats me, well, like *me*. Not what he expects me to be. Just me."

Even to Jenny's own ears, that particular speech had sounded more than a little incoherent. But her mother nodded, as if in comprehension. "And that's what we all want, isn't it? Someone who treats us like us. Of course," she added, smiling slyly, "it doesn't hurt when they're as nice-looking as this Colin of yours."

"He is not mine."

"He isn't?" Without waiting for Jenny to respond, Lysette went on, "As to your other question, well, it was after your father and I had been seeing each other for a few weeks. I was up staying in Sedona, and—"

"And you and your friends decided to go slumming and come up to Jerome," Jenny broke in. She'd heard this story many times before. The only detail Lysette had left out was exactly when Marcus had revealed to her that he was a warlock, and that roughly half of Jerome's inhabitants were all members of one big extended witch clan.

"I never said slumming," Lysette said, giving her daughter a mock-severe look. "But Jerome was a lot different in the late eighties. It hadn't been gentrified, so to speak. There were a couple of bars, and a couple of restaurants, and a few galleries. For a group of girls from Phoenix, it was more about saying we'd gone there. Anyway, my friend Alison was the one who was into all the woo-woo Sedona stuff, and the rest of us weren't going to argue about it, since she was letting us crash at her parents' cabin up in Oak Creek canyon for most of July that year. But we got restless and decided to come up to Jerome."

"And you met Dad."

"Yes, I met your father." Lysette's eyes went dreamy then, as if recalling a day now some thirty years in the past. "He was tending bar at the Spirit Room, and I thought he was the best-looking man I'd ever seen."

Maybe he had been. Objectively, Jenny knew that her father was a very attractive man, and she'd seen pictures of her parents from right after they were married. In those photos, Lysette had ridiculous big eighties hair with shoulder pads to match, but was gorgeous nonetheless, while there was something a lot more timeless about her father's short-cropped brown hair and button-up shirts. Jerome was the sort of place where people didn't worry too much about fashion trends.

"Anyway," Lysette went on, "I knew I wanted to be around Marcus as much as possible, which was harder than you might think, since we'd all come up in one car because there really wasn't room for more than that to park at the cabin. But I borrowed Alison's Toyota a couple of times, and then Marcus came over to Sedona to see me, and...." She let the words trail off, but from the dreamy look in her mother's eyes, Jenny guessed Lysette was recalling some of the more intimate things that had passed between them.

"Spare me the gory details," Jenny said, and her mother raised an eyebrow.

"I wasn't about to go into the 'gory details,' but I was going to say that your father and I had been seeing each other for not quite two weeks when he told me. I was supposed to go back to Phoenix the next day, and that was the last thing I wanted to do. I told your father that I wanted to stay in Jerome with him. And he…he said he wanted me to stay as well, but there was something he needed to tell me. And he also said that I couldn't tell anyone else, even if I decided not to stay after all."

"So he just…blurted it out?"

"More or less." Lysette shook her head, as if even now she couldn't help being somewhat amused by the way she'd learned that the man she loved was a warlock. "He said his family had been here in Jerome for more than a hundred years, and that they kept themselves isolated because of their particular… gifts."

"And you believed him, just like that?"

A smile. "Of course not. I might have been twenty-two and starry-eyed, but I hadn't taken complete leave of my senses. I told him that I loved him and that he didn't have to try to impress me with made-up stories about powers, or whatever."

"He must have loved that."

"Not exactly." Lysette's smile deepened, her eyes blurry with memory. "He said he wasn't trying to impress me at all, just trying to tell me the truth so I'd know what I was getting into. And then he opened his hands wide, like this"—she spread her arms apart, palms pointed toward the ceiling—"and two balls of orange-yellow flame appeared, just sitting on his palms. Then he snapped his fingers, and they were gone."

"It still could have been a trick," Jenny said.

"Yes, it could. But I knew it wasn't. I knew there was something very different about him, about his whole family. So I tried to laugh and made some crack about not having to worry about starting a fire if we ever went camping, and he laughed for real and kissed me, and that was how we ended up engaged."

"But wasn't it strange for you?"

"Of course it was. Strange to come live in this tiny town after growing up in Phoenix, and strange to be surrounded by people who had all sorts of different magical talents. I could have felt left out, I suppose, but I soon learned I wasn't the only 'civilian' in the batch, so that helped. And your father always made sure that I wouldn't feel inferior just because I hadn't been born a witch."

Yes, that could be the hard part, to play down the differences between someone who was witchborn and someone who'd been born an ordinary, non-magical person. But her father had managed it, as had others in the clan, so at its heart, the idea wasn't impossible.

Whether it would work for her and Colin was an entirely different matter, however.

Lysette watched her daughter, clearly trying to interpret her silence. "I'm not saying it's always easy," she said. "But it's worth it…if you're with the right person."

"But how do I know he's the right person?" Jenny asked, unable to hide the desperation in her voice. "I've screwed up so many times—"

"No, you haven't screwed up," Lysette said, her tone quiet, but still firm enough to cut across her daughter's words. "All you did was try to care for people who weren't ready for it. That's on them, though, not you. Maybe you had to go through all that to recognize how good Colin could be for you. I don't know. I haven't met him. But I saw you dancing with him at the reception, and even though I didn't know who he was, I couldn't help thinking that the two of you looked, well, right together."

For a long moment, Jenny didn't say anything, partly because her mother's last sentence had made her throat clench with unexpected tears. She really hadn't been expecting that kind of acceptance, of confirmation. When she did speak, she could tell that her voice was thick, betraying the emotion she was desperately attempting to hide. "Thanks, Mom."

Lysette went to her daughter then and folded her into her arms. "That's what I'm here for, sweetie."

CHAPTER TEN

THE WHOLE TIME HE WAS DRIVING FROM TUCSON TO Prescott, Colin couldn't help berating himself. Not over calling in sick at work; he was about to start losing sick days anyway if he didn't start using them. No, over the whole reason for this trip in the first place. Snooping around about Jenny's family behind her back. Hadn't he already played fast and loose enough with the truth? In a way, this mission only seemed to compound his sins.

But he couldn't stop himself. Something very strange was going on with the McAllisters, and he had to know what it was. That same need to know had pushed him into journalism, even though a lot of people these days thought the profession was on its way out. And that need to know was probably going to get

him into trouble now, but again…he couldn't ignore
the compulsion that was currently driving him.

He'd also tried doing a little snooping into
Alex's family, the de la Pazes, but they'd been in the
Phoenix area—and then Tucson—for literally hundreds of years, dating back to before the time when
the United States were even united. It would take
the kind of work of someone researching a doctoral
thesis to unravel all their tangled relationships and
holdings, and so Colin had abandoned the task after
a couple of wasted hours. The one thing he'd been
able to determine was that there didn't seem to be
anything particularly out of the ordinary about Alex
Trujillo, except that he'd managed to carry a double
major and still graduate in four years. His parents
had been married for almost thirty years and owned
a thriving store, and his little sister was currently
going to UA and majoring in biology. Absolutely
nothing there to throw up any red flags, or to show
that Alex possessed some kind of strange magical
power that allowed him to shoot blue-white light out
of his hands.

The whole thing was crazy-making, which was
why Colin knew he couldn't let it go.

He had decided that his first stop in Prescott
should be the historical society, mainly because their
records went back farther than the county recorder's office and should—he hoped—provide more

jumping-off points for further investigation. If he had time, he could go over to the county recorder's office afterward.

Prescott took its history seriously. The historical society was housed in a converted Victorian house two blocks away from the town's famous courthouse and surrounding park, and he'd been required to make an appointment.

The entire neighborhood was composed of Victorian and Craftsman-style homes, most of them immaculately restored. They didn't look completely alien to Colin's eyes, since there were houses like that clustered in the older parts of Tucson, even if they weren't nearly as well kept up as the ones he saw when he got out of his car and locked it. Still, there seemed to be a weight of history here that he hadn't ever experienced in his hometown, and he unconsciously squared his shoulders as he headed up the front walk—meticulously cleared of fallen leaves, even though the frost-yellowed lawn was studded here and there with bright autumn color, red and orange and gold.

There was a buzzer next to the front door. Colin pressed it, then waited. A moment or so later, a woman who appeared to be in her late fifties, with gray-streaked red hair pulled up into a graceful twist at the back of her head, opened the door.

"Hi," Colin said, holding out a hand and smiling. "I'm Colin Campbell. I have a one o'clock appointment."

She returned the smile immediately. "Of course. I'm Anita Lincoln. Please come in. I've already pulled some documents for you. Jerome in the late 1870s, early 1880s, correct?"

"Perfect," he replied. "Thanks so much for doing that for me."

"Not a problem at all," she said as she led him from the foyer, which was paneled in dark oak and sported some serious stained-glass windows on either side of the door, and then down a short hallway.

The room they entered was a good size, and probably had been a sitting room at one time. Now it was set up as a reading area, with two large tables and their accompanying chairs at the center of the space. On one side was a microfiche reader, and on the other an older-model iMac sitting on a small table. Old black and white and sepia-toned photos of Prescott and the Verde Valley—and yes, Jerome—covered the walls.

One of the tables had a stack of folders sitting on it. Anita pointed to the folders and said, "Those are the materials I thought would be of the most interest. They're from a variety of different sources—old newspaper clippings, excerpts from letters, diaries, real estate records. You weren't completely clear on what you wanted, so I thought it best to give you a range so you could narrow your research down from there."

"Thank you so much," Colin replied. That must have taken a good deal of time, and he was grateful that he wouldn't have to start completely from scratch. "I really appreciate it."

She gave him a small nod. "It's what we're here for. If you need anything else, my office is just down the hall to the right."

That seemed to be the end of the conversation, because immediately afterward she left the reading room, apparently heading toward the aforementioned office. Colin fished his phone out of his pocket and checked the time. Not even a quarter after one. The historical society was open until four-thirty, which meant he had a couple of hours to get his reading done.

He set down his messenger bag on one of the empty chairs, and fished out a yellow pad and a couple of pens. It was always his practice to write things out longhand first, since it helped with his thinking processes. He also hadn't been sure whether the historical society banned the use of electronic devices near its documents, but Anita hadn't mentioned any such strictures.

When he opened the first folder, he saw why. These were all Xerox copies of the original documents. He supposed he should have thought of that; hundred-year-old paper would certainly have started to fall apart if it was handled by too many people, especially ones who hadn't been trained to manage vintage documents.

All right, then.

The first item was a copy of a deed, dated to March 1878, showing that one Joseph McAllister had bought five plots of land in what would later would be incorporated as Jerome. What one person needed with five separate plots that were clearly intended as home sites, Colin wasn't sure, but he surmised that Joseph had bought them for family members.

Beneath the deed was a fragment of a letter, one from a woman named Ida Church. Of course Colin had no idea who this Mrs. Church had been or what she'd looked like, but her tone reminded him of the sort of busybody gossips that seemed to populate sixties-era sitcoms. The first portion of the letter was missing, and so it seemed to open mid-sentence.

...seems there are more McAllisters in Jerome every time one turns around. They're pleasant enough, but keep to themselves. No one even seems to know precisely where they came from, although Mrs. Reverend Talbert told me that she thought they had relocated here from somewhere in New England. What seems strange to me is that they always prosper, no matter what. Why, when that fire ran through town last spring, it burned so many houses to the

CHRISTINE POPE 187

ground, but not a single one that belonged to a McAllister! My own Lewis asked Mr. Joseph McAllister how they could be so lucky, to which he replied that his family could organize a very good bucket brigade. That may well be, but I am of the opinion—

Exactly what Mrs. Church's opinion had been, Colin would never know, because that was where the scrap of her letter ended. Still, even that snippet gave him some food for thought. He'd known vaguely that Jerome had suffered more than one catastrophic fire during its life, due mainly to the wooden construction of many of its early buildings. And he'd spent enough time either covering or reading about local catastrophes that he knew disasters could be like that, leveling one side of a street and leaving the other intact. Still, he wasn't sure whether having *all* the McAllister homes survive one of those fires exactly passed the sniff test.

He laid the piece of Mrs. Church's letter aside and moved on to the next item, which was actually an old photograph of a family group outside a three-story structure with the legend "McAllister Mercantile" painted on its façade. The building even looked familiar to him; he thought he'd been inside it years ago during the one time he'd visited the former mining town. Was it still owned by McAllisters? Probably. If it had been sold to someone outside the family, there would have been a record of the transaction somewhere.

Colin found himself studying the faces in the photo, attempting to see if any of them shared a resemblance with Jenny, or with any of the McAllisters he'd glimpsed at Alex and Caitlin's wedding. None of them looked like anyone he'd met or seen, which didn't mean a lot. More than a hundred years separated the people in the photo—it was annotated as having been taken in 1908—from anyone he would have met at the wedding. Yes, their coloring seemed similar, in that their hair appeared to range from light brown to blond, but he couldn't see an echo in their features of the woman he'd come to care for against his better instincts.

Exactly why falling for Jenny should be a problem, he wasn't sure. Well, except for the way he'd lied to her. But if he put that aside—and also put aside the extreme geographical undesirability of someone who lived hundreds of miles away from him—then on the surface there wasn't anything to keep them apart. He was a few years older, but three years certainly didn't constitute a gap of any significance. And yeah, he had that whole alimony thing hanging over his head, but again, he'd be free of that particular ball and chain in just a few more months. So really, what was the problem?

No problem at all, except all these niggling little bits that didn't seem to add up. He stared at the facsimile of the photograph for a long moment, then put it aside. The next few documents were of little interest to him—manifests of items that had been delivered to "McAllister Mercantile," a list from the Presbyterian church showing the McAllisters as members in good stead. That last little bit surprised him somewhat, considering that slip where Jenny had sworn by a goddess. But maybe she was the only pagan in a family of good Protestants. It was hard to say, because the Trujillo / McAllister wedding had definitely been Catholic, something the groom's family had probably insisted on.

Or maybe the McAllisters had been something else all along, and had only gone to the local church as protective camouflage. No, that sounded ridiculous. He'd seen Jenny's relatives at the wedding, and they all looked like more or less upstanding and prosperous members of society. A lot more sober than he would have expected a group from bohemian Jerome to be, all things considered. The little town had survived the sixties with a good deal of that decade's sensibilities intact; when Colin and his friend Matt had visited some ten years ago, they'd managed to score some pretty spectacular weed from a guy who looked like he'd been wandering around Jerome ever since surviving Woodstock.

But again, maybe they'd toned things down so as not to attract too much attention. Colin imagined having your relatives show up to your wedding in tie dye and fringe might be fairly cringe-inducing.

The next document appeared to be a selection from someone's diary. There was no name, but the delicate copperplate writing appeared feminine, and the content soon left little doubt in Colin's mind.

...quite the scene at McAllister's Mercantile, one so dreadful that Papa put his foot down and said I should not see Charles McAllister again. Up until yesterday, he had not been terribly enthusiastic about Charles courting me, but because the McAllisters have been in Jerome almost since the town was founded, and are certainly very prosperous, Papa did not try to interfere. But now I know there shall be nothing more of it, and indeed he is grumbling about sending me off to stay with my Aunt Tillie in Prescott "until I have gotten this nonsense out of my head."

It is most definitely not nonsense, and Charles McAllister is nothing like his father, who is, I fear, rather hot-tempered. Of course, I was not there, as I was home with Mama, measuring the sitting room windows for new curtains, but there were enough eyewitnesses to make me believe that they all saw the same thing—or rather, they all think they saw the same thing. I am sure there must be a rational explanation for what happened, although I must confess that I cannot think what it might be.

Unfortunately, there are quite a few rough types in this town. It is what happens when a mine is as rich as the United Verde, I suppose. Henry McAllister had stepped out from behind the counter to assist Mrs. Turner in getting a lamp base from a high shelf, and apparently a miner who had recently been fired thought that was the perfect opportunity to sneak behind the counter and take what he could from the cash register.

Well, imagine the miner's surprise—and Mrs. Turner's, and everyone else's in the store—when Mr. McAllister turned around, saw what he was doing, and then snapped his fingers. At once the miner found himself hanging upside down in midair, suspended from nothing. No one could figure out what the trick was, although Mr. Clancy claims he saw something just like it in New York when he saw the great Harry Houdini perform. The miner—a Mr. Oswald Peale—remained like that until Sheriff Gordon, Mr. McAllister's brother-in-law, arrived to take him away. And then Mr. McAllister went back to work as if nothing had happened.

But everyone had seen, and there were a few dark mutters about witchcraft and some such nonsense, although most people were of the opinion, like Mr. Clancy, that it was only a trick, something Henry McAllister had been planning for some time, only waiting for the perfect opportunity to come along so he might make an example of some unfortunate miscreant.

Whatever Mr. McAllister might or might not have done, it certainly should not reflect on Charles, who is a very sober young man. Indeed, I went to Mama and begged her to intercede on my behalf, but I very much fear that—

Again, Colin would never know if the unnamed young woman's fears had been borne out. Had she been sent off to Prescott to her Aunt Tillie? He supposed he could look up Mr. Charles McAllister, who probably would have gotten married in the early 1920s, and see who his wife had been. But again, since Colin didn't have the diarist's name to go on, that wouldn't be of much help.

What got his spider sense tingling, though, was that mention of witchcraft. Now, he didn't actually believe in such things, but still….

Houses that remained intact when everything else was burning down around them. A shopkeeper snapping his fingers and sending a would-be thief to hang upside down in the air with no visible ropes or wires holding him up.

A young man standing in a parking lot, shooting blue fire from his hands at a murderer and rapist.

All right, Alex Trujillo was definitely not a McAllister, but there had to be a connection beyond his marriage to Caitlin. Just as there was some sort of connection between the Wilcoxes and the McAllisters, something Colin hadn't quite been able to figure out yet.

Back in college—before he'd met Shannon—
Colin had briefly dated a girl he sometimes referred
to in his mind as the "woo-woo queen." Her real
name had been Brittany, and she'd earnestly believed
in just about anything and everything paranormal.
Psychic powers. UFOs. Witchcraft. Ley lines and
vortexes and God knows what else. Their relationship had by necessity been short-lived, since he'd
always considered himself a natural-born skeptic,
but Colin couldn't help but think of Brittany now.
He knew if she'd been confronted by this evidence,
she'd be swearing up and down that the McAllisters
were obviously witches. Well, and warlocks. And
she'd probably be saying that the de la Pazes and the
Wilcoxes were, too.

"There's so much going on that you know nothing about, Colin," she'd told him one time in that
horribly earnest way of hers, the one that seemed so
persuasive until you stopped to really analyze what
she was saying. "Going on right under your nose.
And everyone else's, too. The world is so much bigger than you could ever imagine."

In a way, he'd kind of admired her airy-fairy
world view, because it was a lot more hopeful than
his own. Not that he'd ever suffered any kind of
severe trauma in his life, unless you could count his
marriage, but still, working as a reporter, or even

studying journalism, did tend to expose you to the darker side of things.

Anyway, he had no doubt that Brittany would have gone marching up to Jerome, equipped with her PKE monitor or whatever the hell she called it, bent on discovering how much psychic energy was floating around the former mining town.

The image of Brittany, in her tie-dyed skirts and beaded earrings, running into the goddess-like Jenny McAllister and demanding of her whether she was a witch, amused him for a second or two. There was something about Jenny that seemed eminently down to earth. No airy-fairy there, that was for sure. Or witchy.

Then again, even Jenny had claimed that Jerome was populated by ghosts. Colin doubted the phenomena was ghosts—more like creaking old buildings and earth subsidence—but stories like that were the sort of thing that tourists got off on, and Jerome needed tourists for its very survival. Besides, Jenny had sounded earnest, but for all Colin knew, she'd been teasing him, trying to see if he'd fall for her tall tales or not.

Or maybe the former mining town really was haunted. And populated by a family of witches.

Jesus.

He scrubbed a hand over his face and wished he'd brought a bottle of water in with him. There was one sitting in the cup holder in his car, getting warm in the sun, no doubt, even though the temperature up here in Prescott was at least a good ten or twelve degrees cooler than it had been in Tucson. But no, he doubted that he would have been able to bring water in here, even if the documents he'd been given to read were only facsimiles and not the real thing.

Better to look at all this rationally. He took a breath and shifted in his seat so he could see the oak tree outside the window, decked out in autumn gold, but with definite bare patches where its leaves had already begun to fall. Usually, looking at nature calmed him—maybe because he spent so much of his life shut up inside, whether it was in the office or at his apartment—but right then he could almost feel the tension ratcheting up in his neck.

He was already hiding a huge secret from Jenny. Or rather, it hadn't been that big a secret in the beginning, but in the days since Colin had told her that one lie, it had begun to balloon and take on massive proportions, like a tumor you hoped would go away on its own. And now he was supposed to go to her and say, "Oh, yeah, let's put all those lies about why I was there and what I do for a living aside for now. What I really want to know is whether your family is a bunch of witches and warlocks."

Either she'd want to kill him, or she'd laugh at him. Probably both.

Attempting to distract himself, he paged through the rest of the materials Anita Lincoln had gathered for him. Clearly, she'd just plucked anything that had the name "McAllister" prominently mentioned in it. Colin doubted she'd actually read any of the entries, or she might have heard her own alarm bells. At any rate, he didn't find anything nearly as spectacular as the letter from Mrs. Church or the diary entry from the unnamed young woman who had been so in love with Charles McAllister.

Colin did find it interesting that several McAllisters had been heavily involved in setting up the Jerome Historical Society, as well as securing national landmark status about fifteen years after that. So they liked to keep a low profile, but not *too* low. And he supposed it wouldn't have been in their best interests to have the town fall completely into wrack and ruin once the mine shut down. They would have had to start all over again someplace else, and he doubted that prospect would have been too appealing to a family that had been in the same place for nearly a hundred years.

Well, they'd definitely survived. And seemed to be thriving, although there wasn't nearly the physical evidence of their wealth as there was with the Wilcoxes. Still, Colin couldn't help wondering how much of Jerome was owned by the McAllister family.

Not all of it...but a chunk. A chunk that never left the family, apparently.

He glanced over at his phone. Almost four fifteen. It didn't feel as if he'd been sitting here for nearly three hours, going through the documents, taking notes, but apparently he had. No time to send out for anything else—if there even was anything else. If he really wanted to get further into the meat of things, he'd have to go to Jerome, which wouldn't work at all. He might not have been there for nearly ten years, but he knew the town was small enough that his chances of escaping being noticed by Jenny McAllister were pretty slim.

As he shoved his notepad and pens back into his messenger bag and then began recompiling the historical society's documents in as close to their original order as he could, Colin suddenly wondered if that unknown young woman's diary fragment had ended up in the society's archives because she had in fact been banished to her Aunt Tillie's here in Prescott.

If so, tough luck for both her and Charles McAllister. Colin had to hope his relationship with Jenny wouldn't suffer a similar fate.

CHAPTER ELEVEN

JENNY KNEW SHE SHOULDN'T BE THIS NERVOUS. IT WASN'T as if this was some kind of blind date where she was meeting Colin for the first time. Besides, they'd spoken on the phone several times since he'd headed off for work on Monday morning, and those conversations had been relaxed and easygoing enough, just trivial talk about their days and what they might do once he got to Jerome. Even with all that, Jenny found herself far too restless to simply sit and wait for him to show up, and kept roaming around her apartment, making sure that everything was in place. Was the vase of frilly yellow alstroemeria on the bookcase a bit much? She liked to have fresh flowers around, and alstroemeria were cheap and unassuming enough that she didn't think it was making too much of a statement to have them out...but was it?

He probably won't even notice, she told herself. *How many guys have you had over here? Have any of them ever commented on your flowers?*

Well, no. But then, Colin was different from any of the other men she'd dated. He did tend to notice things. It was a quality she respected in a person, even though she found herself worrying about exactly what he might notice while he was here in Jerome. She'd told her mother that Colin was coming for the weekend, and Jenny knew she could trust Lysette to get the word out that her daughter would be having a civilian guest for a few days. However, just because people had been told to be on their best behavior didn't mean they actually would.

It wasn't that Jerome's witches and warlocks rode through the streets on broomsticks or had magical duels outside the Spirit Room, or anything like that. That kind of behavior just wouldn't fly in a place that had literally hundreds of thousands of tourists passing through it every year. But sometimes people would get excited or upset, and something a little out of the ordinary would happen...and if you were lucky, the incident was something that could be attributed to ghost activity or a building settling or what-have-you. People came to Jerome expecting ghosts because the town had been featured on numerous shows that dealt with the supernatural, and a lot of tourists were actively disappointed if they didn't have at least one experience they could blame on Jerome's spectral citizens. Witches, on the other hand, were something completely different.

She glanced down at her watch. Twelve forty-five. Colin had said he should be up around one, and then they could have a late lunch. The flat was spotless, and if he got here in the next couple of minutes, he might even be able to snag the parking space that had just opened up in front of the gallery. Once again her cousin Susan was watching the store, and Jenny knew she owed her cousin big-time for giving up two weekends in a row to work at the gallery. Maybe a spa day in Sedona as a thank-you? That could work.

Standing and waiting on the porch in front of her apartment was way too obvious, so Jenny had settled for peering out the kitchen window, starting a little every time a black car appeared. Which was silly. She was acting like a kid waiting for Santa Claus to show up and claim his milk and cookies.

It did help that the building which housed both the gallery and her flat was located in the lower stretch of Jerome, before you got into the heart of all the shops and restaurants. Parking there wasn't as much at a premium, and so several cars went by without even slowing to take a look at the empty spot out in front.

But there it was—that shabby old Honda Accord, coming slowly up the hill. It slowed down even more as it approached her building, then made a highly illegal U-turn to pull into the open space at the curb. Jenny had to shake her head at the maneuver, but then, Jerome was kind of a free-for-all when it came to that sort of thing. And no one had been coming in the opposite direction, so she supposed it was no harm, no foul.

She watched just long enough to see Colin get out of the car and head back toward the trunk, then made herself step away from the window. It would look terrible for him to catch her peering out at him like the neighborhood snoop, so she went and sat down on the couch and picked up her iPad, pretending to be reading a favorite fashion site, but in reality just waiting to leap up at his knock.

It came only a minute or so later. She laid down the tablet and went to the door.

The quick glimpse she'd caught of him at his car had told her he was wearing a worn leather jacket, but up close, she got to see how really good he looked in it, the way it settled on his broad shoulders and gave her just a glimpse of the dark T-shirt he wore underneath. Likewise, his jeans were faded and even a little ragged around the hems, and he had on a pair of hiking boots that looked as if they'd seen some real use.

Well, she'd told him Jerome was super-casual, and not to worry about getting dressed up. It seemed as if he'd taken that advice to heart.

"Hey," she said.

"Hey yourself," he replied, bending down so he could kiss her on the cheek.

It was a very chaste kiss, but even so she could feel a surge of thrilling warmth flood all through her. This whole week she'd been trying to tell herself that it was silly to be this worked up about him, and that when she saw him again she'd probably be disappointed. That didn't seem to be the case, however. If anything, he was better-looking than she'd remembered, the effect he had on her even more pronounced.

"Come on in," she said, stepping out of the way so he could enter the apartment. She noticed that he held the same overnight bag he'd brought with him when he'd come to visit her at the hotel. "You can put that down in here," she went on, then led him through the living room and up the two steps that led to the level with the two bedrooms and the bathroom.

They went into the master bedroom. Jenny had known from the start that she wasn't going to bother with any foolishness about him staying in the guest room slash office. They both knew exactly why he was coming up here to visit, so why bother to beat around the bush?

He set his bag down on the floor next to her dresser and said, "I knew it."

"Knew what?"

Straightening, he glanced around her room with some approval. "Somehow I knew it would look just like this."

A bit of a flush touched her cheeks. So Colin had been fantasizing about what her bedroom was like? She loved the space, with its warm western light and high-beamed ceilings. It was decorated with antiques she'd sourced both from relatives and from shops here in Jerome and down in Cottonwood, along with Mexican tin mirrors on the walls and block-printed fabric from India framing the windows. Eclectic, sure, but she thought it worked.

"So, I'm that predictable?" she teased him.

His hazel eyes were very sober. "No, just the opposite. You have a lot of sides to you, Jenny McAllister, and so I figured your room must be just as complicated."

Now she knew she was blushing. "Oh, I'm not that complicated," she said lightly. "I just find it hard to pass up a sale."

"So I noticed," he returned, eyes flicking toward the closet on the opposite wall. "Did you ever manage to fit it all in?"

"Oh, yeah. I just had to donate a few odds and ends."

"Odds and ends?"

"Something like that." She wasn't quite ready to confess that her Tucson shopping spree had resulted in her having to clear out a whole garbage bag's worth of stuff to take down to Goodwill. "Anyway, you hungry?"

His mouth turned up, setting off that not-quite dimple in one cheek. "I've been driving for more than three hours. What do you think?"

"I think I'd better take you to Bordello's and get a burger inside you."

"Bordello's?"

"It's a restaurant just up the street. It's awesome." He still looked like he was trying to process the name of the restaurant, so she added, "Jerome had an *extremely* thriving red light district back in the day. I think 'Bordello's' is a perfect name."

Colin put up his hands. "Hey, far be it from me to turn down a chance to eat at a bordello."

All Jenny could do was shake her head. "Let me get my jacket."

It was a lot cooler up here. Colin had noticed that as soon as he got out of the car. True, Jenny had warned him about the difference in temperatures, and so he'd worn his battered and beloved leather jacket, the one Shannon had kept telling him to get rid of because it looked so disreputable. But it hadn't really sunk in that the air here would have a definite nip to it, that it would definitely feel like fall, with Thanksgiving only a few days away.

They had to walk less than a block to get to the restaurant. True, it was an all-uphill block, and Colin began to have a new appreciation for the way Jenny kept herself in shape. It was probably a lot easier when you had to make a hike like this just to get to the closest place to eat.

The restaurant was small and not very bordello-like, unless you counted the hanging beads that hid the alcove where the cash register was located. And it was crowded, which made Colin wonder if they would even get a place to sit. However, Jenny threaded her way through the cramped space, heading unerringly to a small table near the back that was unoccupied but hadn't yet been bussed.

"Hey, Jenny. With you in a sec!" the waitress—who also seemed to be handling busboy and hostess duties as well—called out to them.

"No problem, Eden," Jenny called back.

Of course they were on a first-name basis. Jenny had to know everyone in this town. The thought made Colin vaguely uneasy, as if he had just ventured into enemy territory or something. Which was foolish. Jerome was full of McAllisters, true, but not everyone there was part of Jenny's family. A quick glance around the crowded restaurant told him that if appearance was anything to go on, at least half the people in here were probably tourists.

"Sorry about that," Eden said, appearing next to their table with a damp cloth in one hand. With quick, practiced gestures, she wiped down the table-top, then plucked a couple of paper menus out of the pocket of the black apron she wore tied around her waist. "Something to drink to start?"

Colin hadn't been able to look at the menu, but he could see the small bar off to one side, which meant they must have wine and beer at least. "Something local on tap?"

"Oak Creek Brewery brown ale."

"I'll take it," he said.

"Same for me."

Eden nodded. "I'll have those right up for you."

Colin picked up the menu and gave it a quick perusal. Mostly burgers, as Jenny had said, but some salads, too. Not that he was terribly interested in a salad right then.

Apparently, Jenny already knew what she wanted, because she didn't even look at her own menu. "So… you're in Jerome. What do you want to do first?"

There was a loaded question. All he'd done was kiss her quickly on the cheek, and that was enough to get him hot and bothered all over again. Suggesting that they go back to her flat after lunch for a little afternoon delight sounded kind of crass, though. Anyway, they'd discussed a few things on the phone but hadn't really hadn't made any concrete plans. "Well," he hedged, "I'm having lunch in a bordello. I figure that's a good start."

She grinned. "True. I did make us some reservations for dinner up at the Asylum. Hope you don't mind, but they book up pretty fast, and I figured you should see the place."

"Why would I mind?"

Her shoulders lifted. "Some people might have thought I was presuming."

By "some people," he got the feeling she meant some of her past boyfriends. Lovers. Whatever. He had to wonder what kind of assholes she'd allowed into her life. But at least she was single now, had scraped them off her shoe.

Unfortunately, a good number of her friends and family probably wouldn't view him as much of an improvement.

"I don't think it's presuming," he said, glad to see a bit of the tension leave her jaw. "You know this place—I don't."

"Well, that's true."

They had to pause then as Eden came back with their beers, and then they placed their orders. For exactly the same thing—the Cuban Mary burger.

Bleu cheese and caramelized onions? Colin wasn't about to pass that up.

"She was a famous madam here," Jenny explained as she picked up her pint glass. "Well, not *here,* here. Her brothel was one street over and farther up the hill. It's been for sale forever."

"Someone's trying to sell a brothel?" Colin asked, unable to keep the amusement out of his voice.

"It's not a brothel anymore, obviously. It's a 'historic building.'" Colin could practically see the air quotes Jenny put around the phrase. "Anyway," she continued, "her family wants to offload it, but the land it's on is so unstable that it keeps sliding a few inches every year. So no bank will finance it. Cash-only deal."

"That's unfortunate." Unable to stop himself, he said, "Maybe one of you McAllisters could buy it?"

Jenny gave him a peculiar look. "'You McAllisters'?"

Damn, he'd really put his foot in it there, hadn't he? Backpedaling, Colin said, "Well, that is—your family kind of owns this town, doesn't it?"

Instead of appearing offended, she shook her head and chuckled. Long strands of dark blonde hair fell over her shoulders, and Colin found himself suddenly not caring all that much about her family and its real estate holdings. "I wish," she told him. "Maybe that way we could get a signal installed at the corner of 89A and Hull Avenue. It seems like someone gets creamed there at least once a month while trying to make a left. But no, we don't own this town. We've lived here a long time, and here are a lot of us, but there are just as many ci—people who aren't remotely related to the McAllisters here."

There it was again—that slip where she'd meant to say something else and then checked herself. Ci… what? Citizens? That didn't make much sense.

"Anyway," she went on, "the property would need so much rehabbing that it's not really worth the effort. But if you're that interested in it, we should go on the ghost tour. Cuban Mary's place is on the route."

"'Ghost tour'?" he echoed, not sure if she was teasing him or not. "That sounds like sort of a touristy thing to do."

"Aren't you a tourist?" Jenny replied. Her eyes were wide and guileless, but he thought he could see a teasing glint in them. "Besides, even if you don't believe in ghosts, it's a great way to get more familiar with the town and learn a little bit of local history. I checked, and Frankie has a few spots left in her six o'clock tour. We could do that and still make it to dinner at seven-thirty with no problem."

A ghost tour. Colin could just see Ryan Ortiz getting a good laugh out of that one, should he ever find out. But, as Jenny had said, it probably was a good way to get some more local history under his belt.

What he would do if he actually saw a ghost, Colin had no idea. He figured he was fairly safe from that eventuality, however.

And if you do see one, he thought, *well, that proves there are more things in heaven and earth, Horatio. Which also means that gorgeous woman sitting across the table from you might actually be a witch.*

That seemed to settle things. He picked up his beer and said, "Tell Frankie I would love to go on her ghost tour."

It was funny how you got a different appreciation for a familiar place when you were looking at it through a newcomer's eyes. Jenny knew she probably could have been blindfolded and sent to wander Jerome's streets, and would still have unerringly found her way home—or to the Spirit Room, or to the Mile High Grill, or the Passion Cellars wine-tasting room, or any one of a hundred other points of interest— but on that day her hometown felt like something new and fresh, a place where she was setting foot for the first time.

The reason being, of course, Colin Campbell.

He didn't mind going to the obviously touristy places like the Jerome Museum or the national park that housed the mansion that had once belonged to

William Clark, the man who had financed the United Verde mine. The streets were steep, but Colin seemed to enjoy going up and down them, all the way from the head shop at the top of the hill down to the Guadalajara Grill, where they stopped in briefly for margaritas before sallying forth once again. And the whole time he asked questions that weren't insulting but seemed genuinely curious, showing an appreciation for her crazy little town that Jenny, quite frankly, hadn't been expecting.

More than once the thought crossed her mind: *Maybe this could work.*

Was she being stupid? She didn't know, but a small hope began to grow inside her. The hours passed with ease, and Colin never seemed to get bored, or tired, and the people he met in the shops and the restaurants and the tasting rooms all appeared charmed by him, whether they were witch-folk or civilians. For some strange reason, it was almost as if he fit in, as if the strange little town suited him far better than the hustle of Tucson.

Or maybe she was thinking that because it was what she wanted to believe. That this would be a magical—pardon the pun—weekend where everything would go perfectly and he'd turn to her, declare his undying love, and say that he wanted to quit his corporate communications job and go to work for the local chamber of commerce or something. How that would even work, Jenny really didn't know, because the "chamber" in Jerome was her cousin Pete and a civilian named Rosa, with whom he'd been carrying on a casual affair for at least ten years. But they must have a chamber of commerce down the hill in Cottonwood....

"...where do they do the ghost tour?"

"What?" Jenny blinked, all too aware that she'd been woolgathering. Luckily, they'd stopped at one of the numerous overlooks around town, and Colin had been busy taking pictures with his phone, so maybe he hadn't noticed her distraction.

"It's a quarter to six," he said, showing her the display on the phone. "I was just wondering if we should head over there or not. I don't know how much of a hike it is."

Since they were down on Hull Avenue, just a block past Spook Hall, where all the town's large gatherings were held, they would have a bit of a climb to get to Frankie's office. It was located nearly at the end of Main Street, just on the other side of Rachel McAllister's store.

"It's a ways," she confessed. "You're right—we probably had better get going."

He smiled at her and slipped his phone into his pocket. "Show me the way."

They headed up Hull Avenue and then hung a left so they could go past the Spirit Room on the way to the Jerome Ghost Tours office. Although they'd already gone by once before, Jenny couldn't help noting the way Colin cast an appreciative eye at the row of Harleys and Indians in front of the bar.

"You ride?" she asked, a teasing note in her voice. He was hotter than hell, and she loved being around him, but he didn't seem much like the biker type.

"No," he replied, a note of regret in his voice. "That is, I had a friend in college who did, and he taught me. I thought about buying a bike, but it just never seemed to be in the budget."

Jenny thought of his old Honda Accord, several years past its expiration date, and tried not to wince. No, she guessed he probably didn't have much spare cash for extravagances like motorcycles, not while paying off an expensive divorce. She did her best to dismiss a wild fantasy of Colin moving up here and her giving him a Harley with a big red bow on it for his birthday.

Come on—she didn't even know when his birthday was.

"The Spirit Room is kind of a hangout," she said, trying to keep her tone light. "Especially on the weekend. These mountain roads are really fun to ride when the weather is good."

"You've done it? Ridden up here, I mean."

"A little. I mean, I had an ex-boyfriend who had a Road King. He loved that thing." *A lot more than he loved me,* she thought with some bitterness. Of course, she left off that particular tidbit.

But Colin still seemed to pick up on something. He half turned toward her as he walked, one eyebrow lifted slightly as he glanced down at her for a few moments. To her relief, however, he didn't say anything except, "Well, if the road up over the mountain is anything as twisty as the one to get here to Jerome, I can see why people would have fun with it."

Jenny didn't quite let out a breath. "It is pretty gorgeous. I like it during monsoon season. Not when it's actually raining, I mean, but just because everything turns so green around here at that time of year."

"I hadn't thought about that. We green up a little in Tucson, but it's so hot that things have to be pretty robust to survive."

She wasn't a fan of even the more moderate summers here in Jerome, so she really didn't want to think about how hot it must be down in his part of the state. They passed Rachel's store, and Jenny caught a glimpse of her cousin inside, beginning her ritual of tidying up as the closing hour of six o'clock approached.

For some reason, Colin cast a curious glance up at the storefront as they went by, his brows pulling together as if trying to process something he half-way recognized.

"What is it?" Jenny asked. "Did you want to go in?"

He didn't quite startle, but his shoulders did give an odd little twitch, right before he smiled at her and shook his head. "No. It just looks kind of familiar to me. I think I might have gone in there when I came up here that one time in college."

She wondered what would have happened if they'd bumped into each other all those years ago. But no, that wouldn't have worked at all. He was just enough older that she probably would have still been in high school during his one and only visit to Jerome.

"Rachel's been running the store a long time," Jenny said lightly. "So yeah, you probably did go in there. Anyway, here we are."

Even as she was reaching out to open the door to the tour's office, Colin moved past her to push on the handle and let her in. "Ladies first."

She had to grin and shake her head at his unexpected chivalry. Having guys open doors for her wasn't something she expected, but she had to admit that she kind of liked it. "If you say so."

They headed in, and saw that there was already a group of four people waiting in the space just outside Frankie's actual office. Two couples, both of

whom looked to be in their late forties or early fifties. Definitely tourists. One of the men wore a nota-
ble frown, which meant he'd probably been dragged
into going on the tour and wasn't too happy about it.

Colin noticed the man's expression as well, it
seemed, because his mouth quirked in that way he
had when he was desperately trying to hold back
a smile. And then, probably because he knew that
standing there and trying to avoid eye contact would
be even more awkward than making an unprompted
introduction, he said, "Hi—I'm Colin, and this is
Jenny."

The woman standing next to the scowling man
looked almost pathetically relieved. "Hi, there. I'm
Barbara, and this is Alan."

Alan's scowl decreased a fraction. "Nice to meet
you." The words were just barely above a mumble.

The other couple chimed in, saying they were
Dennis and Kathy from Lincoln, Nebraska, and
how it was very nice to meet everyone. Jenny could
tell that Alan had his own opinion about that, but
right then Frankie emerged from her office, carrying
a stack of the EMF readers she used for her ghost
tours.

"Hi, everyone," she said briskly, ignoring the side-
eye Alan gave her magenta-hued buzz cut and the
big turquoise feather earrings she had hanging from
her ears. "I'm Frankie Lynch. I've lived in Jerome my

whole life, and believe me when I tell you that I have seen a lot of crazy stuff go on around here."

As she delivered that line, her laughing blue eyes met Jenny's, and she didn't quite wink.

Oh, no, Jenny thought then. *You'd better leave me out of this, Frankie.*

But Frankie, being Frankie, wasn't going to miss her opportunity for a joke. "And I'm not the only one," she went on. "You can ask Jenny here as well. She's seen her fair share of, shall we say, phenomena."

"Oh, are you from Jerome, too?" Kathy from Lincoln, Nebraska, inquired.

"Um, yes," Jenny replied, knowing she was blushing. "But Colin wanted to go on the tour, so…." She trailed off then, praying that he wouldn't point out her lie. After all, it had been her idea for them to go on the ghost tour, not his.

From the glint in his eye, he was amused by her discomfiture, but had decided he'd better play along. "Oh, yeah," he said. "I wasn't about to come up to Jerome and miss out on a chance to see some of its famous ghosts."

"About that," Frankie put in, moving from person to person so she could hand them their EMF meters. "Jerome is a very haunted place—we like to say the most haunted place in America, although New Orleans is close. But in terms of ghosts per square yard, I think we have them beat. Anyway, these EMF meters read electromagnetic energy, which spikes when we're in the presence of spirits, ghosts, entities…whatever you want to call them. However, the ghosts are on their own schedule, and they appear when they want to. This isn't a séance, and we aren't calling them to us."

"Sounds like an excuse to me," Alan muttered under his breath, but Frankie pinned him down with a quelling look.

"Just setting expectations, Mr. Lundquist. The ghosts in Jerome do tend to be sociable sorts, so you'll usually see some evidence of their presence, whether it's the EMF meters spiking, or a sensation of cold, or something brushing past you—"

"You mean they touch you?" Kathy from Lincoln asked, a slight quaver in her voice.

"I'm not sure if 'touch' is the right word," Frankie said. "They're moving in their own world, and most of the time they're not really thinking too much about those of us still here on the physical plane. But that doesn't mean some of them don't have a sense of humor." She paused there, her eyes meeting Jenny's for a moment before flicking away. Jenny wondered if her cousin was thinking about Angela, their *prima,* who really could see ghosts just as if they were people, and talked to them like they really were standing right in front of her. Angela did tend to refer to Jerome's ghosts as if they were just another group of residents in the small mountain town.

For herself, Jenny had never seen an actual ghost. Felt them, sure. Cold spots, and air moving when it should have been completely still. None of the town's spectral inhabitants seemed to do anything, though, and ghosts had been such a fact of life for her ever since she could remember that she'd long since given up being afraid of them.

All the same, she'd fervently prayed that Roslyn had moved on, hadn't stayed to haunt the shabby apartment where she'd been murdered. Angela had actually gone there at the clan's request, just to make sure, and she'd said she hadn't sensed anything, hadn't seen or heard from Roslyn or anyone else. That had been the end of the matter, but even so, Jenny had awakened from nightmares more than once where she swore that her sister was calling out to her, begging her to release her from her earthly prison.

A shiver went through her, and Colin gently touched her arm with the hand that wasn't holding the EMF meter. "You okay?"

"Fine," she said tersely. That was a subject she definitely didn't want to get into here.

Or anywhere, actually.

He nodded, but his expression still looked troubled, as if he could tell there was something she was keeping from him.

If Frankie had noticed the tense little moment, she didn't say anything. "All right, so these EMF meters are pretty basic. They're already switched on, but you can adjust the gain when we get to a hot spot—so to speak. And have your phones and cameras ready, because you'll probably be able to get some good orb pictures, too."

"Orbs?" Dennis asked, speaking for the first time.

"We're still not entirely sure what they are," Frankie replied. "But they do seem to manifest in places where there's spectral activity. And they do show up nicely on camera. Just make sure to turn off your flashes. You won't need them. It'll look as if you're shooting into the dark...but you aren't."

After delivering that remark, she paused and surveyed everyone, a broad smile on a mouth painted almost the same magenta as her hair.

"All right, then. Let's go find some ghosts."

CHAPTER TWELVE

COLIN DIDN'T REALLY BELIEVE IN ANY OF THIS STUFF. Pretty much all so-called "ghostly" phenomena had its basis in science, if you drilled down and took a hard enough look. But it would be fun to walk around Jerome in the gathering dusk, and the tour promised some fun historical facts, so he didn't mind spending an hour or so pretending to look for ghosts.

Something was troubling Jenny, though. While they were surrounded by a group of tourists certainly wasn't the right time to ask her what was wrong, so he put the matter aside for later. Maybe during dinner. After she had a glass of wine, maybe she'd be more willing to tell him what had made that shadow pass over her face while they were listening to Frankie give her spiel about ghosts.

Jenny definitely hadn't been kidding when she'd told him that Jerome had been lousy with brothels back in the day. It seemed as if almost every place they stopped used to be a brothel at one point in its existence. Many of them were now hotels—all right, a few rooms above a storefront, in most cases—or restaurants. At the inn attached to the Mile High Grill, everyone swore they could sense something moving around their legs—supposedly the former proprietress's ghostly cat—but Colin didn't feel a damn thing.

The little group made its way down to a vacant lot dominated by an old, old, oak tree, now nearly bare. Frankie explained how the lot had been the scene of a shootout between two quarreling miners, and that they were known to haunt the place.

"It's also one of the best spots in town to see orbs," she added helpfully.

Almost as one, everybody in the group lifted their phones or their cameras and started shooting. Colin didn't bother. He sure didn't believe in orbs, and the battery on his phone was starting to get low. Standing next to him in the semi-gloom, Jenny lifted an eyebrow, but she didn't say anything.

"Oh, my gosh!" Kathy from Nebraska exclaimed. "There are *hundreds* of them!"

What the—?

Everyone crowded around her as she held up her phone. On the screen was, presumably, the last photo she took. Even though she stood several feet away, because it was so dark and the screen fairly bright, Colin could see an image crowded with hundreds of pale glowing spheres in various sizes.

It would be easy to dismiss those strange spheres as an artifact of using her flash in the darkness...but she hadn't. Everyone had, per Frankie's instructions, turned off the flash function on their various devices.

Colin shot a questioning look at Jenny, and she raised her shoulders.

"They've always been here," she said simply.

A creepy-crawly sensation started somewhere around the base of his neck and proceeded to work its way down his spine. There had to be a perfectly logical explanation for those palely glowing spheres that crowded the screen of Kathy-from-Lincoln's phone...but he was damned if he knew what the hell it might be.

The other people in the group started shuffling through the images they had taken, and, sure enough, every single one of them showed more or less the same thing, although not all of the photos were as crowded with orbs as the one that had startled Kathy so much.

"They must like you," Frankie said with a grin. "But we're getting to the end of our tour, so let me take you to say hi to Maisie before we call it quits for the night."

"Maisie?" Colin inquired.

"Oh, she haunts the side street next to Spook Hall—Lawrence Auditorium, I mean. Before the hall was built, that piece of land had a brothel built on it." As she spoke, she was guiding the group away from the vacant lot and down a not very well lit street. "Poor Maisie had a jealous customer, and he cut her throat one night. She's been there ever since."

That's a heck of a way to spend eternity, Colin thought grimly as he followed the other ghost hunters, Jenny at his side. Once again she wore that closed-off, tight-mouthed expression, and he wondered what was going through her head.

Well, he could guess. Joking about ghosts and ghost tours was one thing, but if she believed in ghosts at all, maybe, just maybe she'd also found herself wondering from time to time whether her own sister, also the victim of a gruesome murder, had decided to remain on this plane like the unfortunate Maisie.

No way would he ever ask, though. If she wanted to talk about it, he'd be there for her, but he certainly wasn't going to force the issue. Right then he wished they weren't surrounded by strangers. Judging by the expression she currently wore, he thought she could use a hug.

They paused next to a nondescript building with a large display window that was currently filled with leftover Halloween decorations. *They'd better get a move on that,* Colin thought. *Thanksgiving's next week.*

Or maybe they left the Halloween stuff up year-round. Jerome did seem like a very Halloween-ish kind of place. If Pumpkin Jack and Sally and the rest of the gang from *A Nightmare Before Christmas* ever decided to live in the real world, the former mining town was just the kind of place where they'd take up residence.

"A New York paper once referred to Jerome as the 'wickedest town in the West,'" Frankie said, hands on her hips as she seemed to inspect the blocky outlines of "Spook Hall." "A term that no one really disputed, considering this tiny scrap of land boasted thirty-seven saloons and twenty-nine brothels at its peak. There was—well, you couldn't really call it easy money, what with the way these girls had to earn it, but they flocked here. Maisie Templeton was one of those girls, and she died here when she was just nineteen years old."

"And she's still…here?" Kathy-from-Lincoln asked, a definite quaver in her voice.

"Oh, yes. The building itself has a long history of manifestations—cold spots, knocking on the walls, objects moved from one place to another. Part of the reason why the committee in charge of the decorations in the front window likes to leave them there for so long is that they have fun checking to see what's gotten moved around and when."

Frankie had to be kidding...didn't she? Colin sent a questioning look at Jenny, but she only gave another of those shrugs.

Well, rack that up as another one of roughly a hundred things he wanted to ask her about during dinner.

"Has anyone...." Barbara began, a definite quaver in her voice. She studiously avoided looking at her husband as she went on, tone a little firmer, "I mean, has anyone tried to help these ghosts move on?"

"Oh, sure," Frankie replied. "Sometimes it works. But some of them, for whatever reason, seem very rooted to this place. They don't want to leave. Maybe being here helps to remind them of when they were alive. What's beyond—that next place—it frightens them."

"Frightens a ghost?" Alan said, clearly not bothering to keep the contempt from his voice.

"Ghosts used to be people, Mr. Lundquist," Frankie said. "Just because they're no longer alive doesn't mean they can't still be scared."

An uneasy silence fell after that remark. None of the ghost tour guests seemed to want to look at each other, and even Jenny stepped a few feet away from him so she could stand there, arms crossed, as she stared at Spook Hall. Colin didn't want to know what she might be thinking.

"Anyway," Frankie went on, obviously realizing she'd just thrown a major damper on the tour, "we've got one more stop on the way back to my office, so if you'll follow me—"

They all moved after her as she began to head back up the steeply sloped street. Jenny moved quickly as well, as if glad to be away from the building that stood on the site where another young woman had been murdered.

For some reason, though, Colin didn't feel inclined to begin walking right away. If they were headed toward the Jerome Ghost Tours office, he knew basically where they were going and could catch up soon enough.

Instead, he stood there, arms crossed, looking at the glass-fronted façade of the building. Why, he wasn't really sure. It wasn't as if he expected to see the drippy candles and fake cobwebs and hanging bats in the Halloween display start moving around on their own.

But then he did catch a pale flash out of the corner of his eye, and he startled, pulse beginning to race…until he realized that the pale flash had only been a young woman who was walking up the street toward him. She looked to be around twenty, with curly blonde hair piled up on top of her head. Her clothes were strange, a high-necked white blouse and a long dark skirt, but he thought maybe she worked in one of the shops here and had adopted the turn-of-the-century dress to enhance the old-time atmosphere of the town.

The strange young woman paused a few feet away from him and planted her hands on her hips. This close, Colin noticed that she had very fine, pale skin, and big blue eyes framed with thick gold lashes. Very pretty, if nowhere near as striking as Jenny.

"You better tell her," the young woman said, speaking to him as familiarly as if they were long-time friends, rather than two strangers who'd never seen one another until this moment.

"Excuse me?" he responded, not sure what else to say. Maybe she'd mistaken him for someone else.

The blonde girl jerked her chin up the street, as if to indicate the rest of the ghost-hunting group. They'd disappeared around a corner, but Colin fancied he could still hear Frankie's voice echoing off the tall brick buildings.

"She don't like it when people lie," the strange young woman—girl, really—said. "So you'd better come clean, Colin Campbell."

At her use of his name, he did startle. How the hell could she know who he was? Well, he supposed it was possible that Jenny had talked up his trip here so it was common knowledge among the McAllister family. For some reason, though, he didn't think the young woman standing a few feet away was a McAllister. He couldn't even explain the difference, only that there was something in her features which didn't seem at all similar to theirs.

"I'm afraid I don't know what you're talking about, Miss...." He trailed off, hoping she would supply her name.

But she didn't. She only crossed her arms and sent him a penetrating blue stare, one he could see clearly even in the half-lit gloom of the narrow street where they stood. "Oh, yes, you do, even if you don't want to admit it to yourself. Miss Jenny McAllister has been through enough already without you lying to her. Why, when she finds out, it's going to break her heart."

He went cold. Dimly, Colin noted how he'd never actually experienced that sensation before, and yet, he might as well have been a block of ice in the shape of a man right then. But here was this girl telling him he was a liar, and how the hell could she have known that? He hadn't said anything about the McAllisters and his involvement with Jenny to anyone. The closest he'd come was mentioning to Ryan that he'd met a woman at the wedding reception and that he was going to Jerome for the weekend to visit her. That little bit definitely wasn't enough information for anyone to go on, even in the unlikely event that Ryan had started snooping and had somehow made contact with the strangely dressed woman who seemed to know far more than Colin believed she should.

"Who are you?" he demanded, his tone rougher than he'd intended. But damn, this girl had shaken him up.

She smiled, an enigmatic Mona Lisa sort of smile. Her eyes flicked toward Spook Hall and then back to him. "Oh, I think you know exactly who I am, Mr. Campbell."

And then...she was gone. It wasn't as if he'd blinked and she'd taken off running down the street or anything like that. No, one second she'd been standing there, clear as day, and the next she had disappeared into thin air. On stage, it would have been a pretty good trick.

On a gloomy street in Jerome, where the air felt thick with memory, it wasn't such a good trick after all. In fact, Colin was pretty sure it hadn't been a trick. It had been….

A shiver went over him, followed by another. His mind wanted to reject the explanation, wanted desperately to come up with something that would explain the young woman and her strange prescience and the way she'd blinked out of existence as if she'd never been there in the first place.

Colin realized then that he'd seen his first ghost. The ghost of Maisie Templeton, to be precise. As a woman who'd been betrayed by a man, she no doubt had very personal reasons for making sure that Jenny McAllister could avoid experiencing that same betrayal.

And if the strange girl really had been a ghost, then that quite possibly meant....

No, he refused to believe that. He just wouldn't. Jenny McAllister was the most amazing woman he'd ever met. She couldn't be....

But what if she is? his mind pushed at him, and he didn't have an answer.

It would definitely be a joke from the universe that the perfect woman for him just happened to be a witch.

Something was up with Colin, but Jenny couldn't figure out what it might be. He'd lagged behind a little bit after the group stopped at Spook Hall, but he'd caught up soon afterward, looking as pale as....

Well, as pale as if he'd seen a ghost.

Which was ridiculous. Not that there weren't ghosts around, only that Colin, a civilian, certainly wouldn't have been able to see one. The only person in Jerome who could actually see a ghost was Angela, the *prima,* and she wasn't even here right now. She'd be down in a little less than a week for Thanksgiving, but until then, not a single one of Jerome's denizens, witch or civilian, should have had the dubious pleasure of seeing a ghost.

He'd mumbled something about wanting to look at the display in the windows at Spook Hall, and Jenny had let it go. After all, it wasn't as if he'd ditched her or anything, only allowed himself to get distracted for a few minutes.

Still, she was glad that the tour was over. She managed a smile for Frankie as she handed over her EMF reader, and Colin also smiled and thanked the tour operator for a very educational experience.

Again, it was probably her imagination, but Jenny could have sworn she heard a special inflection in his voice as he said "educational."

There really wasn't time to do anything except head up the hill to the Asylum restaurant. It was quite a climb, but Colin seemed to manage well enough. However, the exertion required to get to one of Jerome's highest points was sufficient that neither one of them was too inclined to talk.

Just as well, Jenny thought. It was probably good for them to have a bit of decompression time after the ghost tour. She still wasn't sure why the whole experience should have bothered her so much. Was this what she had to look forward to—having every little thing set her off about Roslyn?

Goddess, she certainly hoped not.

Because they had reservations, they didn't have to wait at all. The hostess led them to a quiet table in a corner near one of the fireplaces, a welcome spot on a chilly November night.

"You're sure I shouldn't have gone back to your place and changed?" Colin asked in low tones after giving quick glance toward a very young couple seated a few tables away. The boy had on a tie, and the girl a nice dress.

"You're fine," Jenny replied calmly. "I'm pretty sure they're going to the homecoming dance down in Cottonwood after this. You'll notice most people aren't nearly as dressed up."

Another glance, one that seemed to take in the remainder of the diners, most of whom were wearing sweaters or long-sleeved T-shirts. His shoulders dropped slightly—from relief, Jenny guessed. "You're right, of course."

She liked that "of course" but decided it was probably better not to make too big a fuss about it. Instead, she said, "Any of the wines look good?"

"Um…all of them?"

She couldn't help chuckling at his comment. "Well, we might want to narrow it down just a little."

They settled on a local wine from the Pillsbury vineyard, and decided to get some soup because they'd done enough walking on the ghost tour to justify the extra calories. Besides, soup sounded good on a cold night like this. After they'd given their order to the server and she'd gone off to get things started, Colin settled back in his chair and smiled across the table at Jenny.

"That was quite the tour," he said.

"I didn't work you out too hard, did I?" she asked, letting a teasing note just barely enter her voice. Better to lighten the mood a little after the ghost tour.

"Nah." He shifted slightly, then gave an exaggerated wince. "Well, except maybe that last leg up the hill to get here. I thought I was going to dinner, not mountain climbing."

"Wimp."

A grin then, his hazel eyes dancing in that way which made her thighs feel all warm and tingly. "Hey, it's nothing that a little muscle relaxant couldn't cure."

As if on cue, the server came back with their bottle of wine, along with assurances that their soup would be along shortly. That sounded great, but right then Jenny was more concerned about the wine. Colin had the right idea about that "muscle relaxant."

In no time, though, she had a nice measure of wine sitting in her glass. After the server headed off toward the kitchen, Colin raised his own wine glass.

"Here's to Jerome."

She knew she could drink to that, so she lifted hers and clinked it against his glass. "So you liked it?" she asked, trying not to sound too hopeful.

"Absolutely. It's got a great mixture of history and funkiness, the people are friendly, the views are amazing—I can see why you'd want to live here."

Not like I had much choice, Jenny thought then. But true, she did love it here. There were some in the clan who'd moved down to Cottonwood or Clarkdale or even Page Springs or Cornville, but she knew she wouldn't feel quite complete if she couldn't get up in the morning and see all of the Verde Valley spread out before her, the warm red rocks of Sedona, the distant purple of the mountains along the Mogollon Rim. "I'm glad," she said, and decided she'd better leave it there. Anything else, and she might end up sounding too needy.

He seemed to understand, though. His expression grew serious, and he leaned forward slightly, fingers clasped around the stem of his wine glass. "And I can also see why you weren't that thrilled with Tucson."

She hadn't been expecting that response. "I liked Tucson just fine. That chimichanga was amazing."

Most guys probably would have made a crack about the chimichanga that had absolutely nothing to do with Mexican cuisine. As she'd learned already, however, Colin Campbell was not most guys. "Okay, the food and the shopping are pretty great. But I saw your eyes widen once or twice when we were stuck in traffic or when an emergency vehicle went by, or whatever. It's crowded, not really your kind of place."

"I had no idea I was being that obvious."

One corner of his mouth lifted in a lopsided smile. "Maybe you weren't...but I have keen powers of observation."

He looked so goofy—and cute—right then that she just had to grin back at him. "Oh, naturally. Well, you're probably right." She hesitated for a second, then realized she'd better be honest. This wasn't a matter of not liking him or not being attracted to him, but more that she didn't want to set up false expectations. "I guess I'm just a small-town girl at heart. My cousin Caitlin was happy to go off to the big city, but even though I'm glad for her, I can't help thinking about what she gave up."

Colin's smile faded, and the expression he took on looked almost too neutral. "Maybe she didn't look at it that way."

Damn. Jenny knew she probably should have kept her mouth shut. Unfortunately, there wasn't much she could do about it now. "I doubt she did. But then, even before she met Alex, she'd gotten out of Jerome, was going to school up at NAU in Flagstaff." Along with a whole bunch of other

McAllister cousins, all of whom had been thrilled when relations between their clan and the Wilcoxes had been mended, allowing them to go to college in Wilcox territory. Jenny had heard the tut-tutting and witnessed the head-shaking, but she wasn't going to group herself with the older generation, who were still not altogether happy about the new normal when it came to the Wilcox clan. At the same time, she'd been forced to admit that her particular ship had sailed. She really hadn't wanted to start college at twenty-seven, not when most entering their freshmen year were nine or ten years younger.

"Oh, that's right," Colin said after taking a sip of his wine. "I'd forgotten about that."

Jenny's eyes narrowed. Had she mentioned Caitlin going to NAU before now? She really couldn't recall; she and Colin had discussed all sorts of things while on their "date" down in Tucson. And it seemed that half of what they'd talked about had been sort of erased by the amazing sex that followed. It was probably better to let it go. "Mostly we stick around here, though. I guess Jerome kind of gets in your blood."

"That doesn't surprise me."

He said the words in such a neutral way that Jenny wasn't quite sure how to take the comment. Was he agreeing with her, or was he only trying to hide his disappointment at realizing that the world's biggest crowbar couldn't get her out of Jerome? Well, if all she was going to get was this one last weekend with him, she figured she might as well enjoy it while she could.

Something seemed to curdle in her stomach, despite her inner vow to have as much fun with Colin as she could. Hoping she looked casual, she picked up her glass of wine and took a large swallow. There. That was better. A few more of those, and the edges would start to get nicely blurred.

"So," he went on, in a very different tone, "we've gone all over Jerome today. What's left on the docket for tomorrow?"

"It depends," she replied, glad that he'd recognized it was time to change the subject. "What time do you need to head back?"

"Not early. Sunday traffic is light, so I could still hang out here for most of the day and make it home in time to get my beauty sleep."

Jenny couldn't help shaking her head at that comment. "Well, then, we could drive up Mingus to one of the picnic areas there, or we could take the Clarkdale train if you want to do something sort of touristy. I'd say we could also go wine tasting, but that might not be the best idea when you have a three-hour drive ahead of you."

"True." He paused, fingers tapping on the base of the wine glass in front of him. "How about we save that for my next visit?"

Sagging with relief wasn't really an option, but that was what Jenny wanted to do right then. So she hadn't put him off with all her talk about how much she loved Jerome and was a small-town sort of person. He still wanted to see her again, which meant he had to be at least slightly open to the idea of living somewhere other than Tucson.

Whether he'd be equally open about having a long-term relationship with someone who just happened to be a witch was an entirely different question.

She decided she'd better leave that problem aside for now. "Sure. That would be great. There are a couple of wine-tasting rooms right here in Jerome, and then more down in Cottonwood and Clarkdale—"

The waitress came back right then with their soup, so Jenny stopped there. But after they'd ordered their entrees and the server had disappeared again, Colin picked right back up on the thread of the conversation.

"That sounds like fun. I've been hearing some good things about the wines from around here. Haven't they been winning a lot of competitions?"

"Yes, quite a few," Jenny replied, unable to keep the pride from her voice. Business in her hometown was booming, in no small part because of all the accolades that northern Arizona wines had been receiving lately.

They chatted about wine and tourism in the area, nice safe topics that wouldn't get her in trouble or cause any awkwardness between them. The whole time, Jenny couldn't quite keep herself from watching him, his long, strong fingers as they lay on the tabletop or gestured when he wanted to make a point, the way one lock of sandy hair kept falling forward over his forehead. Everything about him seemed to have been made exactly the way she liked it, even though she wouldn't have thought of him as her type if she'd met him anytime earlier in her life. Maybe it had taken getting through a parade of jerks for her to recognize the sort of man who really was best for her.

After dinner—and port with dessert—they descended the town's steep streets in a sort of dreamy haze. The night air had a definite bite to it, but Jenny hardly noticed. She'd brought a wrap, and besides, she held Colin's hand, his strong fingers entwined around hers. Something of his warmth seemed to travel up her arm and fill her whole body.

Or maybe that was only anticipation at what she knew was going to come next.

They'd barely made it inside the door before his mouth was on hers. He tasted delectable, of the sweetness of port and the cherries jubilee that had been made table-side for them. Jenny wrapped her arms around him, pulling him close, their bodies touching from shoulder to hip. It felt so good, as if they'd been made to embrace like this, their proportions carefully sculpted so her hips would meet against him right there, feeling how hard he was even through his jeans.

She let go of him just enough so she could lead him into her bedroom. Once there, she grabbed the jacket he wore and pulled it off his shoulders, then tossed it onto a chair. The T-shirt he had on underneath followed next, and for a moment she paused, running her hands over his body, feeling the lean muscles against her skin, the faintest brush of his chest hair. She liked that—just enough that he seemed entirely masculine, but not so much that she felt as if she was going to bed with a bearskin rug or something.

He tugged at one end of the wrap she wore and pulled it loose, then took hold of her sweater and drew it off. Since she didn't have anything on underneath except her bra, his hands were on her bare flesh at once, warm, strong, caressing her as if he'd never touched her before.

In a sense, maybe he really hadn't. The two other times they'd had sex, they'd both been pretty wasted.

Yes, they'd had wine with dinner, but just enough to feel pleasantly elevated rather than actually drunk.

His fingers found the clasp of her bra and unhooked it. At once he was cupping her breasts, caressing her, and she moaned—loudly, because the only thing below her was the gallery, and no one was around to hear or care. And oh, Goddess, he bent then, his mouth closing on her nipple, and she wanted to collapse into his arms right then and there. Maybe it was the buildup of having to wait for this all week, or maybe it was only that he really was that damn good, but she knew her knees were going to buckle at the waves of sensation of sweeping over her.

Colin seemed to realize something of the effect he was having on her, because he gently guided her over to the bed and then pushed her down on top of it, shoving the quilt and the sheet and the blanket out of the way as he did so. As soon as they were lying down, his fingers found the button on her jeans and popped it loose. And then he was tugging down those jeans, along with her underwear, and he was touching her again, sinking into her, stroking her.

The orgasm burst over her like storm-driven waves falling on a beach. She clung to him, her breaths coming in quick gasps, her entire body shaking. How the hell was he able to do that to her? She'd never climaxed so quickly with anyone else.

But she didn't have much time to think about that particular puzzle, because his mouth was now between her legs, his tongue touching her, and oh, Goddess, it was going to be hard to figure out where one orgasm ended and the other began. All Jenny knew was that she never wanted him to stop, never wanted to experience this with anyone except him ever again.

And then he was in her, their bodies locked together, finding their rhythm, fingers intertwined, their breaths seeming to come as a single gasp. He held off, she could tell, trying to lengthen the moment as much as he could, but at last he couldn't hold back the tide, had to release in her, his warmth filling her, his body hot and sweat-slick against her own.

Afterward, they lay next to each other for a long while, dozing in satiated silence. Finally, Jenny got up and went to the bathroom to get herself more or less in order, which also meant pulling on her sleep shirt and a fresh pair of panties. Over in the bedroom, she could hear the bed springs creak as Colin got up, presumably to retrieve his underwear. When she returned to the bedroom, however, she couldn't tell for sure, as he was already tucked back beneath the covers.

"That looks snug," she said, glad of the darkness in the room so he couldn't see her expression. Even though she'd been looking forward to making love with him all week, something about having to look a man in the eye after sex always got to her.

"It is," Colin replied. "Come on in and find out for yourself."

She didn't need any further urging. Moving quickly because it was cold in there—the wall heat didn't work so well, and she'd forgotten to turn on the space heater—she climbed into bed next to him and snuggled close so she could lay her head on his shoulder.

It should have felt strange to have him in her bed. Usually she'd preferred to go to the homes or apartments of the men she dated, keeping her own flat as her private sanctuary. But she hadn't thought twice about inviting Colin over.

What precisely that meant, she wasn't sure she wanted to analyze right then.

"Comfy?" he asked, and she nodded.

He reached over to stroke her hair, and she didn't know whether she'd ever felt so safe and warm and happy before. If she had, it must have been a long, long time ago.

And then....

It always came on her in much the same way a severe migraine affected some people—crushing pressure, and the flickers of rainbow auras at the edges of her vision.

Oh, no....

That was her last rational thought, because the dark curtain which usually blocked her mind from the minds of others was torn out of the way, and she could see everything around her—her cousin Kirby wondering if he could convince his boyfriend to go with him to California to get married, and Henry Lynch worrying that the ruby ring he'd bought his wife for their fortieth anniversary wouldn't be fancy enough, and Maggie, the girl who'd sublet Adam's old apartment over the fudge shop, hoping the guy she'd gone out with the night before would call her, and...

...and Colin, happy and sated, but worrying underneath that every hour he let pass without telling her the truth was an hour that was making the whole thing worse, and how the hell was she going to react when she found out, and—

The words were out of Jenny's mouth before she could stop them. "You're a fucking *reporter?*"

He started, then pulled away from her slightly. Even in the darkness of her bedroom, she could see how his eyes had widened. "I—what?"

"Don't lie to me!" she snarled. It was intolerable to be sitting next to him in her own goddamn bed, so she pushed herself over to one side and then stood up, arms crossed over her breasts as she glared down at him. "You—you crashed my cousin's wedding!

You lied about who you were! You—you're the one who wrote all those articles about that bastard who killed my sister!"

During this onslaught, Colin had sat quietly, as if knowing that to interrupt would be to make things worse than they already were. When she paused for breath, however, he said, his tone low but desperate, "Yes, I did all those things. I wanted to tell you. I really did. I just—I couldn't think of the right time to do it. You were just so amazing, and I didn't want to screw things up—"

"Well, you have screwed them up!" she burst out. "You have fucked them up royally! So do me a favor and get your lying ass out of my house!"

"Jenny, I—"

Something about hearing her name on his lips only enraged her that much more. She grabbed his jeans from where they lay draped over the chair and flung them at him. They hit him in the chest with a slap, but all he did was grasp them by the waistband, then push back the covers so he could pull them on.

During this procedure, she watched in silence, arms still crossed. How could she have been so stupid? She should have known something was up, because he'd seemed too good to be true from the very beginning. But digging around, trying to find out more about the McAllisters—she'd seen it all in a flash, all his guilt, all the lies and machinations.

And underneath it, worry and a dawning wonder. Because it seemed he really had met a ghost. Met her, and talked to her. And if that was possible, then it wasn't that big a leap to begin to believe that the McAllisters might really possess strange powers, that the woman he'd begun to care about just might be a witch after all....

Jenny went cold. Her family had survived all these years because they'd kept their abilities and their heritage a secret. And now she'd put all of them in jeopardy, just because she'd gotten drunk and slept with a *reporter,* of all people. The elders were going to have a fit when they found out.

Grossly misinterpreting her silence, Colin said, "Jenny, please let me explain—"

"You don't need to explain anything," she snapped. "All you have to do is finish getting dressed, and then get your sorry lying ass out of my house." She pulled in a breath and added, "And if you mention anything about me, or the McAllisters, or—or anything you've seen here in Jerome to anyone else, I'll—"

"You'll what?" he cut in, reaching for his T-shirt so he could pull it on. "Put the whammy on me? Stick pins in a voodoo doll?"

Gritting her teeth, she said, "Worse." Which was really a hollow threat. The McAllisters had always used white magic, their powers ones that weren't easily subverted to the left-hand path. The Wilcoxes, on the other hand....

But Colin didn't know that. He didn't say anything else, only continued to get dressed in silence. Once he was done, he picked up his overnight bag, which he'd never had the chance to unpack. Then he stood there, weighing it in one hand, just as he was clearly weighing what to say next. Maybe he was perceptive enough to feel the waves of rage pouring off her, because after a long pause he only said, "I'll let myself out."

He went out into the living room, and a few seconds later Jenny could hear the front door open and shut. Quietly, though; he didn't slam it.

The silence in the apartment thundered in her ears. She stood there for a long moment, then sank down on the bed and let the tears come.

CHAPTER THIRTEEN

DAMN. DAMN, DAMN, DAMN, DAMN, DAMN, DAMN, DAMN.

Colin took the turns down the side of the hill way too fast, tires screeching on more than one curve. When he hit Cottonwood, however, he retained just enough of his senses to realize that he'd better not be calling attention to himself like that, not when he was still processing half a bottle of wine, not to mention the glass of port he'd had with dessert. Ending up in the local drunk tank would really be the cherry on the cake of his evening.

Where the hell had *that* come from?

Because apparently Jenny McAllister was a witch who could read minds. Or something like that. Why she hadn't learned the truth about him long ago, Colin had no idea. Maybe her powers weren't completely consistent. Or maybe she could only see into his mind after they'd been intimate. No, that didn't sound right. Otherwise, she would have discovered exactly who and what he was after the first night they'd spent together.

All he knew was that it had been perfect—except for his little visit from Maisie the ghost—and now that whole bright sparkling day had shattered to pieces around him. And it was all his fault. He couldn't and wouldn't blame anyone but himself. The first thing he should have done when he got to Jerome was tell Jenny the truth, but he'd been too much of a chickenshit. And man, had those chickens come home to roost.

He saw an all-night convenience store coming up on his right, and pulled off into the parking lot. As much as he wanted to keep driving and not look back, he knew he had more than three hours to go before he got home, and that meant a lot of hot, cheap coffee to fuel the drive.

The man behind the counter—well, boy really, since he barely looked old enough to drink—didn't even make eye contact as he counted out Colin's change. Just as well. Colin didn't really want to know what might be reflected in his expression just then, and he didn't want anyone else to see it, either.

The coffee sucked. Probably had been sitting on the warmer all day, but that didn't matter. All that mattered was it was strong and hot, and enough to keep him from nodding off on the way to Tucson and ending up in a ditch. Then again, maybe that would be better. If he managed to knock himself unconscious, then maybe he wouldn't have to keep seeing the bitter recriminations in Jenny McAllister's glorious blue eyes.

God, he'd been an idiot. All right, there was a very good chance she might have told him to get lost the second he confessed all to her, but even that would have been better than continuing to lie basically every moment they'd spent together since he'd arrived in Jerome. Maybe then, once she'd had some time to cool off, she would have thought things over and decided to forgive him. There probably would have been a good deal of groveling involved, but Colin didn't think he would mind that too much if it meant she might have given him a second chance.

Now, though....

He shook his head and downed another swallow of acrid, lukewarm coffee. From the way she'd been shooting daggers at him with those big blue eyes of hers, he'd be lucky if he got twenty feet in sight of her before she started throwing real-life knives at him. Or curses, or whatever it was that witches did.

If she really was a witch.

Psychic? Maybe. He didn't know which was worse, admitting that witches were real, or that the woman he'd hoped would become a permanent part of his life had some sort of strange psychic abilities. A few days ago, he would have dismissed both possibilities as equally unlikely. But something very strange had just happened, something that had given Jenny McAllister the ability to see directly into his mind, to see everything he'd kept hidden from her.

Computer hacker, he thought then as his brain attempted to come up with something that made sense. *That's nice and plausible.*

And equally unlikely. He hadn't brought his laptop with him this weekend, just his phone. Besides, most of the notes he'd put together while investigating the McAllisters and the puzzle of their existence, he'd written longhand, an artifact from his days in college when he'd done most of his work with pen and paper. The computer he'd had back then was old and unreliable, and after losing a term paper—and almost getting an F in the class because of it—he'd always done his first drafts the old-fashioned way, only putting them in the computer when they were more or less finished.

Anyway, there really wasn't anything for Jenny *to* hack. All right, she could have done some investigating on her own and discovered that he worked for the *Daily Sun,* but that was the only thing she would have been able to find out. He didn't even have his photo posted on the paper's website, due to a request he'd made when the divorce had started to get ugly. So all she'd have was a name, and "Colin Campbell" wasn't all that unique. There were two other men with that name in Tucson, and seven more in the greater Phoenix area. He knew, because he'd checked.

So that put him back more or less to the beginning, and the possibility that the girl he thought he might be falling in love with just happened to be a witch.

A witch who hates your guts, he thought, and drank some more bitter coffee. It seemed to be a perfect match to his mood.

All he could was hope, as he swung down out of the darkness and into the glitter of the Phoenix suburbs, was that she wasn't planning some sort of spectacular revenge.

They all sat in the living room of Bryce McAllister's big restored Victorian. Jenny really wished this meeting could have taken place almost anywhere else, because ever since she was a little girl, she'd been intimidated by Bryce. Part of her reaction to him was due to his brusque manner, she knew, but she'd never felt comfortable around him. For all she knew, the three elders had decided to meet here exactly because it was the one place in Jerome that Jenny was least likely to feel at all comfortable.

Not that she would have felt comfortable even if they'd gathered at her Aunt Tricia's house. Tricia was definitely in "elder" mode, mouth tight and blue eyes worried, the laugh lines around them more pronounced than usual. Allegra Moss looked more distracted than anything else, but Jenny hadn't expected much more than that from her.

With the way the three elders sat on the floral chintz couch—something that had to have been chosen by Bryce's wife Meg—with Jenny in the armchair opposite and staring at them across the coffee table, she felt all the more as if she was facing down a tribunal.

In a way she was, she supposed, although there wasn't that much they'd really be able to do to her. It wasn't as if they could throw her out of the clan. But being ostracized and ignored often worked just as well at letting a wrongdoer know how much they'd truly screwed up.

The day outside was gloomy and cold, threatening rain. Maybe that was why a shiver worked its way down her back, even though the room itself felt warm enough.

"A reporter," Bryce said, then shook his head. The amount of disgust he'd been able to inject into that one simple word was actually kind of impressive. "What were you thinking, Jenny?"

Well, she hadn't been thinking. Not really. She'd let herself succumb to her attraction for Colin without doing any due diligence. Yes, people in witch clans got involved with civilians, but not without performing some background checks first to make sure there weren't any red flags that might make such a connection dangerous. And she hadn't even asked the name of the company where Colin worked, for Goddess' sake.

Not that it really mattered, she supposed. He would have just handed her another lie.

"I didn't know he was a reporter," she said, and despite vowing to herself earlier that morning as she got dressed that she wouldn't lose her temper, would be calm and controlled and utterly dispassionate, even she could hear the edge to her voice. "You know how my ability works—or, more to the point, *doesn't* work. It's not as if I can just dip into people's minds whenever I feel like it. He told me he worked in corporate communications, and I believed him." She paused, then added, "I didn't have any reason not to."

Silence. The three elders exchanged glances, but Jenny couldn't read much from their expressions. Even Tricia's pretty face was blank and cold. Jenny supposed she'd been hoping for a little more compassion from her aunt. Then again, elders had to be impartial. True, everyone here was related to everyone else in one way or another, but some connections were closer than others. Tricia McAllister couldn't allow her feelings for her niece to get in the way now.

"Besides," Jenny went on, even though she knew the argument she was about to present wouldn't earn her any points, "it wasn't as if anyone at the reception pointed him out as a gate crasher. He was sitting there in a room full of McAllisters and Wilcoxes and de la Pazes, and not one person seemed to notice that he shouldn't have been there."

"So you're saying it's their fault?" Bryce's eyes were positively glacial beneath his heavy gray-flecked eyebrows.

"Of course not," Jenny replied. "I'm just saying that expecting me to think he was anything except what he said he was, when no one else seemed to notice anything strange about him, is a bit much."

Allegra Moss spoke then. "Maybe it is. And I'm sure we'll have some questions for the Trujillos and the de la Pazes before this is over. But I think—and I'm sure Tricia and Bryce will agree with me—that the most important thing right now is to do some damage control before we start casting blame on anyone."

From the way Bryce scowled at her remark, Jenny got the feeling he was all too willing to start assigning blame, even if in the end that sort of activity wasn't terribly productive. But Tricia gave a weary nod, saying, "Allegra's right. Did this Colin Campbell give any indication that he was planning to publicize what he'd learned?"

"No," Jenny said. At least that was one thing she hadn't seen during that blazing lightning-flash look into his mind. She'd seen a lot, but absolutely nothing about trying to do anything with the information he'd gathered so far. "I got the impression that he was just trying to satisfy his own curiosity."

"And it was the incident in the parking lot at that mall in Phoenix that set things off?" Bryce asked, picking up the thread of what Jenny had told her aunt on the phone earlier that morning, when she called to tell her what had happened with Colin.

"I think so. I guess whatever that de la Paz detective—"

"Jack Sandoval," Tricia supplied, surprising Jenny a little. But then she told herself it made sense. Caitlin was a de la Paz by marriage now. It was only natural that her mother would know a good deal about the various members of the family.

Jenny nodded. "Right. So anyway, I know he did something to the two women who were in the next parking row over, something to make them forget they'd seen or heard anything. Luckily, they were the only ones close enough to have noticed something strange was going on. But whatever he did to them, obviously it didn't last forever. One of the women approached Colin at his paper because she saw the wedding announcement, and something clicked. I guess she went to him because he was the one who covered the trial." She stopped then, because every time she remembered sitting in the courtroom at Matías Escobar's sentencing, she felt physically ill. There hadn't been a single speck of remorse in those cold black eyes of his.

Whereas Colin had been all remorse. And regret. And a good deal of self-directed anger for not just biting the bullet and telling her the truth. Which Jenny supposed was all well and good, but it didn't change what he'd done. Every single moment they'd shared, every smile and embrace...and more...was now tainted because of the lies he'd told her.

"I'll talk to Luz about that," Tricia said. "I know she assured me afterward that any witnesses wouldn't be able to remember anything of what they'd seen. Jack is supposed to be very good at that sort of thing."

"Not good enough, looks like," Boyd grumbled.

Allegra and Tricia both frowned. The effect of them frowning in tandem might have been amusing if the situation hadn't been so serious, since other-wise they were a study in contrasts, Allegra with her messy gray-blonde topknot, and Tricia with her per-fectly styled bob. Brows still pulled together, Tricia said, "Well, there could be extenuating circum-stances. If the woman who went to see Colin was sufficiently strong-willed, it's very possible the effects of the forgetting charm might have begun to fade with time. We just don't know for sure, and it's not as if we can go talk to her…or to Colin Campbell."

For some reason, Tricia's words calmed Jenny a bit. She'd been worrying that the elders would make her confront Colin or, worse, that they would go see him themselves to get to the bottom of his intentions. However, it seemed as if they were willing to go on the intelligence provided by the quick flash Jenny had had into his mind.

"Maybe," Bryce said in grudging tones. It seemed clear enough that he wasn't willing to give Jack Sandoval the benefit of the doubt. "Even so, that's a serious breach of security right there."

"Oh, for heaven's sake, Bryce," Allegra said. "You make it sound as if we're working at the Pentagon or something." Wearing what she probably thought was a reassuring smile, she shifted toward Jenny and went on, "Did Colin actually witness anything that would provide positive proof that we're not your ordinary family?"

"You mean besides me being able to tell him everything about himself, including what he had for breakfast?" Jenny replied dryly.

"Well, yes, besides that."

Jenny folded her hands on her lap. There wasn't much, but…. "He talked to Maisie."

"The ghost?" Tricia asked, eyes widening slightly. "But how—"

"I don't know," Jenny said. "From what I saw in his mind, he talked to her like she was really there. The same way that Angela talks to our ghosts. I can't explain it, because I know that Colin Campbell is one hundred percent civilian. He's not witch-kind, and he doesn't have any sort of psychic abilities. Yet he managed to do something that none of the rest of us—except Angela—are able to do."

Once again the three elders exchanged eloquent looks. It seemed obvious enough to Jenny that they were more or less flummoxed but really didn't want to admit it to her—or each other.

"Anyway," she continued, "because he saw Maisie, and because she disappeared right in front of his eyes, meaning he couldn't explain her away as a reenactor or someone who just liked dressing up in Edwardian clothes, he could tell something completely outside his regular experience had happened. He's not the type of person to believe in the paranormal. But Maisie was proof that the world was a much stranger place than he thought. And because of that particular realization, it wasn't that big a leap to realize something was a little off about us McAllisters."

"That's…unfortunate," Tricia said after a long, uncomfortable pause. "But still, it's not as if he has any concrete proof."

"What does that matter to places like the *National Enquirer* or the *Weekly World News?*" Bryce shot back. "All they need is the smallest whiff that something is a little strange, and they're plastering it all over their ridiculous papers. And then the damage is done. Everything we've tried to keep secret all these years is displayed for the whole world to see."

"Colin doesn't work for the *Enquirer,*" Jenny pointed out, a little surprised at herself for coming to Colin Campbell's defense. "He works for the *Tucson Daily Sun.*"

"I don't see much of a difference."

Jenny sent a beseeching glance in her aunt's direction, and Tricia appeared to relent slightly. "Bryce, I think there's a very big difference." She hesitated, then went on, "Still, how sure can you be, Jenny, that he won't change his mind about letting other people know what he's found out? You said you threw him out in basically the middle of the night. That sort of thing could make him want to retaliate in some way, even though of course you were completely in the right."

Would Colin retaliate, betray her family's confidence because he was angry with her? Jenny wanted to think that he'd just let the matter go, but she wasn't sure. After all, he'd had the balls to crash a stranger's wedding, just to investigate whether there really was more to the groom than met the eye.

After a long pause, she lifted her shoulders, feeling more helpless than ever. "I don't know what he'll do," she said. "I just don't know."

Monday mornings generally sucked enough on their own. A Monday morning after being thrown out on your ear by the girl you were falling in love with—that really sucked. As in super-massive black hole kind of sucking.

Colin had woken up long before the alarm on his phone was programmed to go off. Thinking it might be better to get to work early and therefore escape any unwanted chitchat with his coworkers in the break room, he'd gone ahead and showered and dressed, and arrived at the *Daily Sun*'s office a good forty-five minutes early.

That strategy had worked...up to a point. At approximately ten minutes after eight, Ryan Ortiz came and propped himself up against the doorframe to Colin's office and said, "So, how was the hot date?"

Colin threw a balled-up piece of paper into the trashcan in the corner. About all he'd accomplished so far was to doodle all over the yellow pad he kept on his desk, the one where he was supposed to be writing down ideas for his next in-depth investigation. Tucson's criminal element had been relatively quiet over the weekend, and so he didn't have anything assigned in terms of what he mentally referred to as the "ambulance chaser" type of article. At slow times like this, he'd go pitch something a little more involved to his editor, see what Ned was on board with. Unfortunately, Colin's mind was a perfect blank this morning. He'd never been less motivated to do the work that had once been his passion.

Without looking over at his colleague, Colin said, "She hates me and wants me dead."

"In other words, a typical Saturday night for you."

If his current dire situation hadn't involved Jenny McAllister, Colin might have laughed. Instead, he scowled and said, "Not helping."

"Sorry, man." Ryan paused and watched Colin for a long moment, as if attempting to glean more information from his expression. "You want to talk about it?"

"Not really." After all, what in the world could he say? *I lied to her about who I was, and she found out because she's a psychic from a family of witches. The usual.* That wouldn't fly, for several reasons. First of all, he knew he'd never utter one word about the real truth behind the McAllister clan to anyone. He might have betrayed Jenny already, but he wasn't going to compound his sins by revealing the secrets her family had worked so hard to hide. Second, even if he was the kind of asshole who would go telling tales out of school, Ryan would never believe him.

His friend was even more hardheaded about that sort of thing than Colin was. Or rather, than he'd been up until Saturday night. Talking to ghosts and seeing your would-be girlfriend exhibit insane psychic powers tended to blow that whole "skeptic" thing out of the water.

Ryan shifted his weight from one foot to another, and appeared as if he intended to press the issue. But then he took another look at Colin's face and seemed to realize that way led madness, or at least the kind of argument you didn't want to have in the workplace. So he shrugged and said, "Okay. But I'm willing to listen if you want to talk about it later."

Then he headed off toward his own office. Colin couldn't relax, though. He kept replaying his time with Jenny McAllister in his head, stopping at key moments to ponder whether that had been the perfect time when he should have told her the truth, or whether it would have been better the next day over breakfast, or—

He shut that line of thought down. What good would it do now to continually keep second-guessing himself? All he could do as this point was try to get his head screwed on straight so he could do his work. The last thing he needed was to put his job on the line because he was so completely preoccupied with Jenny McAllister.

Because he knew he didn't currently possess the sort of analytical skills required for anything more demanding, Colin pulled up the list of leads that the overnight team had put out on the server. Nothing terribly spectacular, but following up on a string of vandalism incidents in the upscale neighborhood of Skyline Estates would at least keep him occupied for a while. He knew he needed to keep busy. Otherwise, he'd be far too tempted to plead the sudden onset of a migraine or food poisoning, just so he could leave work, get in his car, and drive all the way back to Jerome. Pound on Jenny McAllister's door until she was forced to come out and listen to him...and then have him arrested for stalking. For all he knew, local law enforcement was filled with their family members so anything unusual could be kept off the public record.

Even if that wasn't true, he had a feeling that Jenny and the rest of her witch family would probably blast him all the way back to Tucson.

Sighing, he pulled up the meager info on the vandalism story, and started to make some calls.

CHAPTER FOURTEEN

SHE HADN'T THOUGHT IT WOULD BE LIKE THIS. AFTER ALL, she'd been through plenty of breakups. It always hurt for a while, and then she'd be back to drifting through her life as if the relationship had never happened. A few tears, a few days of self-recriminations, trying to figure out what she'd done wrong this time, but it never lasted.

Now, though....

Jenny tried to tell herself it was stupid to feel this way. She'd only been with Colin for a week—if you could even call the few times they'd been together being "with" someone. A couple of dates did not exactly constitute a relationship.

Problem was, she knew that what she'd felt for him, what she'd allowed herself to feel, was utterly different from what she'd experienced with anyone else.

She'd dared to let herself hope that he might be the one.

Pesky thing, hope. It usually ended up screwing you over in a spectacular fashion.

The elders weren't happy with her, but as the week had worn on and nothing about the McAllister witches ended up splashed on the front page of the *National Enquirer,* they seemed to relax a bit. Besides, Thanksgiving was the very next day, and they had more important things to deal with. She got the impression that they were primed to do damage control if necessary, but in the meantime had decided it was better to get on with the business of the clan.

Jenny couldn't think of anything she wanted less than to deal with the overwhelming family togetherness of the holiday, but she knew there wasn't much she could do about it. This would be the first Thanksgiving since they'd lost Roslyn, which was bad enough, but this whole mess with Colin had just made the whole situation that much worse.

The *prima* and her family had come to stay in the big Victorian up on the hill, and Angela had texted Jenny, saying that she wanted to talk to her. It was definitely a conversation she would rather have avoided, but Jenny knew she didn't have much of a choice. You didn't turn down a direct request from the *prima,* even if you had a good five years on her.

At least Angela was coming down to Jenny's flat, rather than saying that the audience must be held up at the big house that had once been their Great-Aunt Ruby's. That particular request had probably been made in order to avoid having Angela's twins interrupt their discussion than out of any concern for Jenny's feelings, but she still couldn't help feeling grateful. Way better to get raked over the coals in the comfort of her own home.

Angela came up the walk, dark hair shining in the bright sunlight. It was a gorgeous day, crisp and clear, with only a few big white clouds to mar the perfection of a sapphire sky. Jenny had closed the gallery for the day; the town got huge crowds the day after Thanksgiving, but the Wednesday before was always a total graveyard. No point in hanging around and pretending to work when there was nothing to do.

"Hi, Angela," Jenny said as the *prima* came up the steps. There might not have been anything natural about this situation, but she figured she might as well try to act as normal as possible.

"Hi, Jenny," Angela replied. She was dressed casually, in jeans and a dark green sweater and her beloved black cowboy boots. At first glance, she probably wouldn't have attracted much attention. It was only when you looked a little closer that you noticed the way she carried herself, confident without being arrogant, as well as the keen light in those brilliant green eyes of hers. She didn't look like a girl anymore, which was how Jenny still tended to think of her. But being *prima*—and a mother—could definitely change a person.

"Come on in," Jenny said. There didn't seem to be much point in idle chitchat, since she knew Angela was here just to give her an extra helping of grief for her indiscretions with Colin Campbell. Even so, she had to add, "Do you want some water, or coffee? I just made a fresh pot."

"Coffee would be great. Thanks." Angela went ahead and settled herself on the couch in the living room while Jenny got busy in the kitchen, pouring two big mugs of coffee, then setting a pitcher of cream and a bowl of sugar on a tray.

She brought it out and set it all down on the coffee table. Angela picked up one of the mugs and got busy doctoring her coffee with cream and sugar, then settled back against the couch as Jenny sat down on the accent chair to the right of the sofa.

What the *prima* said next startled her. "So...tell me about Colin Campbell's interactions with Maisie. I just spoke with her, but I wanted to hear your—or rather, Colin's—side of things."

It still seemed strange to hear Angela refer to "speaking" with Maisie in such a casual way, as if the ghost was just another ordinary citizen of Jerome.

Maybe to the *prima*, she was. "Well, this is all just from one of my 'flashes,' but—"

"It's okay," Angela said as she picked up her mug, but only cradled it in her hands rather than lifting it to take a sip. "I know you can't give me a blow-by-blow. But I'm just curious how she looked to him."

Jenny paused, doing her best to sort through the barrage of images and thoughts and impressions she'd received during that one brief burst. When she had one of her psychic flashes, oftentimes what she "saw" didn't remain with her for very long—just as well, since she often was bombarded by memories and feelings that she really didn't want to retain. In this case, though, she'd done her best to keep going over what had come to her from Colin's mind. It hurt to know how he'd lied to her, but on the other hand, the future of the clan might just depend on what she'd seen and absorbed.

"He didn't see her appear," Jenny said then, leaning over to pick up her own mug of coffee. "It was more like he glanced back and saw her walking toward him. So of course he just thought she was someone who lived here. And he did notice a number of details about her—the way she wore her hair piled up like this"—Jenny scooped up her own long hair and approximated a messy Gibson Girl hairstyle as best she could—"and the lace on the high collar of her blouse, and how fine her skin was. She definitely looked like a normal person to him, except for the way she was dressed. But he just thought she was a reenactor or something."

Angela nodded. "That's how she always appears to me, too. Every once in a while the color of her skirt will change—sometimes it's dark blue, sometimes gray—but her hair and her blouse always look the same. I know she's a ghost because I just know, but I can see why a civilian like Colin would have been confused."

"He saw her disappear, though," Jenny said. "That was when he realized she couldn't possibly be a normal person. It kind of freaked him out."

"I can imagine," Angela replied, her mouth lifting a bit at the corners. It wasn't quite a smile, but her amusement was fairly obvious. "Nothing like having your entire view of the universe upended."

Jenny hadn't really thought about it that way. Yes, she'd felt the blast of his remembered shock and astonishment. At the time, though, she'd been far too overwhelmed by his betrayal to spend much time dissecting his feelings about being confronted by a ghost. He was a practical person, though, not the type to come to Sedona to experience the vortexes or to have his palm read or whatever. Coming to the understanding that ghosts were real—and therefore the world contained far more in it than he'd wanted to believe—had to be difficult.

"Anyway," Angela went on, "Maisie was worried that she'd upset him. She wanted to know if he was all right."

"Seriously?" Jenny demanded, not bothering to keep the annoyance out of her voice. "She's worried whether *Colin's* all right? What about me?"

The *prima's* mouth quirked again. "I'd tell you to talk to her yourself, but I know that isn't possible. I did try to tell Maisie that he'd come here under false pretenses, but she only shrugged and said she knew that. She said she'd told him he needed to make things right with you."

"She did?" Jenny's head was swimming. That particular piece of dialogue had been missing from the explosion of memories and feelings and thoughts that had hit her. She'd seen that he'd talked with Maisie, had felt his utter disbelief when she dematerialized right in front of him, but it had all been visuals and sensations, with no real words attached.

"Yes," Angela replied. "I asked her why she thought it was so important. That is, I pointed out that Colin hadn't exactly been truthful with you, and that wasn't the best way to begin a relationship."

"That's for sure."

An awkward pause. Angela looked as if she wanted to say something reassuring but didn't know the best approach to take. They'd never been close, after all. Cousins, sure, just like they were cousins with half the population of Jerome, but that wasn't the same thing. They weren't friends in the way Angela was best buddies with that civilian, the one who used to live in Cottonwood but now had a winery in Page Springs with her new husband, or the way the *prima* was friends with Mason, Jenny's own sister-in-law.

"I don't know what to say about that," Angela continued after a noticeable hesitation. "I mean, what Colin did was crappy, no doubt about it. On the other hand, Maisie seemed to think it was very important that the two of you patch things up."

This was getting better and better. "So now she's bored with the afterlife and has decided to play matchmaker?"

A lift of the shoulders. "I think it's more than that, but when I pressed her as to why it was so important for you to be with Colin, she just shook her head and said it was, and that she knew a time when people didn't ask questions when they were being given advice from beyond."

"I wasn't aware that she was this great spirit guide." Jenny took a sip of her own neglected coffee. Actually, it hadn't cooled down that much, and sent a flood of welcome warmth down her throat and into her stomach.

"Well, she isn't. She's just a ghost who's bound here because she's afraid of what lies ahead for her.

I've tried to explain to her that there is no hell, just a new sort of life for her to experience once she lets go of this world, but she won't listen to me. Product of the Victorian age, I guess. She was a prostitute— through no fault of her own—but she thinks because she died while she was still living that life and never had a chance to repent or reform, then she's going to go straight to hell if she doesn't stay here."

Poor girl. Jenny supposed there were worse places to spend eternity than Jerome, Arizona. Even so, all the McAllister witches believed in the power of the otherworld, and the enlightenment that came with passing beyond the veil to that next place. It seemed tragic to her that Maisie wouldn't let go because of superstitions that had no place in the real world.

"But I know there isn't anything else I can say that will make a difference, so I don't bother anymore," Angela continued. "As to why she's suddenly acting like she has messages or directives from beyond, I have no idea. I'm just telling you what she said to me."

"As arguments go, this one isn't very convincing," Jenny said dryly.

"I know. But I also know that Maisie isn't a liar. She can be difficult to deal with sometimes, just the way all ghosts can be difficult. Their priorities are different from ours, and they see the world very differently from how we see it. Once you get past that, though, you can tell when something is important to them. And you being with Colin is important to Maisie, for whatever reason."

"Maybe she just thinks he's cute or something." As soon as Jenny made the remark, she wished she'd kept her mouth shut. Not because Angela suddenly looked judge-y or anything like that, but more because Colin's face appeared in Jenny's mind's eye, the laughing glint in his hazel eyes, the nice lines of his jaw, the mouth with that half-buried dimple at one corner. Strange how clear he was to her, when guys she'd spent six months or more with had now become blessedly hazy memories.

"Maybe," Angela said, her tone carefully neutral. "And maybe at some point Maisie will stop beating around the bush and will actually tell me what's going on. But I wouldn't hold my breath."

"So...what now?" Jenny couldn't believe she was asking advice of this girl who used to be her little brother's major crush, but desperation knew no shame, apparently.

The *prima*'s expression held no judgment, how-ever, only worry and possibly a little pity. "I guess that's up to you. I'm not worried that Colin Campbell is going to say anything to reveal who we are, even if he is a reporter."

"You're not?"

"No." A quick flash of a smile before she added, "Which makes me absolutely crazy in Boyd's eyes.

But I'm not as paranoid as Boyd. Anyway, I've got a feeling that everything is going to be okay."

"A psychic flash?"

"No. That's Caitlin's thing, not mine. And I'm sure if she'd seen anything, had any weird premonitions, she would have contacted me, even when she was on her honeymoon." Angela paused, fiddling with the turquoise ring she wore on her right hand. "She was very apologetic about the wedding announcement when I talked to her a few days ago. She said it was mostly Alex's idea because of his work, and that if she'd had any idea of the trouble it would cause, she would have put her foot down."

"It's okay," Jenny said wearily. The last thing she wanted was to be putting a guilt trip on her cousin over something as silly as the wedding announcement. True, it had been the thing that got Eileen Kosky's spider sense tingling, but something else just as silly could have set her off. Seeing Alex at the grocery store, or his photo on the TV station's website. Goddess only knew. Sometimes events got set in motion, and there wasn't a damn thing you could do to stop them. "Shit happens."

"That it does," Angela agreed, setting her half-drunk mug of coffee down on the cocktail table. "Well, I need to get over to Spook Hall and check on a few things for the shindig tomorrow. You going to be okay?"

"I'm fine," Jenny said, her tone stiff. Of course she was far from fine, but no need to turn this into a pity party.

Angela gave her a searching look, green eyes keen under the finely arched brows. But she only said, "I'm glad. We'll see you at Thanksgiving tomorrow," and then stood up.

Jenny rose as well so she could see the *prima* out. Once she was gone, Jenny shut the door with a weary sigh. That had gone better than she'd expected. No recriminations, no blame. Angela appeared willing to let the whole thing go.

As to why Maisie was so insistent about making sure things worked out between her and Colin, Jenny couldn't begin to guess. He was a civilian. It wasn't as if being with him would patch up a feud and break a curse, the way Angela's relationship with Connor Wilcox had. Colin was just an ordinary enough man, and Jenny knew she was a very ordinary witch. A kind of sub-par one, when you got right down to it. So what was so earth-shakingly important about making sure she had her own happy ending—assuming she could even find it in herself to forgive Colin?

Right then, she wasn't feeling very forgiving.

Thanksgiving might have been a national holiday, but it wasn't a given that Colin would have the day off. Someone had to be on shift in case anything catastrophic happened. This year, however, Ryan was the one who got the short straw and had to watch the store.

"I hate turkey anyway," he announced, fooling absolutely no one. "And I can watch the games on the break room TV."

Well, that part was probably true. They had the full cable package in there, mostly to keep an eye on any breaking national news. Still, unlimited football didn't seem like a fair tradeoff when it came to spending time with your family. Ryan was divorced, true, but he had a large extended family here in Tucson, and would probably be missing out on homemade tamales in addition to the turkey he supposedly scorned.

As Colin headed toward Phoenix on Thanksgiving morning, he couldn't help wondering if maybe he should have volunteered to take on holiday duty. His parents and sister would have been disappointed, but something about having to work on Thanksgiving appealed to him, as if by depriving himself he could somehow do penance for what he'd put Jenny McAllister through.

Which, he knew, wasn't very logical. Problem was, a lot of feelings didn't have to be logical.

He'd brought his overnight bag with him, since his mother always insisted on him staying after Thanksgiving dinner. "Too many drunks on the road," she said, which wasn't entirely inaccurate. She didn't bother to mention that she wanted to make sure her son wasn't one of those drunks. The wine did tend to flow freely at the Campbell holiday get-togethers.

This year would be small, though, just his parents and his sister, since his Aunt Lynne and Uncle Rob were cruising in the Mediterranean, and their three kids had conveniently scattered to visit friends. Just as well, because Colin didn't think he could put up with a crowd this year. It was bad enough that he had to socialize at all. His mother was sure to notice that something was wrong—and Kate, too. She'd always been a bit too perceptive for Colin's comfort.

Too late to back out now, so he'd just have to make the best of it, and try very hard not to think about Jenny McAllister and what she must be doing about now. Did they have an early Thanksgiving dinner, or did they wait until it was dark to sit down and eat? And was it a huge clan gathering sort of thing, or did the individual families have their separate dinners in their own homes?

You might as well stop wondering, he told himself as he pulled into the driveway of the big two-story home his parents owned in Tempe. *Because you're never going to be able to find out for yourself.*

He dismissed that self-pitying thought as best he could while he got his bag out of the trunk and

headed up to the front door. It was a nice neighborhood, but his parents always made sure to keep
the house locked up, and he didn't have a key. Why
would he? This wasn't the place where he'd grown
up, just a house that his parents had bought after
relocating to the Phoenix area.

After he rang the doorbell, he waited and took
a quick look around the covered walkway. A fall
wreath hung on the front door, and chrysanthe-
mums in autumn hues were clustered to either side.
His mother's handiwork, trying to make it look as if
they were enjoying a traditional Thanksgiving, even
though temperatures had hit the mid-eighties today.
Colin was wearing a short-sleeved polo shirt. Not
exactly Thanksgiving attire.

It wasn't his mother who opened the door, but
his father, also wearing a polo shirt, although one in
a warm rusty-red shade that Colin knew his mother
had chosen because it looked vaguely autumnal.
"Come on in," Liam Campbell said.

Colin smiled and went inside, glad that it was his
father who'd first greeted him. That would give him
a little more time to get his bearings. Liam, an engi-
neer, was probably the last person to start quizzing
his son as to how he was feeling. No, he'd offer him a
beer and ask if he'd been following the game on the
radio on the way over, and that would be it.

They headed into the house, passing the dining room on the way to the family room, where, as he'd anticipated, the football game was blaring from the sixty-inch TV. Kate's husband Jeff was in there already, holding a bottle of Heineken and staring intently at the television.

"Hey," he said absently, waving with his bottle.

Colin nodded in reply but headed on toward the kitchen, wondering as he did so how long that particular relationship was going to last. Not that he wished divorce on anyone, but he couldn't help thinking that his little sister could have done a lot better. She was bright and bubbly and pretty, and Jeff had always seemed like sort of a lump.

Oh, well. Colin had enough romantic woes to deal with at the moment. He certainly didn't need to be borrowing any for his sister.

Both she and his mother were in the kitchen. Naturally. Liam Campbell was not the sort to help out with the cooking, although he did unbend enough to load the dishwasher on occasion. And Jeff took his cue from his father-in-law, only too glad to exploit that particular gender gap.

Vowing to be nothing like either of them, Colin said, "Need any help with anything?"

His mother turned from the sink, where she'd been peeling potatoes. Her hazel eyes, so like Colin's own, glinted with laughter as she asked the standard question. "How are you at potatoes?"

"Awesome," he replied, moving toward the sink. They shared this same exchange almost every year, although sometimes he ended up slicing yams instead of peeling potatoes.

She smiled and handed over the potato peeler, even as Kate, who was standing at the kitchen island and setting rolls on a cookie sheet, frowned slightly and said, "Hey, what's going on with you?"

"What do you mean, 'what's going on' with me?" he asked. "Don't I always offer to peel the potatoes?"

"That's not what I meant." Kate finished with the last of the rolls and crossed her arms as she surveyed him with a critical eye. "You look like crap."

"Thanks, sis."

Lynda Campbell paused in front of the refrigerator and glanced back at her son. "Well, I think 'crap' might be a little harsh, but you do look tired, Colin."

"Long hours lately," he replied as he turned on the water and started in on the remainder of the potatoes.

"'Long hours,' my butt," Kate said. "You live for that kind of thing. I smell girl trouble."

"I'm not even dating anyone," he protested. Well, that was true enough, now that Jenny had dumped him like a bag of dog shit. Actually, that simile was more apt than he wanted to admit. He was dog shit for lying to her the way he had.

"Uh-huh."

"Children," Lynda said mildly. That was all she had to say. When she sounded all calm and placid like that, you knew you had to watch out. Colin's mother was not the sort to lose her temper, but neither was she kind of person who would allow you to mess with her Thanksgiving.

Kate subsided, but, judging by the narrow-eyed look she was giving him, Colin knew that she wasn't buying his story. Sooner or later she'd corner him and get the truth out of him. She always had been good at that kind of thing.

Well, fine. As long as he could make his confession while everyone else was passed out in front of the TV in a turkey and pie coma.

After that, Lynda told Colin about her sister's cruise, during which one-sided conversation he nodded at the right intervals but didn't say much. It felt good to stand there and peel potatoes and feel vaguely useful. And then of course, some time afterward, things in the kitchen devolved into the usual last-minute chaos involved in getting any sort of elaborate meal together—Liam was rousted to get the turkey out of the oven, since it was too heavy for Lynda to manage, and Kate took over the potatoes, since she announced that she didn't trust Colin to get the proportions of milk and butter right. And Lynda kept carrying serving bowls and trays out to the dining room—cranberry sauce and stuffing and sweet potatoes and green bean casserole and ambrosia salad and a few other things Colin soon lost track of. Good thing the dining room here was so large, and the table had extra leaves put in it, or there would have been no way all of that stuff would ever fit. As it was, he couldn't help wondering if his mother had forgotten that it was only the five of them this year.

Through it all, Jeff didn't lift a finger to help. Once all the food was on the table, though, he pried himself out of his recliner with some reluctance, then ambled into the dining room and took a seat, eyeing the bounty before him with anticipation all over his meaty face.

Asshole, Colin thought. And when had he thickened up like that? He'd always been a big guy, had played football in high school and college, but the muscle seemed as if it was rapidly turning to fat. He looked as if he would squash Kate if he rolled over the wrong way in bed.

There was a mental image Colin really didn't need. He waited as his father spoke a brief prayer—and wondered if the McAllister witches offered up any kind of grace before they sat down to their own Thanksgiving meal—and then was quiet as the food was passed around the table.

"Everything looks great, Mom," Colin said, since he knew Jeff didn't possess the social skills to offer even that rudimentary a compliment.

"Thanks, sweetie," she replied, her cheeks pink. But maybe the flush was a result of her exertions in the kitchen.

"And the table is beautiful," Kate added. "You always make everything look so perfect."

Which was true. Lynda Campbell could set a table that would make Martha Stewart jealous. But his mother had always taken pride in her house. She'd worked before he and Kate were born, but after that she'd been a stay-at-home mom for many years. Now she had a part-time job at the local library, although Colin knew that was more for her to have something to help keep her busy rather than because she needed to work. His father had always possessed a knack for holding down well-paying jobs, even through recessions and reductions in the work force.

Too bad he didn't pass that knack along to me, Colin thought with a mental grimace. But then, whose fault was that? He'd known journalism would be tough, but he'd stuck with it anyway. If he really wanted to, he could've tried for a cushy corporate communications job like the one he'd lied about to Jenny McAllister.

And there was someone he really didn't want to be thinking about. He did his best to concentrate on the conversation, which was mainly Kate trying to convince their parents to go on a cruise the way Lynda's sister and brother-in-law had. True, Colin knew his parents were not big on traveling, but even so, he wasn't sure a cruise was the best way to entice them out of the house, not with so many cruise ships turning into modern-day vomitoriums, thanks to fun things like the norovirus and good old-fashioned food poisoning.

He knew better than to bring up food poisoning during Thanksgiving dinner, though, and so mostly didn't say much at all, passing food when asked and offering a tidbit here and there when asked about the Cardinals' chances of making it to the playoffs this year. Neither Liam nor Jeff seemed to notice anything off about his replies, although Kate kept giving him those sidelong glances when she thought no one else was looking. His mother also seemed more or less oblivious, probably because she was focused on making sure that everyone at the table had enough to feed a small village in Africa.

Afterward, Colin jumped up to help clear the table before his mother could even begin to move. She made a small protest, but he just shook his head and said, "It's the least I could do. You just relax, Mom."

A grateful smile was her only answer. Both Liam and Jeff got seconds on pie but carried it out to the family room, clearly hoping to catch the last bit of the game.

Kate followed Colin into the kitchen, her hands also filled with dirty dishes. He knew that wasn't her only reason for being there, though. After she'd set down her burden, she turned toward him, hands on her hips. "Okay, spill."

"There's nothing to spill," he said calmly as he began running the hot water and rinsing off plates. Thank God that his mother had finally relented a few years ago and agreed with Colin that her precious china could survive a bout in the dishwasher, as long as he promised not to use the heat dry setting.

"Uh-huh." Kate leaned up against the counter, one brow tilted at an ironic angle. "I haven't seen you look this emo since you and Shannon first split up. So what happened? I didn't think you were seeing anyone."

Damn it. He was feeling full and tired after the big meal, even though he hadn't drunk all that much, just two glasses of wine. But he knew his sister would keep pecking at him, especially since she knew she had a captive audience. Neither Liam nor Jeff would be coming in the kitchen anytime soon, not when they had pumpkin pie to keep them occupied, and Lynda had probably followed them into the family room to keep up appearances as hostess, even though Colin knew his mother had absolutely no interest in the outcome of the football game.

"I'm not seeing anyone," he said evenly.

Another of those eloquently lifted eyebrows.

"All right," Colin told her. "I met someone, and she's pretty amazing. But I screwed it up before we could really even get started."

"Screwed it up how?"

He hesitated. The best thing to do would at least attempt to dodge the question. On the other hand, he was getting tired of not being able to talk to anyone about Jenny McAllister. Colin knew his sister would keep anything he told her in confidence. She'd never been the kind of girl to gossip, knew how to be discreet when the situation warranted it. That quality was one of the many things he loved about her.

Problem was, he didn't know if she would believe him even if he told her the truth.

"I lied to her."

"Ouch. What about?"

"What I do for a living."

A flicker of confusion passed over Kate's features. "Since when are you ashamed of being a reporter?"

"No, that's not why. It's—" He flailed for a few seconds, not sure of the best way to explain. "That is, I knew of this girl because I covered her sister's murder."

"Holy shit." His sister's hazel eyes narrowed, and she gave a small nod, as if confirming something to herself. "The Escobar case?"

"Yeah, that one." Colin moved on from rinsing the plates to the silverware, carefully segregating the sterling pieces from the stainless serving items so they wouldn't get spots. "It was dumb of me. I should have told her. But I could tell she was still having a rough time—"

"I'd think so." Kate shuddered, then crossed her arms as if to ward off a sudden chill. Suddenly, she looked very small and thin, and Colin thought again of what in the world he would have done if it had been his sister who'd been Matías Escobar's victim. "Still, I don't see why you had to lie. It might have been awkward at first, but—"

"Well, there was also how I met her."

"What, were you stalking her?"

Colin let out a humorless chuckle. "No, but I might have been crashing her cousin's wedding."

"Um…what?"

"You heard me. Not one of my prouder moments. But I was given a tip, and I wanted to investigate it. Meeting Jenny was sort of an accident. That is, I saw her at Escobar's sentencing, but I would never have approached her then."

"But it was okay when you were gate-crashing a wedding?"

He wanted to flinch at the skepticism in his sister's voice. "Well, I don't know about 'okay,' but the circumstances were completely different."

"So you hit it off."

"You could say that." No way was he going to tell his sister that he'd had a one-night stand with Jenny McAllister. Besides, you couldn't really call it a one-night stand when the two of them had gotten together the next day, and then again the following weekend.

"But she found out eventually."

"Um, yeah. I went to see her last weekend, and it just sort of…came out." Well, that was one way of putting it.

Kate seemed to sense he was leaving something out of the narrative. "How'd she find out? Did you finally confess all, or were you talking in your sleep again?"

He shot her a pained look. Unfortunately, he knew all the pieces weren't going to line up unless he told his sister of his suspicions about the McAllister family and the very real evidence of Jenny's psychic powers—or whatever they were.

Not to mention his conversation with the ghost of a dead prostitute.

"This is probably going to sound crazy—"

"Try me."

For a long moment, he hesitated, and only continued to rinse off serving utensils and flatware and put them in the dishwasher. How in the world was he supposed to broach that particular subject? *Oh, I think the girl who dumped me might just be a witch?*

Right.

Kate tapped her fingers on the granite countertop. From her posture, it seemed fairly clear that she was fighting the impulse to tell him to spit it out. But she also appeared to understand that something was going on here that went way beyond a simple breakup. She waited quietly, letting him gather his thoughts.

At last he said, "In general, you'd call me a sensible person, right?"

"Well, yeah, except when you're crashing weddings, apparently."

He didn't bother to respond to her comment. It would have been nice to chalk that particular indiscretion up to temporary insanity, but he knew it had really been his innate curiosity getting the better of him. "Let's just say this girl—and her family—are unusual."

Kate's neatly arched brows pulled together. "Like, former hippie kind of unusual, or Texas Chainsaw Massacre kind of unusual?"

"Neither, but probably closer to the hippie thing." He let out a breath, then said, "I think they might be witches."

She didn't blink. "I seem to recall you saying more or less the same thing about Shannon."

"Not that kind of witch. I mean, really... witches."

A long, long pause. Kate flicked a lock of shiny brown hair over one shoulder and then sent a glance toward the kitchen door, as if attempting to reassure herself that no one was going to barge in and hear what they were saying. "Are you sure you haven't been working too hard? Those stupid pamphlets of yours—"

"This has nothing to do with any of that." He hesitated, stalling for time as he rinsed off the last of the serving pieces, then laid it down on the top rack before closing the dishwasher door. "Let's just say I overheard a couple of things that didn't sound right, and I did some digging."

"And?"

"Well, what I found isn't anything that could be proved in a court of law, but it did seem to indicate that there's something a little off about the McAllisters."

"That's her family?"

"Yes. They live up in Jerome. Anyway, add that to Jenny suddenly picking things out of my mind, things she couldn't have known any other way, and that conversation with the ghost—"

"Whoa, whoa." Kate held up her hands. "Back up a little. A ghost?"

Colin started to run a hand through his hair, then remembered it was damp from washing dishes and stopped himself at the last minute. "She didn't look like a ghost. She looked like a reenactor or something. Although I doubt most reenactors can disappear into thin air right under your nose the way she did."

"You saw that."

It wasn't a question, but Colin answered anyway. "Oh, yeah. I saw it. I wish I hadn't. Up until that moment, all I had was suspicions. But you can't have an experience like that and not begin to think that there are more things in heaven and earth, Horatio. You know what I mean?"

Beneath her carefully applied makeup, Kate looked a little pale. She swallowed, but she didn't glance away from him. He loved that about her. He'd just said something that must have seriously shaken up her world view, but she wasn't arguing with him or trying to tell him he must have just thought he saw a woman disappear.

"Yeah," she said after a moment. "I guess I know what you mean." Another pause, and then she added, "So the girl you were seeing had some kind of vision and saw that you hadn't told her the truth about being a reporter?"

"More or less." Colin couldn't say much more than that, because he still didn't know exactly what had happened, just that it had led to Jenny McAllister throwing him out of her life. "Like I said, I know it all sounds crazy. And I keep having this little voice in the back of my head tell me that I'm crazy, that I'm putting two and two together and getting five because I don't want to admit that I did this to myself. Again, I know what I saw, but that doesn't mean I have any concrete evidence about the McAllisters. Not really."

Kate was silent for a moment, clearly going over what he'd just told her. "There's no one else who might know anything about the McAllisters? You said the wedding was for Jenny's cousin. Who was she marrying? You'd think her fiancé must know something."

A good suggestion, but Colin had a feeling that the de la Pazes were also not exactly what they appeared to be. They'd close ranks the second he came poking around. Same for the Wilcoxes. What he needed was someone who'd been involved in that world, but who was now no longer inside it. Someone who might have a grudge....

Of course. He knew exactly who he needed to talk to.

"What is it?" Kate asked. "You suddenly lit up like a Christmas tree."

"You just gave me a great idea. And it's even better, because I'm staying over tonight and won't have to drive as far."

The look of mystification on Kate's face only deepened. "Go where?"

"The Arizona State Prison in Lewis."

CHAPTER FIFTEEN

JENNY KEPT TRYING TO TELL HERSELF THIS WASN'T SO BAD. She sat with her parents and with Adam and Mason at a table off to one side of the crowded hall. Maybe she'd gotten the side-eye from a couple of clan members as she'd entered the building, but no one had said anything to her directly. For all she knew, Angela had decreed that everyone should leave her alone. In general, the *prima* tried not to interfere too much in the goings-on of the clan, but she also didn't like to see people get bullied. If this mess with Colin had blown up into a full-on catastrophe, that would have been one thing, but so far the only real casualty appeared to be Jenny's heart.

At least her parents had had the foresight to choose someplace to sit that wasn't out front and center. This way she could face away from most of the hubbub, and pretend to be interested in Mason and Adam's conversation about the house he was restoring, and the plans she was making for her graduation in late May. It had taken a little longer than she'd planned, but she'd be getting her master's degree in education then.

And after that, I'm sure she'll take over the world, Jenny thought, knowing her inner voice sounded especially cranky right then. No, that was just sour grapes. Mason had worked hard for her degree, and Jenny wished her every success. But seeing her brother and his wife together and happy only made Jenny think about what a loser she was. Almost thirty, no husband, not even a steady boyfriend, and a make-work job that existed basically to justify her living in the flat.

She didn't even bother to point out to herself that a good number of the McAllisters living in Jerome didn't have what anyone could call true vocations. They ran shops or restaurants, or lived off the stipend they were sent every month. Nothing wrong with being a slacker in Jerome, she supposed. But Mason seemed so driven, and Adam so happy in his fledgling carpentry career, that Jenny couldn't help feeling even more dissatisfied with herself than she'd been when she woke up this morning.

Well, she'd put in her time, shown her face. Maybe she should have walked into Spook Hall with a big letter "A" embroidered on the front of her sweater. Boyd probably would have liked that; he was one of the people who kept giving her the stink-eye, even though he sat tables away.

Luckily, her own Aunt Tricia and Allegra Moss appeared serene and unconcerned, and Angela, seated with her family at the main table at the front of the hall, was laughing and leaning close to Connor, stealing a quick kiss while the twins were occupied with smearing mashed potatoes all over their faces. Watching them, Jenny couldn't help but experience a swift, sharp pang of jealousy, followed by a deep, deep ache somewhere in the pit of her stomach. She was still angry at him, but she wanted Colin with her right then, wanted him to sit close enough so he could push her hair aside and give her a swift, secret kiss on the neck before anyone noticed.

She removed her napkin from her lap and set it down on the table, then pushed back her chair. At once, her mother gave her a startled glance. "You're going? But they haven't even served dessert yet."

A lift of her shoulders, and Jenny replied, as carelessly as she could, "You know I don't like pie. Anyway, I have a headache from all this noise." She summoned a smile, one she knew probably wasn't fooling anyone. "You all have a nice night."

Then she walked away before anyone could offer a protest. Adam and Mason hadn't even looked startled—they knew just as well as she did why she wanted to leave early—but the look of disappointment on her father's face did sting Jenny a little. Well, he should be used by now to having a total disaster of a daughter.

By then it was almost five, and the short, sharp dusk of a mountain evening had begun to fall. It was only a walk of a few blocks from Spook Hall to her flat, but something about the dim purple shading of the streets around her made Jenny shiver and wish that she'd brought something warmer to wear than the wool shawl she'd wrapped around herself. Maybe it was just that the town was so quiet, the streets empty of tourists, nearly everyone else inside the hall, enjoying their Thanksgiving dinner.

But then she saw it up on Main Street—a shadowy figure moving quickly, a streetlight catching a shimmer of dark golden hair. At first Jenny thought perhaps she was seeing the mythical Maisie, but that had to be wrong. In the flash she'd caught from Colin's thoughts, the long-dead young woman's hair was a pale, almost flaxen, blonde, not the warm honey color Jenny had just seen. Her own hair was almost that shade. The only other person in town with hair that color had been Roslyn.

Roslyn. Jenny stopped dead for a moment, and then began to run, a wild impulse driving her up the street to chase after the specter she'd just seen. When she reached Main Street, however, it was utterly deserted, nothing moving except some fallen leaves on the sidewalk, propelled by a cold November wind.

Even knowing she must look like a madwoman, she couldn't keep herself from turning from side to side, staring in every direction, certain she must be able to see something of the strange vision that had brought her running up here. But there was nothing, only the empty street, and the dry, skittering sound of dead leaves on cement.

She stood there, panting in the cold, dry air. Tears stung at her eyes, and she blinked them away.

She's dead, she told herself. *She's gone. She's not like Maisie. She's not here.*

And then, fighting the lump in her throat and the ache in her breast, Jenny began to walk home.

The drive out to Lewis only took about forty-five minutes. Traffic was light, most everyone already where they planned to be for the long holiday weekend.

His parents—especially his mother—hadn't been happy when he announced that he needed to make a trip for work today.

"On a holiday?" Lynda asked, but Colin only shrugged.

"Yesterday was the holiday. And the news doesn't stop just because it's Thanksgiving."

She hadn't protested after that, although the disappointment remained in her eyes. Colin was just relieved that he'd actually managed to wrangle an interview with the prisoner at such short notice. But after he'd rattled off his credentials and said he was doing a follow-up article on the Escobar case, he'd been given an appointment.

This could all be a wild goose chase. But better to try than sit around eating turkey sandwiches and pretending to be interested in one of those interminable football games his father loved to watch. Kate and Jeff-the-Lump had headed off to their condo in Peoria the night before—funny how it was okay for Jeff to drive on Thanksgiving, but not for Colin to do the same thing—and it would have been a quiet day anyway.

Liam had actually seemed proud that his son had something work-related to do the day after Thanksgiving. They didn't talk much, but Colin knew his father still secretly hoped he would pull some latter-day Woodward and Bernstein maneuver, or do some kind of meaty investigative journalism of the type that had been publicized in *Spotlight*.

Well, if he'd been harder-hearted, he could have tried to expose the McAllister witches, but Colin didn't have that in him. Whatever strange talents and abilities they might possess, they just seemed like a bunch of people who were trying to live their lives without bothering anyone else. Who was he to go messing around with that?

And this trip…this was only to satisfy his own curiosity, nothing more. He knew what he'd seen and experienced, but he wanted outside corroboration.

Even if said corroboration came from a convicted rapist and accessory to murder.

Colin had visited prisons enough times that he knew the drill by now. Walk through the metal detector, get patted down. Tell the guard on duty who he was there to see.

"Tomas Aguirre, got it." The guard made a notation on the clipboard he carried. "He's on his way down to the visitation room."

At that comment, Colin let himself relax slightly. He'd put in the request, but he couldn't make Tomas show up. All he could do was hope that the prisoner might be sufficiently bored by life behind bars that he'd come to talk to someone he'd never heard of just because he had nothing better to do.

As soon as Kate's offhand suggestion had started ideas pinging around in his head, Colin had first thought of going to talk to Matías Escobar. He was the one Alex Trujillo had blasted with that blue-white light, after all; it made sense that Matías must have some kind of powers as well. There'd been all kinds of ritualistic crap in the apartment the trio had used to torture the girls they'd kidnapped. But then

Colin realized that Escobar would most likely not be very cooperative. He'd been cocky to the end, even when the judge had pronounced a life sentence and he'd been hauled out of the courtroom in manacles.

But Jorge and Tomas—

Jorge got ruled out as soon as Colin discovered he was locked up in Safford, which was halfway across the state. Whereas Lewis, where Tomas had been incarcerated, was an easy drive from Phoenix. And it didn't seem to matter that much which of the two Aguirres Colin ended up talking to. They'd been willing accessories, but clearly under Escobar's thumb.

The one thing Colin hadn't been able to figure out was why they'd allowed themselves to be captured if they actually did possess any kind of supernatural powers. True, Alex Trujillo seemed to have done something to take out their leader, but Jorge and Tomas should have been able to get away. And if not in the parking lot where Eileen Kosky had witnessed the confrontation, then after they'd been locked up. You'd think a couple of warlocks could manage a spectacular jail break.

Well, he supposed he'd find out soon enough. He sat down on the hard metal chair, which was bolted to the floor, and tried to tune out the conversations around him, the whine of a toddler with his mother a few yards away, the hiccupy crying of a fussy baby held by a tired-looking young woman on the other side of the room.

Happy Thanksgiving, Colin thought, feeling just about as tired as that woman looked.

A door on the other side of the glass partition opened, and a young Hispanic man entered the small cubicle with its single chair. His black hair was pulled sharply back from his face and into a ponytail, when it had been cut quite short at the time of his trial, but Colin still recognized him. He was a good-looking man, but not as handsome as his cousin Matías.

"Hello, Tomas," he said.

Tomas Aguirre scowled as he stared at Colin through the glass. "Who the fuck are you?"

"Colin Campbell, *Tucson Daily Sun.* I thought the guards would have given you that information."

The frown only deepened. "They did, but I thought someone was messing with me. I thought—" He broke off then, as if realizing what he'd been about to say might only get him into trouble.

"Thought what?" Colin asked. "That I might have been someone else, and was only pretending to be a reporter? You expecting someone to break you out?"

"You're crazy, man."

"What, none of your witch friends interested in seeing you a free man?"

At that question, shock flared in Tomas' black eyes. Then he seemed to gather himself, and crossed his arms as he gave Colin a flat stare. "I don't know what the hell you're talking about, *pendejo*."

Colin ignored the insult. Lord knows he'd been called worse over the years. "You don't? Then do you want to explain what eyewitnesses described as a 'flash of blue-white light' in the parking lot of the Dillard's at the Paradise Valley Mall? It seems to have been what took out your buddy Escobar."

The frown returned, digging a deep furrow into the space between Tomas Aguirre's brows. He darted a quick glance left to right, but the people to either side of them were engaged in their own discussions, the woman with the toddler begging the man behind the glass to ask "Andy"—whoever that was—to make sure the problem was handled, while on Colin's right was a hard-faced man apparently attempting to coax the inmate on the other side of the glass to tell him where the "stuff" was. No one was listening to Colin and Tomas's conversation.

Again the inmate said, "I don't know what you're talking about."

But there was a hint of confusion in his expression, as if he was trying to figure out how Colin could possibly have figured out that there was more to Tomas Aguirre—and his crimes—than met the eye. Confusion, and possibly worry.

Good. Colin leaned back slightly in his chair, hoping he looked unruffled and as if he had all the time in the world. Which he sort of did; he wasn't needed back at work until Monday. But Aguirre didn't need to know that. "I'm just curious," Colin said. "You'd think someone with those kind of powers wouldn't stay behind bars for very long. From what I've been able to discover, though, it seems as if you and your cousin and even Matías Escobar have all been model prisoners. What's up—someone tell you to keep quiet? What else could possibly happen to you that hasn't already?"

Tomas Aguirre's mouth twisted. Not in anger, but almost as if at some inner torment, as though he was remembering something too painful to bring up. "You don't know what you're talking about."

Interesting. Similar to his former protests, but not really the same. "So enlighten me."

Once again the other man shot a quick glance from side to side. Since their companions in the visitation room were clearly occupied with their own problems, it didn't seem likely that they'd pay any attention to what he or Colin were saying. "What do you know?"

"I know there's something off about the McAllister family, and probably the Wilcoxes and the de la Pazes as well."

"'Off'?" A bitter chuckle. "You don't know, man."

"So tell me. Or are you scared they're going to still do something to you?"

At that question, Aguirre looked as if he wanted to spit on the floor. He collected himself, though, and shook his head. "Nah. They already done their worst."

"By putting you in here?"

Tomas gave the glass partition separating them a scornful glance. "This place? This ain't nothing compared to what they done."

Colin tried to think of what would be worse than prison and came up short. Well, hanging, probably, but even the great state of Arizona didn't dispose of its death row inmates that way anymore. Besides, Tomas Aguirre wasn't on death row. He'd been an accessory to a capital crime, which meant he'd be in here for a long, long time, but he still could be looking at parole in another twenty-five years or so. He wouldn't be young when he got out, true. But he also wouldn't be the first person to start his life over at fifty.

"So what did they do?"

Another long silence, one in which Aguirre seemed absorbed in staring down at his hands, which had the familiar bluish-black prison tattoos across the knuckles. It also looked as if he had far more complex tattoos on his forearms, strange symbols that Colin didn't recognize, although he couldn't see much of them because of the half-rolled-up sleeves of Tomas's blue denim prison shirt.

Then, almost in a whisper, "They took it away."

"Who took what away?"

True hatred flared in Aguirre's dark eyes. "The *prima* and the *primus*. Stinking McAllister witch and her Wilcox husband."

Prima? The only other times Colin had heard that word used was to refer to either a ballerina or an opera singer, and he had a feeling Tomas wasn't talking about either one of those. More importantly, though, he'd called a McAllister woman a witch. He might have been speaking metaphorically, but Colin didn't think so.

"So what did this McAllister witch and her husband do?"

"Took our powers away—Matías and Jorge and me. Made us into a bunch of civilians."

Civilians. That was it, the slip of the tongue that Jenny had self-corrected on more than one occasion. Civilians must be people without magical powers.

Muggles, Colin couldn't help thinking, and forced himself to keep from smiling. Not that any of the people he'd met in Jerome bore much resemblance to the witches and wizards of J.K. Rowling's world.

"They can do that?" he asked.

Tomas Aguirre shrugged. It was a careless gesture, but Colin thought he could see the pain beneath it, could tell that the other man was trying to appear dismissive because he didn't want to admit how much the loss of his magical talents had hurt him. "Looks that way, doesn't it? I never heard of it before, but then, a *prima* and a *primus* have never been united before. They got ways of using their powers that go way beyond what regular witches and warlocks can do."

And the *primus* was the McAllister witch's husband. No first names, but that wasn't as important to Colin right then as the mere fact that Tomas Aguirre had basically admitted witches and warlocks were real, and that he was one of them. Or at least he used to be.

"Are there a lot of you?"

Another shrug. "Some. Guess it depends on what you mean by 'a lot.' It runs in families. They all got their territories. Mostly they try to keep quiet about who they are."

No kidding. Colin had already known that, but it didn't hurt to get some corroborating information from an insider. "So," he said, "you're with the de la Paz clan?"

Once again Aguirre looked as if he wanted to spit. "Hell, no. I'm not one of them. I'm with the Santiagos."

"They're also here in Arizona?" It sounded to Colin as if witches were kind of thick on the ground, actually.

"No. California." He sat up straighter in his chair and gave Colin a menacing look. "And I wouldn't go poking around there, if I were you. The de la Pazes, they're soft, but old man Santiago would blast the crap out of you and bury you in an unmarked grave if he caught a reporter sniffing into his business."

"Good to know," Colin replied, trying to sound as casual as possible, even though Tomas's words had sent a shiver down his back. "But thanks, I've got my hands full here in Arizona."

"Hmm." An eyebrow lift, and Aguirre added, "What, you going to write about this, put it in the paper? Ain't nobody gonna believe a word of it."

Of that, Colin had little doubt. Luckily, his goal here wasn't to write an exposé, but to get outside evidence that the McAllisters truly were a family of witches. So far, he'd say he'd been successful. Yes, one could argue that Tomas was feeding him a line of bull, but Colin didn't think so. He'd spent a lot of years interviewing people, learning how to interpret their tells, the small twitches and reactions that they probably didn't even realize they were making. But they might as well have been waving semaphore flags for all they good they did at hiding what they were thinking or feeling. Jenny was better at hiding her feelings than most people he'd met, but Tomas didn't even seem to be trying.

"Probably not," Colin agreed. "But I guess that's between me and my editor." He paused, wondering whether he should ask the question. It would be rather like rubbing salt in an open wound. Then again, what consideration did Tomas Aguirre really deserve? He'd helped his cousins kidnap two girls and murder one of them. As far as Colin was concerned, the man sitting behind the glass partition didn't deserve squat. "So...what was your talent?"

The smallest of flinches at the word "was." Colin made sure to look for it, and allowed himself some small satisfaction that he'd managed to get in that verbal dart.

But then Tomas lifted his shoulders, affecting a nonchalance he probably wasn't actually feeling. "I could find people. Witch-kind, that is."

"What...you could sniff them out like a bloodhound or something?"

"Or something." Aguirre shifted on his chair once again, running a hand over his hair so he could smooth back a stray piece that had come loose from its ponytail. "I mean, it started out as just finding stuff people had lost. It's kind of a common talent."

"So they're not all unique? Your gifts, I mean."

"No. There are healers and weather-workers and people who can find things, or people who can see the future. That kind of shit. But then there are people like that *pendejo* Alex Trujillo. Ain't nobody ever heard of a talent like his before, at least as far as I can tell."

Fascinating. Colin wished he could explore that side of things more, ask how prevalent psychic powers were among witch-kind, as Tomas had referred to them. But he didn't want to get too specific, because he didn't know how much the warlock sitting in front of him knew about Roslyn's family. After all, they'd held her for almost a week. They could have gotten her to talk.

He decided he'd better leave that question aside for now. "You said your powers started out as just finding objects. When did you start being able use it to locate other witches?"

Tomas scratched the side of his nose. "Well, we can always tell when we're around other witches if we get close enough. Like, within a few yards, I guess. But it started to be more than that for me when I was in high school. I could tell when witch-folk were within almost a mile radius of me. So that's how I was able to find the girls."

"Danica Wilcox and Caitlin and Roslyn McAllister."

Was that a flicker of remorse in Aguirre's eyes? Maybe. Colin wouldn't allow himself to feel sorry for the guy, though.

"Yeah, them. Matías wanted me to find some witches who weren't part of the de la Paz clan."

Colin didn't bother to ask why. If you were going to use young witches to power your ritualistic spells, best not to kidnap them from the clan whose territory you were currently occupying. He did find himself compelled to say, "And you didn't care about what he wanted them for?"

This time Tomas scowled again. "He said he just wanted their blood. Jorge and I didn't know that much about the kinds of spells he planned to use. We didn't think—"

"You didn't think he was going to murder them?"

"Not at first. See, that was why we needed three of them. Just a little from each one, each day. But then the redhead got away, and we were left with only two, and Matías wasn't going to let that stop him."

No, obviously not. Everything Colin had learned about Matías Escobar during the course of his investigations had shown that the warlock was a very driven man. What no one had been able to adequately explain was why he'd been so driven, what he'd hoped to accomplish by murdering Roslyn McAllister. The D.A. had presented the case as pure ritual murder, with no other real motive, but now Colin had to wonder.

"What was the point of the spells?"

At that question, Aguirre's lips pressed together, and once again he looked down at the tats on the back of his hands. "You don't need to know that. He didn't get what he wanted. Fucking Trujillo saw to that."

So many pieces, and not many of them made that much sense. There had been a girl in the parking lot with Matías, according to Eileen Kosky. Had he been trying to kidnap someone else so he could accomplish whatever he was attempting with those dark spells?

"Look, man," Tomas Aguirre went on. "We didn't mean for it to happen, Jorge and me. But Matías kept using Roslyn instead of Danica, and I figured out he wanted to keep Danica for himself, didn't want to hurt her *too* bad."

"So he killed Roslyn instead."

Was that real grief behind Aguirre's eyes? They did look a little too bright. His jaw went tense as he swallowed. "Yeah, he killed her. Stupid fucking waste. She didn't deserve that."

No, she didn't. And her family didn't deserve to be left behind to mourn her. Colin thought of the grief Jenny tried so hard to hide, the way she somehow seemed to blame herself, even though there was certainly nothing she could have done to prevent her sister's murder.

Voice hard, Colin said, "And you didn't do anything to stop him."

This time, Tomas didn't look away. His eyes looked like scorched black holes in his face. "No, I didn't. You know why? Because Matías could make you do anything he wanted. That was his power. He could make Danica think she wanted to be with him, and he could make me and Jorge hang around and help him, because we had talents he could use. Stop him? There's a joke."

"Why didn't you tell anyone that? It might have reduced your sentence."

"Who would have believed me?" The warlock straightened in his chair, and, just for a moment, Colin could see the man he might have been, if he hadn't fallen in with Matías Escobar. "Anyway, we don't rat out our fellow witches. Ever."

"But you're talking to me now."

"I'm talking to you. One person. I'm not saying anything that's going to be a matter of public record. Or is it?"

For a long moment, Colin didn't reply. He met Tomas Aguirre's defiant but worried gaze, then shook his head and said, "No. This conversation is just between you and me."

Because, as Tomas had just said, who would believe him?

CHAPTER SIXTEEN

Busy was good. Busy kept Jenny from thinking that she might be going crazy.

As predicted, the tourists had swept into Jerome the day after Thanksgiving, filling the shops and restaurants and bars, bringing the traffic on Main Street to even more of a crawl than it already was on non-holiday weekends. Jenny worked with only half her mind on what she was doing, answering questions by rote, directing people up the street to the restaurants or other shops they were looking for. Somewhat to her surprise, considering that most of her customers appeared to be casual browsers, she did sell one of Connor's paintings to a well-dressed couple from Scottsdale. The husband handed over his black American Express card and didn't even blink at the five-figure price after sales tax.

There were days when Jenny would have closed up shop after that kind of a sale, since the gallery's cut of the sales price was substantial, but she knew she couldn't get away with that kind of maneuver today. Besides, what would she have done with her free time? Wander around Main Street in the hope of catching another glimpse of the apparition that had upset her so much the evening before?

Well, actually, she did have something like that planned, but it would have to wait until she closed the gallery at six. The town would still be fairly busy with those who had stayed on to have dinner or who had decided to hang around until the band started to play at the Spirit Room at eight-thirty, but a lot of the people who currently crowded the streets would have packed up and gone back to their hotels in Sedona, or begun the long drive home to Phoenix.

After she made some smaller sales of jewelry and prints, six o'clock finally rolled around, and she was able to lock the front door and turn the sign in the display window around so it read "Closed." Mason and Adam had gone back to Flagstaff, but Jenny's mother had invited her over for dinner, an invitation she'd quietly refused. Lysette only wanted to make sure her daughter was all right, but after Thanksgiving, Jenny had had enough family "togetherness" to last her for quite a while.

She turned off the lights in the gallery, then went out the back and up the steps to her flat. Only long enough to retrieve her coat; a cold wind was blowing from the northeast, and she didn't want to make the same mistake she had the night before, when she'd worn only a shawl for warmth. Anyway, she didn't know how long she might have to be out.

At least the area around Spook Hall should be relatively quiet, as the building wasn't in use this evening, and the wine-tasting room a few doors down also closed at six. People had gathered around the entrance to the Spirit Room, chatting or smoking or merely hanging out, but no one seemed to be looking down toward Hull Avenue.

Jenny walked as casually as she could down the alleyway on the south side of the building, the spot where Maisie was rumored to make her appearances. Making sure she was standing in a location not illuminated by the feeble streetlights on Hull Avenue, she called out in a stage whisper, "Maisie!"

There was no answer, of course. The wind picked up slightly, making Jenny glad that she'd buttoned up her coat all the way before venturing forth. And the voices from the people on Main Street sounded strangely ghostly themselves as they drifted down the hill toward the place where she now stood.

Knowing she was going to be calling herself an idiot and several other choice names when she woke up the next morning, Jenny tried again. "Maisie!"

No reply. Maybe if she'd brought Angela with her....

Which would only have made the whole situation that much worse. The *prima* was up at her house with her husband and family, probably snacking on Thanksgiving leftovers, and no doubt wouldn't have been too thrilled to be dragged out into the cold on such a fool's errand. After all, Jenny knew that she probably hadn't seen anything at all the night before. She'd been worked up and emotional because of the split from Colin and the pressure of being around her family, not to mention missing her sister, and she'd just thought she'd seen Roslyn. What she should really do right now was turn around, go home, and pour herself a big glass of wine. Or two. And then binge-watch *House of Cards* on Netflix or something.

"You called?"

Jenny whirled around. Standing farther down the alley, her white blouse a blur in the shadows, was a young woman with pale blonde hair piled on top of her head. She had her arms crossed, and gazed up the sloping street toward Jenny with what appeared to be an expression of some amusement on her face, although it was hard to tell in the darkness.

Even though Angela had always said that Maisie looked just as normal as anyone else, except for the way she dressed, and Jenny herself had caught a glimpse of the ghost in Colin's memories, now that the moment had come, she couldn't quite believe what she was seeing. Talking to ghosts was Angela's talent, not hers.

"M-Maisie?"

"The same." She came closer, enough so that Jenny could see her skirt was navy blue. Tiny drops of mother-of-pearl hung from her ears, but she wore no other jewelry, not even a pin for the high neck of her blouse. "Seems like you're troubled, Jenny McAllister."

"Well, I—" Jenny broke off there, not sure what she should say next. "How is it I'm talking to you now?"

Maisie's thin shoulders lifted. "Your need was great."

"That's all it takes?"

"For me, yes. Most folks don't know that, though, so they all think the only one who can talk to me is Angela. Your man, though—he needed to hear from me as well."

"He's not my man," Jenny said, her tone flat. And whose fault was that? Not hers.

"Oh, yes, he is, even if you're angry with him. You have every right, o'course, but I can't see how his crime was so terrible that it's not worthy of some forgiveness."

Easy for her to say. Maisie had the perspective of a hundred years, while Jenny felt as if her own wound was very fresh. She crossed her arms and glared at the ghost. "Why do I have to be the one doing the forgiving? I didn't do anything wrong. He was the one who lied to me."

"That's not how forgiveness works, is it?"

Was it permissible to start yelling at a ghost? Because that was what Jenny felt like doing then. The only thing she'd been guilty of was a minor indiscretion…followed by beginning to lose her heart to absolutely the wrong guy. "What difference does it make to you, anyway?" she asked. "Are you bored with the afterlife, and so you decided it might be fun to play matchmaker for a while?"

Rather than being offended by that question, Maisie only chuckled. "Laws, girl, I don't really care one way or another. I'm just trying to do a favor for someone."

"A favor?" Jenny demanded. "For whom?"

"I'm not sure I'm supposed to say. I've probably said too much already." As she spoke, her outline began to turn blurry, and the bricks of the building behind her started to become visible as she went transparent and then disappeared altogether.

"No!"

Her denial rang off the walls of the buildings on either side. Jenny shoved her hands in her coat pockets and looked from side to side, desperately praying that Maisie's disappearance was only temporary. But the street was empty, and the ghost had gone.

Despite that, Jenny stood there for several more minutes, hoping Maisie might return. Jenny needed more answers. She needed to know what Maisie had meant about doing a favor for someone. And did she really expect Jenny to simply turn around and tell Colin it was okay, that she forgave him for being a lying bastard?

No. She had to stop herself there, because while he certainly was a liar, she couldn't go so far as to think of him as a bastard. He'd had his reasons for concealment in the beginning, even if he had allowed the whole sorry mess to go way too far.

Damn it, she thought angrily. *Now you really are just one step away from forgiving him.*

She stomped away from the spot where she'd had her conversation with the ghost. At the same time, she couldn't help wondering what Colin might be doing at that moment.

Colin sat with his sister Kate at a trendy wine bar and bistro in Chandler. She'd chosen it because it had great reviews on Yelp and, although he'd had to drive a good deal farther to get there, it was still more convenient than going into downtown Phoenix or driving all the way into Peoria, where Kate's condo was located. While he might have gone with something a little less hip, the wine bar did have the benefit of being located in a town where no one knew him or his sister. The place was mobbed, but he had a feeling most decent restaurants were packed that night. No one wanted to cook the day after Thanksgiving.

"So you seriously went to a prison?" Kate asked.

"I needed answers."

"Did you get them?"

He paused, looking across the table at her bright, earnest face. She'd taken this whole witch thing with more equanimity than he'd expected, but he could tell that she was slightly shocked by the revelation about his activities earlier that day. "I think so. The guy basically told me that there really were witch families here and in California—and I have to assume that means they're probably all over the place, not just in the Southwest."

"Like Salem?" Kate's hazel eyes were dancing, and he knew she was teasing him. Even so, he felt a stab of annoyance, because he already knew how crazy the whole thing sounded.

"I didn't ask. Anyway, I think it's pretty clear that Jenny McAllister and her family are a little out of the ordinary. I'm just not sure what to do about it."

An eyebrow went up. "Oh, give me a break. You know exactly what you have to do."

"What's that?"

"You like this girl. A lot."

"Is it that obvious?"

Kate's French-manicured fingers tapped on the base of her wine glass. "To me it is. Come on, Colin—you've been basically living like a monk for the past three years. If you've gone on any dates, you sure haven't talked about them. But then you show up at Thanksgiving looking like you've lost your last friend, and you admit you were seeing somebody and you screwed it up and don't know what to do about it. I doubt you would have gone up to see her in Jerome if you didn't think it was worth taking the risk."

Well, when she put it that way.... He didn't know about living like a monk, but he'd definitely been through a long dry spell in recent years. The divorce was final, and supposedly he was a free man, but he still didn't feel much like one. To tell the truth, he'd been marking time until the last of those alimony checks were written. After that, he'd be able to call his life his own again. So he'd seen a few women, even slept with a couple of them, but he hadn't allowed himself to feel that connected. And apparently none of them minded too much, because they'd let things peter out naturally, texts and calls becoming more and more spaced out until they disappeared altogether.

But then he'd met Jenny, and everything had gone sideways. He'd never reacted to a woman like that before, not even Shannon. And he realized that he didn't care if the McAllister family was full of spell-casting witches and warlocks, or that the world was a much crazier place than he'd ever imagined. All he wanted was Jenny. No matter what.

"Exactly," Kate said then, even though he hadn't spoken. But she was his sister, and she'd sat there and watched the shifting emotions on his face, and probably guessed what was going through his mind. "If she's that special, then what are you doing sitting here and talking to me?"

"Trying to get things figured out, I suppose." He lifted his neglected bottle of beer and swallowed a mouthful.

"What's there to figure out? You really like her, don't you?"

"I don't know." He drank some more beer before setting the bottle back down on the table. "I mean, she is *really* pissed at me, Kate."

"Then you grovel."

"Excuse me?"

"Grovel. You're a reporter—I assume you know what the word means."

He grimaced. "Not funny."

"I'm not joking. But seriously, Colin, if you've screwed up as epically as you say you have with Jenny McAllister, then you have to prove that you're willing to do whatever it takes to get her back." She stopped then and took a sip of her pinot noir before continuing, "*Are* you willing to do whatever it takes?"

"Yes. I mean, I think I am."

"Well, that's a half-assed answer."

Great. There his sister sat, looking all pleased with herself, as if this whole thing was so very simple. "You did catch the part about her family being a bunch of witches and warlocks, right?"

"Yeah, and?"

"So what if I go up there to grovel and they blast me right off the side of the mountain?"

"Would they? You made it sound as if they're mostly trying to fly under the radar."

Well, that was true. He doubted that having a reporter disappear was high on the list of things they wanted to happen in their town. Missing persons were bad for business and raised a lot of questions. Anyway, he knew he would be an utter coward if he didn't go up there and do his best to make things right. Jenny might still tell him to go to hell, but that was her prerogative. But at least he'd get his groveling in first. Whatever that might entail.

"Will I have to beg? Go down on my knees?"

"I don't know," Kate admitted. "I've never actually had anyone grovel to me before. But it seemed to work with a couple of my friends who were on the verge of dumping their boyfriends."

It was probably mean to say it, but Colin couldn't help himself. "What, Jeff doesn't grovel?"

She didn't crack a smile. "I think you know the answer to that."

None of his business, but…damn it, she was his sister, and he could tell she wasn't happy, either. She might pretend, might be perky and funny and offhand, but underneath all that was the quiet, gnawing hurt of realizing you'd made an awful mistake and not knowing what the hell to do about it.

He knew what that looked like because he'd been there himself.

"So…what are you going to do about it?" he asked, then held his breath, wondering if she was going to tell him to go to hell, that it was none of his business.

But she let out a strange little hiccupy sound, half laugh, half sob, and then quickly picked up her glass of wine and drank some, as if attempting to cover up what she'd just done. "I don't know. We've been limping along for the past six months or so. I've tried to get him to go to counseling, but he doesn't think we need it. I don't know if he's going to ever get it, even as I'm walking out the front door."

Colin winced. He had absolutely no use for his brother-in-law and would be all too happy to have him out of Kate's life, but he hated to see his sister in pain. "Is it really that bad?"

Her manicured fingers tapped on the stem of her wine glass, and she wouldn't quite look at him, her gaze instead fixed on some point past the booth where they sat. "I think so. I've been trying to deny it, but…." Her words trailed off then, and she let out a very small sigh. "Mom is going to freak when she finds out. Both her kids divorced? She's going to feel like a total failure."

"Our failures shouldn't reflect on her," Colin said. Then he shook his head. "No, I hate that word. We didn't fail—we made a mistake. Sometimes mistakes can be fixed, sometimes they can't. And you know Mom just wants you to be happy. So do I."

Kate didn't reply at first. Her fingers still played with her wine glass, and he could see how she was staring down at the wedding set on her left hand, on the smallish diamond and plain gold band. Jeff wasn't rich, but he probably could have afforded to get Kate something nicer than that. Colin recalled how she'd been so proud of her engagement ring, though, how happy that Jeff had proposed to her and that everything was working out the way she'd hoped.

That feeling hadn't lasted for very long.

"I know," Kate said at last. "And I know I have to do something about it. Only...not quite yet. I figure I'll get through the holidays and see what the new year brings. Anyway, I turned in my thesis before the holiday break, so it looks like I'll be graduating in the spring, and then I can go out and be a real adult, whatever that means." She stopped there, and offered him another of those half-smiles. "Don't look at me like that, Colin. I know what I have to do. Anyway, this shouldn't be about me right now. It should be about what you're going to do next."

"And what if I do manage to get it all worked out?" he asked. "What if I end up going to Jerome? What would you do then?"

She flicked a piece of expertly streaked hair over one shoulder and shook her head slightly. "Contrary to what you might think, Colin, I am an adult. I can handle it, even if things go sideways. In the back of my mind, I've already been planning exit strategies. Anyway, Jerome isn't exactly the dark side of the moon, or even the other side of the country. You wouldn't be that far away if I really needed my big brother to come riding to my rescue."

And that was it, right there. He hadn't exactly asked for permission, but maybe he had been asking for her blessing. But, just as he'd said about their parents, he knew that Kate just wanted him to be happy, to have someone in his life who was important to him. And, as she'd said, being in Jerome wasn't like moving to New York or something. He'd be close if she needed him.

When that thought passed through his mind, he realized he'd already made his decision. He liked his job, but he could find something to do in Jerome or Cottonwood or Sedona, if Jenny would take him back. He didn't want any more hollow days of pretending that the work was enough. Those few hours he'd spent with her had been the happiest of his life. He wanted more of that.

He wanted her.

"Go on," Kate said with a smile, a real one this time. "Don't beat yourself up for trying to follow a dream. Tell her how you feel. We women are suckers for that kind of thing."

"Thanks, Kate," he said simply, but she seemed to understand everything he didn't say.

"That's what I'm here for. Anyway," she added, "if you work things out with Jenny, Mom will be ecstatic that you have someone in your life again."

"Even if that someone takes me all the way to Jerome?"

Kate leaned forward and laid her hand on his. Just for a moment, but he could feel the reassurance in her touch. Her smile didn't waver. "Even then."

CHAPTER SEVENTEEN

IT WAS FAR TOO LATE TO DRIVE TO JEROME. THE CLOCK ON his dashboard read nine-thirty when Colin got back to his car. Even if he'd left at that exact moment, Colin knew he wouldn't have been able to make it to the mountain town before close to midnight, which was a little late to be knocking on someone's door and pleading with them to take you back.

So he'd sat there in the darkness for a long moment, then shook his head and pointed his car south, toward home. Kate was already on her way back to Peoria, since he'd stood and watched while she climbed into her CR-V and then pulled out of the parking lot. At least she'd be home within a half hour or so. Colin had never thought he'd be grateful for Jeff's ritual Friday night poker games, since he knew Kate was less than a fan, but at least the game had given her the chance to get out of the house and come see him.

He wondered how Ned and Ryan would react if he turned in his notice on Monday morning and told them he was moving to Jerome.

Getting a little ahead of yourself, aren't you? he thought as he drove south on I-10, but he couldn't help himself. If he didn't allow himself to indulge in a little magical thinking, he didn't know if he'd have the guts to do what he needed to do. And he supposed he'd have to decide what in the world to tell Eileen Kosky. The easiest thing to do would be to simply lie and say he'd discovered that Alex Trujillo had a permit to carry a Taser, but Colin knew he'd had enough of lying. Anyway, she'd already told him that she knew what a Taser looked like, so that wouldn't have worked. Well, he figured he'd come up with something eventually. For now, he needed to focus on tomorrow.

Which was a Saturday. Normally, that would be perfect, but Jenny had to work. Not into the evening, though; he knew she closed down the gallery at six on Fridays, and he assumed that Saturday hours were probably the same.

Well, he would just have to check. He'd made a note of the gallery's name when he was in Jerome, so it was easy enough to look up the place on the web. East of the Sun. The gallery had an elegant one-page website, with not a lot of detail. That was enough, though. The phone number, address, and hours were listed directly under the gallery's logo, of a sun rising behind the name. And yes, it did close at six. He could leave in the afternoon and get there right as she was shutting things down.

All he could do was hope she wouldn't shut him down as well.

She'd had another flash that morning. Not a horrible one, since it had only lasted for a few seconds before she was able to do her breathing exercises and force it out of her head. Also, because she was alone, she wasn't hit with the sort of brilliant imprint she'd gotten from Colin's mind when he was lying beside her, but only a kaleidoscopic impression of thoughts from those in the buildings within a hundred-yard radius. Luckily, most of those thoughts had been occupied with plans for the day or figuring out what to have for breakfast. It could have been a lot worse.

Still, she was worried by the episode, because she'd been doing her best to meditate each morning, do her yoga exercises on a mat in the middle of the living room. With December only a week away, the temperatures outside were far too cold for her to perform that ritual out on the porch as she preferred, but she'd forced herself to go through the motions even so, knowing that ignoring the only activities which helped to mitigate her brain flashes would only make matters worse.

Problem was, she couldn't seem to focus the way she wanted to, since Colin kept intruding into her thoughts—the quick flash of his smile, the warmth in his hazel eyes as he gazed at her from across a restaurant table. And the way she'd been able to rest her head on his chest and take in deep, calm breaths, as if her body knew what her mind didn't want to accept, that in his arms was the place she was meant to be.

Several times she'd picked up her cell and scrolled through her contacts, then stared at his name and number, her finger hovering over the phone icon, wanting to touch it but not quite daring to. And then she'd mentally cursed her weakness and put the phone away, telling herself that she'd get over this soon enough. Another week, or two, and Colin Campbell would be just another period in her life that she could put behind her.

Right.

A part of her had wanted to wander down to Hull Avenue before she started work today, to see if she could roust Maisie once again and attempt to coax the ghost into revealing who she was supposedly doing favors for, but Jenny told herself that was a silly idea. She couldn't rely on voices from the afterlife to help her now. She'd get through her current pain because she had to.

As for all that nonsense about forgiving Colin....

Would it really be that terrible? All right, he'd lied to her on multiple occasions. But....

No, she told herself as she went around the gallery and straightened a few paintings that had gone slightly cockeyed. Occupational hazard in a place like Jerome, where the ground was always shifting just a bit because of the mines buried deep below Cleopatra Hill.

How can you trust someone like that? Once a liar, always a liar.

Problem was, she didn't know if that was exactly true or not. He'd had very specific reasons for hiding his identity from her. But he'd been telling the truth about his divorce, as well as other particulars of his life that might have been easier to hide. Things that would have hurt her if he hadn't come clean about them.

And they did say that forgiveness was divine.

But then it was time to open the gallery, and the place was even busier on Saturday than it had been the day before. The frantic pace helped the time move along, and Jenny had to be grateful for that. Besides, Alice, the gallery's owner, had it set up so Jenny would get a nice bonus whenever daily sales went over a certain amount, and they'd certainly accomplished that goal this holiday weekend. Not that she really needed the money to survive, but she could spend the bonus on fun things for herself and not feel as if she was being too frivolous.

Attending to the last few customers made her keep the shop open until a little past six, which was all right, as they bought several of Angela's hand-made pieces of jewelry, as well as a vase made by a local potter. Besides, it wasn't as if Jenny had any-place she needed to be. There was a good band playing at the Spirit Room later on, but she thought it would be a lot better if she just stayed at home, drowned her sorrows in some of the leftover pump-kin pie her mother had dropped off earlier that day, and watched more Netflix. Maybe more *Orange Is the New Black* or something.

Just as she was locking the front door, a shadow moved in front of the entrance to the gallery. She began to gasp—and then realized she recognized the hazel eyes staring at her imploringly from the other side of the glass inset in the door.

Colin Campbell.

His voice was somewhat muffled by the glass door, but recognizable enough. "Can I come in?"

Her first instinct was to say *hell, no.* Her heart was pounding, although she wasn't sure whether that was because of the way he'd startled her, or just the mere fact that he stood inches away from her, even if a solid oak door was separating them at the moment.

"What are you doing here?" she asked. That seemed a good way of stalling for time until she could figure out whether or not she really was going to let him in.

"I needed to talk to you."

"Your phone broken?"

"I needed to talk to you in person."

She almost pointed out that he was already doing that very same thing. But something about the pleading look in his eyes stopped her. He'd driven three hours to be here. Maybe some people might have made him turn around and go right back to where he'd come from, but Jenny didn't think she could be quite that cold.

"All right," she said at last, and unlocked the door so he could step inside.

He entered the gallery, giving a quick glance around—to reassure himself that they really were alone, most likely.

"It's okay," she told him as she relocked the door. "The tourists have all gone home, or at least back to their hotels."

Had he always been that tall? She didn't remember having to look up at him. But then, the first time they'd met, she'd been wearing those stupid heels, and for some reason that particular height difference had imprinted itself on her brain, even though she normally wore flats.

He nodded and shoved his hands in his pockets. "I know it's pushing things to come and see you like this," he said. "I thought about calling, but...."

"I probably would have hung up on you," she said frankly. "It's a lot harder to ignore someone on your doorstep."

"That's what I hoped."

An awkward silence descended. Since she knew the gallery probably wasn't the best place for this kind of conversation, she made a vague gesture upward. "Let's go up to my flat. If someone comes by and sees us talking in here, they might wonder why the place is locked up if I still have a customer."

The faintest expression of relief passed over his features, and he nodded. Clearly, he'd been worried that he wouldn't even be able to get that far. "Sure. Thank you."

Damn, now he was looking hopeful. He shouldn't look hopeful...or should he? Jenny didn't even know anymore. It was one thing to be angry with him and want him out of her life permanently when she didn't have to look at him. But when he was watching her with those puppy-dog eyes of his....

Biting back a sigh, she led him out the back exit and up the stairs to her flat. The wind was cold, but she ignored it, since they'd only be outside for a minute. Once they were in her apartment, she went over and turned up the space heater and flicked on a couple of lights.

"Do you want something to drink?" she asked, surprising herself. "I've got an open bottle of pinot in the kitchen."

"Sure," Colin replied, also looking vaguely startled. He stood in the middle of the living room, hands dug into his pockets as if he didn't know what else to do with them.

"Go ahead and sit down," Jenny said, mostly because the sight of him of there, clearly unsure what to do with himself, only made her that much more nervous.

From the corner of her eye, she could see him take a seat on the couch as she went to the kitchen to fetch the bottle of wine she'd opened the night before. Her crystal wine glasses seemed far too fancy for the occasion, so she grabbed a couple of stemless ones, left over from wine tastings gone by, pulled out the cork, and poured a few inches of wine into each glass.

Crazy. This was crazy. She should have told him that she didn't want to talk, didn't want to see him.

But those would have been lies, and there'd been enough lies between them already.

She went into the living room and set the glasses down on the coffee table. No way was she going to sit next to him on the couch, so she settled herself into the accent chair and picked up a wine glass.

Colin did so as well, although he didn't drink, only held the glass cradled between his hands. What nice fingers he had, strong and yet sensitive. She recalled then how good those fingers had felt as they drifted over her skin, and did her best to fight back an extremely unwelcome shiver of arousal.

"I know this is asking a lot, barging in on you like this," he said. "And I'm not going to make excuses for myself."

"Good."

He looked slightly put off by the interruption, but then pulled in a breath and continued. "You were right back then—I was a sorry lying ass. I should have told you the truth right up front."

"But you didn't because I was just so damn amazing." Was that her voice, so cold, so sarcastic? The hurt and shock of discovering what he'd done seemed fresh all over again, and she clenched her hands on her jean-clad knees.

"Yes, you are," he said quietly. "I'd dug myself in deep and didn't know how to get out. If you need me to tell you every single day from here on out how much I fucked up, I will—if it means I get to see you every day. Because I was wrong. I knew it at the time and didn't do anything about it, and I'll say it again now because I don't want to lose you, Jenny. I was wrong. You have every right to be angry with me, but please—please give me a second chance. I swear I'll never lie to you again."

He looked so worried, so strained, and yet there was still that spark of hope in his eyes, because he was here talking to her, and she hadn't thrown him out yet. No, she realized that moment had long passed. If she had really meant to tell him to go to hell, then she should have done so the second she locked eyes with him through the gallery's door.

"I am angry with you," she said, and his shoulders slumped slightly, although he didn't look away, didn't try to break their eye contact. "But I'll give you a chance to put your money where your mouth is. Do you really believe that I'm a witch, that I'm from a family of witches?"

"Yes," he replied without hesitation. He didn't even blink.

"Why? Because you think you saw a ghost, or because I was able to see into your mind?"

"Both those things. And —" He hesitated then, as if wrestling with some inner dilemma. His next words came out in a rush. "And also because I went and talked to Tomas Aguirre, and he told me that there were many families like yours, all with their various abilities."

At the name of the man who'd helped murder her sister, Jenny went cold, the blood in her veins turning to antifreeze. With a shaking hand, she set down her untouched glass of wine. "You *what?*"

A muscle in Colin's jaw tightened, but he didn't try to avoid the question. "I wanted to talk to him because I figured he would be a good outside source who could corroborate what I'd already seen and experienced. And he did. He said he was once a war-lock, but that your *prima* burned his powers right out of him. Is that true?"

"Yes." Jenny could hear her own voice shake, so she swallowed and fought to regain her composure before she spoke again. "The Aguirres and Matías Escobar were dabbling in the very blackest of magic, magic they fueled by taking my sister's blood. That kind of magic has been outlawed for centuries. So Angela—our *prima*, or head witch—and her hus-band Connor joined their own talents and used them to take away the magical powers the three warlocks had been born with. That way, they couldn't hurt anyone ever again."

"And they could be locked up in a civilian prison and not cause any more trouble."

Surprise flickered in her, and she raised an eye-brow. "'Civilian'? Tomas Aguirre teach you that?"

"He used the phrase, and I remembered how you almost said it once or twice and then caught yourself."

She probably had; it was sometimes hard to watch what you said when you were around non-magical people. And really, although she couldn't deny the lies Colin had told her, she had to admit that she hadn't been exactly truthful with him, either. For an entirely different reason, of course, and one that no one in her clan could fault her for. Still, she and Colin had both come to one another under false pretenses.

A tremor went through her, and she retrieved her wine and took a large swallow. Colin did the same, although he showed more restraint in how much wine he drank. "It sounds like Mr. Aguirre was very chatty," she said dryly.

Colin's shoulders lifted. Voice thoughtful, he replied, "Actually, he was. And…." The words drifted off, and she could see the way his mouth tightened, as if he'd thought better of what he was about to say.

"And what?" she asked. "If he told you something about—about Roslyn, then I deserve to know."

"You're right." His eyes were clear and sober and very sad. "You do deserve to know. It doesn't change what he did, but…I think Tomas regrets how things turned out. I think he wanted to save her, but didn't have the strength of will to go up against Escobar."

Jenny's throat tightened. *You will not cry,* she told herself. *You will not cry. Not now.*

"Most people didn't," she said, her voice hardly a whisper. It was about all she could manage right then. "That was the problem. That was his power. Caitlin somehow managed to get away, and Alex had his own defenses, but...Roslyn didn't. Danica didn't. And it sounds like Tomas didn't, either." Which made it all the more horrible. It was so much easier to think of Tomas Aguirre as a monster who'd happily participated in the murder of her sister. Jenny didn't want to see him as someone who'd also been coerced by Matías Escobar.

Damn it. There went a tear, followed by another. She reached up to wipe them away quickly before Colin could see, but she wasn't fast enough. A frown pulled at his brows, and then, before she could move or react, he was coming over to her, lifting her from the chair where she sat so he could put his arms around her, hold her close. He didn't try to kiss her. He didn't even say anything. But it was enough that he was there, his body strong and reassuring against hers, his heartbeat calm and steady, telling her that he was with her, that he would always be there for her...if she let him.

A little sob caught at her throat, and she choked it back. She needed to be able to speak then. She had to tell him—had to—

But he beat her to it. "I love you, Jenny McAllister," he said, his breath warm against the crown of her head. "Please tell me that you'll let me love you."

"Yes," she said. "I want you to love me. I want to be with you. I love—"

The last word was smothered by his mouth as he kissed her, his lips so warm, so strong, so aching with need. She couldn't fight this anymore, couldn't tell herself that it was stupid or wrong. It couldn't be wrong, not when everything in the universe was telling her that he was the only person who could ever make her feel this way.

At last their mouths broke apart, but his arms remained around her, as if he knew that she needed the reassurance of his touch. And because she was unable to stop herself, she said, voice breathless, "But how can we make this work? You're in Tucson—"

"I'm here," he cut in with absolutely no hesitation. "I want to be with you here. I'll work in the gallery with you. I'll flip burgers. I don't care, as long as we're together here."

Laughter bubbled out of her, coming from a spring that she'd thought had long ago gone dry. "I don't think you need to make quite that much of a sacrifice. I heard the *Verde Valley Independent* was hiring. I'm sure they'd love to take on an ace reporter like you."

"Even better," Colin said, right before he bent to kiss her again.

The world spun around, but that was all right, because she was standing there with him, knowing he would always be there for her, solid and safe and true.

Then she heard him say, "My God," and she had to lift her head to see what had made that note of awe enter his voice.

Standing on the other side of the living room was Roslyn, Roslyn as Jenny always tried to remember her, beautiful and pink-cheeked and bright, with her dark gold hair falling down her back. Not the wasted husk that was all Matías Escobar had left behind after he was done with her. Jenny's talent—or curse—had acted up in a moment of stress, picking those horrible images from her parents' minds, from the day when they'd had to go and identify their daughter's body. Now the person standing before her was not the nightmare vision that Jenny had spent many months trying to erase from her memories, but her laughing golden-voiced sister.

"R-Roslyn?" she managed. Was she seeing things? She must be. But no, Colin had made that shocked exclamation, which meant he must have seen her, too.

Roslyn smiled and spread out a hand. Mystified, Jenny looked to see where she was gesturing. There, in the open doorway that led to the bedroom, stood Maisie. She smiled as well, although there was a certain impishness to the way her mouth lifted that was noticeably absent from the beatific-looking Roslyn.

"I told you I was doin' a favor for someone," Maisie said. "It's hard for her to be here long, as this ain't her plane, or some such. But she wanted to drop in so you could see she was all right. And she wanted to make sure you was all right, too." She hesitated, sending an inquiring glance toward Jenny and Colin. A laughing glint entered her blue eyes as she saw the way the two of them stood hand in hand. "Well, I suppose you are all right, after all."

Jenny glanced up at Colin, saw the loving glow in his eyes, and felt the way his fingers tightened on hers. And then she looked at the ghost of her sister— but was she a ghost, really? She seemed far too full of life to be dead. And perhaps she wasn't, not really. She had only moved on from this plane, had left this world to fulfill her destiny elsewhere.

"Yes," Jenny said, smiling at her sister, and seeing how Colin smiled as well. "I am all right.

"We all are."

THE END